Do you want to know what I'm thinking? I'll tell you whether you do or not. It popped into my head all of a sudden. A new idea. Can you imagine? I'm usually rehashing the old ones. It's how love is associated with the loss of willpower. People 'fall' in love, as if they were walking along and suddenly tumbled into some kind of tiger pit. How often are people minding their own business like that? No, they're really wandering around in a forest full of tiger traps hoping to plunge into one.

HALF WIT

CLOWN

CIRCUS MEDIA GROUP

HALF WIT

By clown

A Circus Book

www.circusmediagroup.com

Cover design handcrafted by Luciana Lara Maruca.
https://lucianalaraat.wordpress.com/home

For information about subsidiary rights, please contact the publisher at ip@circusmediagroup.com.

❋ Created with Vellum

1

He entered like a person who has just trekked across a desert, whose eyes flash and whose pace quickens when at last he sees the sustenance he seeks. Weak, feeble, enervated, strong, and driven. He was neither young nor old. Not really any age. The confidence of youth and resignation of middle age balanced on a fulcrum. Chastened, a fine word nobody uses anymore.

When you think you're floating in calm waters, you might be adrift, carried along by the caprices of stealthy breezes. Common problems had displaced and dumped me in a godforsaken town thrown together at a convergence of pleats rippling down from a range of ancient mountains. Not the daring, majestic, jagged snowcapped peaks that make you think of clean, frosty breath, glistening sunlight, and rushing clear water, but rather the lumpy, muddy, and verdant mountains emeritus that over epochs have stubbornly wrestled erosion to an impasse.

You were unlikely to chance upon this village, unless chance resolutely disfavored you. It lay far away from any highway, waterway, or railroad. A single unlined ribbon of asphalt ran through it and dissolved into looming, inexorable wilderness. It was a terminal basin amassing backwardness and dejection. You would like to think that over the years a few souls had had sufficient levity to have wafted themselves away—you know, the classic archetype, the spunky iconoclast escaping a small, ignorant dead-end town. I don't know. I've only been here a few months. I doubt it ever happened.

Every imaginable kind of man-made material contributed to an amalgamated layer of litter strewn across the hillsides. Glass bottles, aluminum cans, cardboard boxes, food wrappers, paper cups, and so much plastic—bags, bottles, containers, cutlery, and innumerable other forms that the material could take. More fascinating was the large trash, the mattresses, microwaves, couches, chairs, tables, televisions, tires, refrigerators, bicycles, lawn mowers, washers, driers, and, not infrequently, stripped-down vehicle chassis so decrepit and rusty that they had almost naturally been recycled back into the raw iron that colored red the creek beds and substratum of slimy clay. It would have been easier to let the large debris rot where it stood, even in your own front yard, and this was certainly not the type of place where you would face the opprobrium of your neighbors for doing just that. You were compelled to admire the extra effort and creativity that went into dumping these relics. The placement of some of them seemed so impossible that you would suppose some enterprising person had airdropped or catapulted them to their final resting places. It was truly inspired. Vandals do indeed take pride in their work.

On a small mound behind the town stood a solitary Catholic church. Inscribed in its stones, pews, and stained glass in equal standing with Latin Bible verses and descriptions of Biblical scenes were a dozen or so rough Germanic names that are still prominent around here, the names of its builders, the founders of this village. They must have been an ambitious, resourceful, and thoughtful people, because they hadn't been content just to pile up stones in the shape of a simple, gloomy Romanesque chapel you usually see in these old country towns. Certainly they could have achieved something suitably imposing and weird—I think it's a requisite that Catholic churches be a little fantastical—while expending fewer resources. Instead, they opted for a sweet, dainty Gothic style, a scaled-down and somewhat simplified version of a grand cathedral that perhaps their ancestors had collaborated to build. I can't tell you the story of its construction, because not a single soul had any idea how it got there. Its builders probably never imagined that their descendants would be too dim-witted to appreciate the passion, care, and ingenuity required for a small number of hands to erect such a structure.

The ancestors of the present population wouldn't have been naive enough to think that their beautiful shrine would ever be guided by some wise, brilliant, enthusiastic counselor sent from the diocese. Undoubtedly they had endured many merely adequate shepherds, like the priest stationed here now, who could more or less paraphrase the Gospels in his homilies, conducted his official duties with sufficient gravity, and didn't cause any scandals. They had correctly assumed that they would need to fulfill their spiritual cravings themselves. They had poured into this structure all of their yearning for serenity and relief from a world that was at worst capricious and cruel, and at best mundane and disappointing.

The interior was as ornately and expertly crafted as one of the finer small cathedrals of the late Middle Ages but had a more unified aesthetic, as a single generation with a shared vision had constructed it over a short period of time. Many virtuoso feats had been demonstrated on this tiny canvas, with tenderness and suppleness that comforted and caressed the worshiper. Its whimsical touches could draw warmth out of even the most stoical hearts. You might easily fall under its spell and feel a surge of several of our noblest emotions—love, humility, compassion, tenderness—all at once. The enchantment couldn't even be broken by the prosaic commentary from their exiled priest.

The exterior was constructed of red sandstone. A single thin spire thrust skyward over the front entrance like a tongue of flame. Its builders had used the minimum amount of stone needed to support the structure while accommodating its massive windows, which were framed in white sandstone and curtained with richly colored stained glass. At the end of each transept, the windows comprised three separate lancets that together bore up an ornate crimson glass rose. In the right passage of the transept, two angels flanked Mary, and in the left, two watched over the baby Jesus. The rectangular windows along the nave and the apse were topped with pointed trefoil arches and depicted the apostles and Joseph. The extraordinary level of skill extended into the third dimension, as the nave was lined with miraculously animated and magnificently colored plaster friezes of the stations of the cross set in gleaming gilt frames. Also scattered throughout the interior were statues of the holy family, apostles, the church's namesake Ambrose, and ingenious discreetly placed motifs of bees and beehives. A small gang of the little golden creatures gathered at the edge of one of the rose windows, and others wandered and made mischief in other pieces of the artwork.

These elders must have harnessed and expended every iota of poetry in their beings on this project, a convergence of simultaneous magnum opuses, and had no talent left to bequeath to their offspring, because there was no other structure in town like it. The five or six other ancient buildings were careless and deformed, and all successive ones were thoughtlessly utilitarian and disposable. The other pillars of the village were a tavern, a bank, and a combined town hall and post office. An incoherence of houses and businesses radiated outward and dissipated into the woods and fields of garbage.

During daylight hours, that dignified structure and its graceful tower seemed to inspire the citizens. They were typical nice small-town folks. They eschewed capital vices and embraced the pragmatic austerity of their forebears, but, if I'm honest, their isolated setting provided few truly perilous temptations. The slightest whiff of misfortune or injustice—an ailing elder, a tragically young widow, an ill child, a job loss, a car accident, or a spurned husband, for example—elicited an outpouring of communal sympathy. Maybe I flattered them because the sight of their chapel nurtured a kernel of optimism in me. In reality, charity is often condescending, an assertion of superiority, and their altruism could have given them a sense of relief that they weren't quite as hopeless as those whom they pitied.

At night, when darkness enveloped their spiritual beacon, the residents underwent a startling transformation, abandoning themselves to licentiousness and drinking. Twilight expands the private domains in which people can reveal their dominant natures. Those of you pinioned by the stultifying boredom of the suburbs need not cram yourselves into the nearest city. Head to the forests, where the evening unfurls immeasurable space into which your constrained essence can swell and enjoy its terrible potency.

I had situated myself near what I believed was the heart of town. My routine was to be outdoors during the day to allow the sun to warm and invigorate me, which it could do even with its pale winter face. At sunset I returned to my room to relax quietly while the daylight yet lingered inside me. I was always a little surprised at the moment when the last ember of feeling burned out and went cold. Then I would shuffle outside, smoke one or two weak, cheap cigarettes, ladies' cigarettes, as they had often been teasingly described to me—I had acquired the habit in the company of women—and walk to the bar.

The tavern consisted of a long counter with video poker

machines at both ends, a pool table in one corner, a dartboard, an ancient jukebox with nothing but popular music from decades ago worn out from having been played so many times that it sounded like you were listening to it through a wall, about a dozen tables, and a few dark recesses where you could in solitude embrace the total stupefaction that came with drinking the hardest liquor.

When my barmates needed listening to, I could be a hub of conversation, congratulations, and complaints. Not always. Many nights I sat by myself. Maybe I mimicked a sage demeanor. I'm a good listener. Really, it's my only skill, and enough to give me purpose. Such a vocation requires little more than to be silent, appear attentive, and occasionally say something that sounds profound, like that there's more to floating in water than being still. To the people who screamed and writhed, or acted out their longings and frustrations, whom existence answered with silence, maybe my calm eyes, cocked grin, and knowing nod were sufficient relief. After months, however, I still had no idea who these people were. They told variations of the same old stories, registered variations of the same old complaints, and appended variations of the same new episodes, as if to make sense of their lives they needed to align themselves as closely as possible with a caricature of the people in their community. Nevertheless, as far as I could tell, nothing ever changed. Life may have been unsatisfactory, but at least it was safely sedentary and relatable.

I took my place on a stool at the bar and drank slowly, considering for the millionth time the rate at which my body metabolized alcohol, and why I always consumed it faster than that. I was never so intoxicated that I lost my lucidity, my ability to question and criticize myself, to see myself sitting there drinking too much for no reason. Extreme drunkenness was common around me and in my opinion ruined the entire experience. I asked myself what engendered such a will to self-impairment. It certainly wasn't fun.

Existential questions were always at the periphery of my consciousness, and drinking could dull my senses and silence distracting stimuli so that my reflections had all of my attention. I thought more, and more clearly, when I was slightly drunk. Simple questions. None of those unanswerable ones about existence itself, but the only three apropos to every situation and condition: "What the hell am I doing? Why am I doing this? What good am I?"

I might be the only person who saw him, who alone observed the fact that he entered, sat, drank, spoke, and left. I wouldn't say it's impossible. Contrary to progressive thinking, it's comforting to believe in the mysterious and impossible. We're all going crazy because we have conspired to take away our fantasies. Logic, facts, and empiricism shackle us. Even meager slivers of possibilities project themselves into the limitless, pull us along with them, and elevate our minds and imaginations. So let him be a peculiar shade sensible only to me. Let me be singled out for unusual experiences, bizarre phenomena, like I was once certain I was.

Lined up alongside other men or women in the room, probably in the entire county, he would undoubtedly have been considered the healthiest, handsomest, and heartiest. Nevertheless, I sensed that a more fulsome man stood somewhere casting the shadow of the one who found me. He wore a ragged black wool frock coat that must have once looked quite smart but was wholly inappropriate for the stagnant freeze that settled into the region in late November. He sat beside me on the stool that I could have sworn had been occupied a second ago by a drunkard babbling to himself and mumbled something about being new in town. Just passing through. Needing to warm his bones. Nice little place. How about the weather. Other stupid phrases that tried to spark a conversation. Not to nobody in particular, but to me, because my purpose is to listen.

I scanned his profile, smiled, and nodded. He stopped his mumbling, stared blankly, and then turned his head mechanically to meet my gaze.

"What should I drink? I don't normally drink. Hardly ever," he said.

"Why drink anything, then?" I asked.

"I came to a bar, so I have to," he responded. "I've never been much of a drinker. Maybe it's something everyone is supposed to experience. I'm trying a little bit of everything."

He might have been joking, but a flash of anguish passed over his face, and then he recomposed himself, suppressing something with his waning reserves of nervous energy. I sensed that he had been subjected to more extraordinary events than the mundane numbing disappointments that the locals continually languished in. He stifled a shiver, either from the outside cold still clinging to him or from his own anxious emotional state. There was something so alien about his manner that most people couldn't process what they were looking at. Strange, dissonant symbols that could do no more than elicit indifference.

"The bartender has one bottle of cheap brandy," I said, adding sarcastically, "For special occasions." And, with a barely noticeable relaxing of his brow and jaw, I was allowed into his confidence. "It's been sitting so long that it may have matured into something of higher quality, or evolved into a whole new species of liquor."

I beckoned to the bartender, who was hesitant and unsure what I wanted, having developed, like all of those who were condemned to a career in rather than passing through the occupation, an instinctual timing for when, what, and whom to serve as the evening progressed. "Get this guy a big glass of brandy, on me."

Without actually acknowledging the man, the bartender asked, "Special occasion?"

"Sure, why not?" I replied.

He roughly set down a whiskey glass and poured a stingy amount of this particular bar's uppermost-shelf spirits.

"I used to think I would just take a break here. But as you can see, I found a comfortable spot," I told my new companion.

"Yep, it sure looks that way," he responded. "It seems like there's someone like you everywhere. Someone who has one foot stuck in the mud—you know, that thick, slimy, oozy kind that sucks itself onto you. The world keeps marching on while you're trying to get that leg out, and when you finally do, you just step in it again or trip over something else. Always behind and out of sync."

I stared at my beer and didn't react to his observation, which was pretty accurate.

"Don't mind me or be insulted," he said.

He drank half his brandy and inhaled deeply. The remaining anxious, almost frantic, energy in his smooth emerald eyes disappeared. I now beheld a face that perfectly comprehended and commanded its wearer's own existence, and perhaps mine. He smiled, an explosion of straight white teeth to accompany those dazzling, unblinking eyes. A sight sobering and intoxicating.

"I'm sure you've heard a lot of stories, but you should listen to mine, if you have the time. You would be the first person I've told," he said.

WHAT YOU'RE reading is a long, discursive conversation, a dialogue in which I at times played both parts, molded into a story. The man wasn't a naturally gifted talker. He composed and recomposed his tale as he went. When he became frustrated with his inability to communicate his thoughts, I could usually find the one or two right words that coaxed the narrative forward, or else I simply nodded my understanding. And when it comes to emotions, can anyone accurately explain them? I've done my best, guided by my own limited knowledge. They're inexpressible psychological experiences, impossible to articulate as they happen. If they're intense enough, you might later think about and describe them to yourself, but most are discarded and quickly subsumed under waves of new sensations. I don't think you can truly remember your feelings. All you're left with are dim impressions of poorly preserved memories of badly perceived events. I can only tell you my story of his story, what I thought he meant or would have wanted to say. You might later relay your own version of mine.

I can't relate verbatim what my strange companion told me. That would be unreadable. The longest sustained structured story I've ever heard lasted perhaps no more than five minutes. A writer conspires with an audience to impose order. Not only do readers resist acknowledging the illusion, they protest being confronted with anything of the randomness, incoherence, false starts, anticlimaxes, futility, regular failures, and unexpected successes of an actual human life. Honestly, I have no idea if anything I'm writing is real, but you shouldn't care. The suppleness of the truth is what allows our spirits to evolve. Those who would rigidly demand objective facts imprison our souls. Imagine not being able to reinterpret and rewrite the past.

The hero in a story needs a name, but he never told me his, so I called him David.

2

———

David came from somewhere that had been one of the obvious points through which to run a major high-way. The land had been cheap and the locals hadn't appeared to be worth worrying about. Several factories moved in, attracted by written agreements for huge tax breaks and unwritten ones that workers would accept low pay and never unionize. His parents arrived when the first new housing developments were springing up around the old weather-beaten village. By the time he started school, communities were being crammed in everywhere, each one designed to outdo its predecessors, along with shopping centers and supermarkets catering to every income level and lifestyle. A city emerged from the chain reaction of income, allowing consumption to generate more income to allow more consumption.

David had been an exceptionally delicate and beautiful child. His father, who had been slapped together from whatever crude leftover parts had been lying around, doubted his paternity, and even his maternity. He himself was dark, short, blocky, and covered with hair so coarse and black that it made him look persistently filthy, and no amount of shaving and trimming could change that. His mother was fat and red—red hair, freckled red skin that always looked sunburned, as attractive as a plump ripe apple. She craved sex as much as she craved cheap snacks. His father, however, was repelled by the nude human form, having had to endure his own misshapen body for so long, and avoided intimacy as much as possible, only until he could no longer endure his wife's nagging. As the relief of old age seemed imminent, they accidentally had a son.

Neither mother nor father could identify any probable alternative progenitor from among the other men she caroused with. Not that they tried; this beautiful baby flattered his peculiar lineage. Upon closer inspection—the nose! Don't you see it? Simply a rough jewel in the father, but here in the boy, cut, polished, and set more attractively. The eyes, shaped and colored like his mother's but without the bulging, frog-like placement, fixed more deeply like his father's. Mother's long legs and father's long torso. The complexion and the hair also balanced the extremes of both parents. They had no idea where this child had come from, but didn't care—oh! if only you could see how much he really was their own son.

Since his childhood, David had a full head of golden hair always about to extend its soft tendrils down his neck and over his ears. Constellations of swirling ringlets. Each little coil seemed to be its own entity, and they all accommodated each other, slinking and twisting however they liked, in defiance of any artificial arrangement. They saw to their own affairs and didn't trouble him for attention.

His skin was smooth, unblemished, and delighted in the sunlight; even that wan, bashful winter sun could induce a golden glow. His physique effortlessly remained lean and fit and in its every movement exhibited tremendous strength and grace married to a childlike suppleness.

Even with all of these endowments, you noticed his eyes first. Colored a bright, smooth green with a touch of milkiness, like peridot. The stroma radiated from the pupils as regular, symmetrical spokes. Perfect eyes that appeared to have been crafted with an expert artisan's steady, precise hand. But their perfection rendered them somewhat artificial and lifeless. They lacked any of the lively organic warmth of the artist's touch. If he looked at you with a wide, unblinking stare, his eyes seemed to hover in front of you like two mesmerizing amulets.

He was never known for cleverness, or even so much as a dash of wit, but his looks tended to excuse him from any sort of intellectual demands, which would have struck a discordant note anyway. He got away with putting minimal effort into his school assignments. His teachers forgave his apathy and distractions, his staring out the window for hours, his fixating on some object in the classroom, and his not-quite-innocent infatuations with every pretty girl. Although his teachers did their best to play their parts as earnest educators, when they considered how his face shone with such intensity during his quiet, aimless contemplations, even the dourest of them inwardly berated themselves for their own tediousness. Nevertheless, he had a natural aptitude for the apparent and easily retained basic information, which was sufficient to carry him with little effort, although not exemplary success, through primary and secondary school, and onwards to university.

What were his little raptures? Merely the surfaces of objects, albeit in extraordinarily high resolution. He delighted in things as they were. The extent of details available in plain sight is something most of us miss. As soon as our senses detect something interesting, our pitiful brains begin chattering to themselves about their ideas, associations, emotions, and memories. Soon, the impetuous little conversations we have with ourselves distract us from whatever started the whole process. I suppose that's why we take so many photographs and videos and then never look at any of them very carefully.

David was fortunate to have a relatively empty, clear head.

His senses, however, were like microscopes. He could observe the beating of a bumblebee's wings, millisecond by millisecond, examine them filament by filament, scrutinize the fragile membranes drawn over the delicate veiny structures. He could study something so thoroughly that if you gave him piles of crude elemental materials and miraculously precise instruments, he might from memory reconstruct that bumblebee, the sound of a pretty girl's giggle, or the smell of a withering lily about to shed its petals.

Inverse to his thorough knowledge of exteriors was his ignorance of interiors. He was aloof, untouchable, his childlike eyes constantly searching for new stimuli. He was completely deficient in romanticism and had almost no imagination. He generally understood emotions only insofar as they were reflexes, reactions, effects of sometimes discernible causes.

The affections he withheld from others, he never lavished on himself, though. He was impeccably polite, not from self-consciousness, the underbelly of egotism, but just so. He spoke freely to whomever he met without ulterior motive or guile, stating the truth completely and clearly just for its own sake. His power over people was tremendous.

The other boys, obsessed with determining who ran the fastest, tackled the hardest, cursed the loudest, spat the farthest, or pissed the most, were circumspect, even a little afraid of him. They recoiled at how effortlessly and lazily he excelled at physical activity, as if it were second nature, sullenly debated whether or not he was mocking them, and seemed to make some kind of compact to steer clear of him, thereby depriving him of male camaraderie.

As he grew up, girls became his main interest, and most of them prized and coveted his attention. Young women, preoccupied with nonsensical ideals of masculine sensitivity amidst the melodrama of abrupt maturation and surging hormones, quaked before his unaffected ease and directness. He told me about the first girl he had sex with—rather, who was bold enough to offer herself to him—Joanna, one of the few whose name he never forgot, the most desirable, although, as is usually the case, not the most attractive girl in school, a seventeen-year-old two years ahead of him and already being spoiled by the attentions of college boys. Despite having had no intention of courting her, he had won her over with a frivolous comment about her wardrobe, something like, "You're the best dresser among all the girls in school." He then added suggestions about what clothes best accentuated her hips, her breasts; how the length of a particular skirt revealed the shapeliness of her calves while still being modest; that she should avoid wearing jeans because they could make her look childish and less feminine; which hairstyle best complemented the steep angle of her jawline, her high cheekbones, her slightly bulbous nose, and her full lips. If you attend to such specific details of a woman's form, to many of them, it's as if you're caressing them. You've certainly been doing so with your eyes.

Such a waste of talent! Men like me spend most of our lives being caring and sensitive to the interior lives of women but are tragically blind to the colors that warm them and deaf to the tones that charm them.

He easily nurtured the young woman's vanity without her realizing it was vanity that was pulling her toward him. After she had taken off her clothes, and taken off his, doing her best to mimic the playful eroticism of a sexually mature, confident adult, he quietly remarked how the perfect placement and slightly large size of her areolae helped round out the shape of her pleasantly symmetrical and exaggerated breasts that swelled beneath her golden skin, and how they reminded him of two enormous drops of honey. He complimented the moderate amount of her soft, sandy-hued pubic hair and praised countless other details of her anatomy. This woman, wherever she is and whatever she looks like now, must still feel giddy remembering his meticulous private examination. Like most women in David's life, she must also have mistaken his frank, precise, and delicate utterances for the passionate poetic outpourings of a sensitive soul. To him, they were just data.

Without revealing everything about their intimacy, Joanna let slip what a delicate artist this young man was, which inflamed many other girls, including several devout nonconformists who ridiculed juvenile female behavior, to compete for his attention. Giggling, gossiping cliques of rivals shared their fantasies about him but were still ever ready to fight, insult, and malign for advantage. The hint of sweetness often attracts those that sting the worst. David wound up with a choice selection of other sexual encounters. He found most of this unremarkable other than that he was able to become acquainted with a variety of women's bodies.

He noticed the ones who ignored him, too. They were all the more fascinating for their unaffected indifference and preoccupations with things he couldn't see, smell, hear, touch, or taste. In late May of his final year, when old anxieties and injuries were being put to rest and new hopes and fears loomed, a girl named Becky, who was always listening to music, reading, or deliberately avoiding people, approached him in the hallway.

"I probably will never see you again, but I wanted to tell you that I've never seen anyone who looked as bored with people as you do. It's actually kind of amazing, man. I guess it's cool that you're sort of out there, daydreaming all the time. I don't think most people see that."

David screwed up his face in thought, something few people caused him to do, and replied, "Thanks. I'm not sure I daydream, but I think people probably don't understand me."

Daydreaming was definitely something he didn't do. Speculations? Hopes? Expectations? How could you not find the concrete reality of the present, the moment you were in, thoroughly engrossing? Why did this make him different, so noticeably different?

That could have been the end of the story, and David could have been another unambitious man stranded in suburbia claiming to have once been remarkable. However, a few months before graduation, serendipitously weeks after he turned eighteen, a lawyer contacted him to inform him that he was the sole heir of his paternal grandfather's estate. He left vehement instructions that his only child, David's father, should get absolutely nothing, and that his wealth should pass to his grandchildren, should any exist, and if they didn't, then to a young woman who had a window across the street from his apartment whom he probably had been spying on for years. It had taken the lawyer a year to track David down, during which time he had liberally deducted his fees. Nevertheless, David received a sum sufficient to apply toward his immediate future.

While David's parents devised ways to get the money, such as by charging him for his room and board, his literature teacher, Miss Something Common, Smith or Jones or something, found out about his good fortune and urged him to get away and go to college. Despite his apathy and generally poor grades, she had favored David and taken an avid interest in his development. She cited his exceptional ability to quickly complete perfect grammar assignments and his peculiar talent of instantaneously picking out the meter, the rhyme scheme, and the most subtle instances of alliteration, assonance, consonance, and other sound and word patterns in poetry, even free verse. When it came to reading comprehension and interpretation, explaining plots, settings, characterization, themes—the contrived elements literature teachers are taught to pester and ruin children's love of reading with—he was utterly hopeless. Not that his grade reflected his deficiencies, because she coaxed him into allowing her to tutor him after school and gave him plenty of extra credit assignments.

This was Miss Something's first year teaching and she wasn't much older than David. She was one of those typical young teachers who tried to relate to students by using their slang, humor, and references to popular culture, which his classmates loved but didn't do anything to help him appreciate the point of what he was being forced to learn. She had a small triangular face and tiny eyes, ears, mouth, and nose. She preferred old-fashioned floral print dresses, wore her auburn hair in a loose bun, and smiled all the time when she was in front of the class. However, during his tutoring sessions, he could smell the cigarettes she had sneaked off somewhere to smoke, and sometimes alcohol on her breath when she brought her lips unnecessarily close to his ear to explain something. She frequently shot bolts of lightning, gesticulating like an orchestra conductor, stomping, and slapping her desk while explaining a text. He liked it. Violence definitely suited her. She should have cut her hair short, never worn flowery dresses, avoided smiling, and certainly never been around children.

Miss Something helped him fill out his university application materials and write his essays, or rather, she did these things for him. She also drafted glowing recommendation letters and convinced several of his other teachers to do the same, and coached him on his college entrance exam. She surprised and perhaps thwarted herself with how successful her campaign had been, because he was accepted to a prominent university on the other side of the country. Nevertheless, she dutifully drove David to the airport and was the sole person to see him off.

"I'm so proud of us, David. We did it. Promise me you'll write to me often and tell me how you're doing. And don't forget to call me as soon as you get a phone line set up so we can talk. If you want to come visit, you can stay with me instead of your awful parents. Or I can visit you. Whatever you want," she said.

"OK," he replied.

She embraced him tightly and held him for what might have been a minute or two. He couldn't hug her back because he was holding two large suitcases. He never contacted her or saw her again.

David discovered that he continued to have an aptitude for language and linguistics. Their systems revealed themselves to him almost instantly. He set about knowing the nuances of tones, the shapes of sounds, accents, the incredible diversity of noises that the human mouth was capable of producing, the fluidity of syntax, the scope of morphology. How in totality, language was such a capacious medium that it should be able to describe every microscopic detail of the physical world. Of course, his laziness and ignorance of semantics limited his success in the discipline to merely average grades.

One day, he met a fierce and haughty woman, the type who indiscriminately rejected and reviled things, people, ideas, and places as a substitute for genuine insight. Eccentric in an extremely common way, with a personality that if present in a man would have been considered extremely boorish. She assumed control of David, defying and denying him, demonstrating ages of experience he was lacking, falsifying every position she presumed he would hold. A person so preoccupied with her opinions was in many ways a suitable complement to him. She relieved him of most decision-making responsibilities.

It began from their first meeting. "Excuse me. Your name is Lindsey, right? I've been wanting to tell you that I think you have really fantastic hair." Lindsey, Lindsey. I named her Lindsey. He called her, "something beginning with an *L*, I think. Libby? Linda? Lilith?" There was always something about hair, he admitted, that entangled him. Uncountable, unknowable numbers of strands, individually free and chaotic, but together conforming to some kind of ordered system of shape, movement, light, and color.

I NODDED ENTHUSIASTICALLY, and interjected, "The Greeks believed there were precise mathematical principles for the perfect placement and proportions in the human face and figure. But no matter how flawless a person might be, hair, ranging freely and organically as life should, always makes a difference."

He responded, "Hair moves after you do, like an echo. All your movements last just a second longer, like where you've just been has been briefly traced in the air. It's an interesting effect," he said.

THIS LINDSEY, however, was congenitally incapable of accepting compliments or kind words. "Who do you think is in charge here?" she responded slightly scornfully and pointed to her absolutely magnificent mane. "If I let it go, it turns into a fuzzy bird's nest. Every day, I have to spend tons of time dealing with it. It will probably add up to years wasted, lost forever from my life, like dying younger than I should. It's a parasite. I would be better off cutting it all off, shaving my head bald."

These responses were standard form and didn't present obstacles to their dating. David was unflappable and said whatever he felt like saying. He continued to politely observe and analyze the physical world, and Lindsey continued to abruptly deconstruct it and note its deficiencies. When he pointed out that he liked how the trees were dispersed along a hillside in a park, how the shape and colors of their collective mass mutated with the position of the sun and the strength and direction of the wind, she challenged him. They weren't real nature. They filled in gaps where people let them, and otherwise were hacked out of the way. Even entire forests had been engineered by people. If he called her attention to some bird, or hare, or butterfly, or spider, she challenged him. Weren't mild little animals like that the worst conspirators in the artificiality propagated by humanity? Somewhere there were wild, untamable beasts who were a threat to and threatened by people. These others were nothing more than glorified pets.

All the other natural and artificial features of modern life were similarly abused. Ground under her heel with wicked, unrestrained satisfaction. Clothing? Your natural self is hidden underneath, and it's either beautiful or it's not. Why is nudity considered profane? The real perversion is all this clothing, designed to reshape and lie about our bodies. She, of course, joylessly endured the expensive, fashionable clothes, the makeup, and the jewelry she was obliged to wear. Food? It was supposed to be utilitarian, not entertainment, but people had been brainwashed or bred, probably during the Industrial Revolution, to have overly sensitive taste buds. Not that this stopped her from agonizing over the preparation of their meals and which restaurants they should dine at.

David never learned what Lindsey's preconceptions actually were, only that nothing met them. So confident were her condemnations that he began to wonder if there was an objective reality that he was deficient in perceiving. Maybe her insights were due to a unique gift.

David learned that Lindsey had left behind a wasteland full of men worn down by her skepticism, infected with anxiety and doubt over opinions they had once believed to be sound but that had been revealed by her to have been hopelessly idiotic. She blamed her past relationship failures on their being intimidated by her confidence and intellect. David's not having philosophical insights insulated him from these psychological shock waves, and, in fact, he was relieved not to be trusted with anything important. However, he himself was never a target of Lindsey's complaints, and she expressed a genuine affection for him. They never fought or harmed each other. Although neither of them was in the thralls of infatuation, they had sex often and vigorously and enjoyed the rush of hormones and endorphins and the postcoital feeling of refreshment, as they would from any strenuous physical activity, like a brisk run. Their shared intimate life was adequate, perhaps more satisfying than was typical.

Lindsey justified moving them in together after graduation as a simple logical progression. An appliance company that was frequently in contact with the linguistics faculty offered David a job writing user instructions. He was an unambitious, mediocre student, so he was a perfect fit. The wording needed to be clear and natural-sounding, but also easily translatable into several other languages. He was satisfied with the thoughtful, monotonous work. After several months of letting him support her, Lindsey found a job at a local cultural affairs magazine that covered a mix of arts and entertainment, celebrity news, community interest stories, gossip, and sometimes a little sports or science as long as it could support some social commentary. Often all these themes showed up in the same article. A magazine written and read by people with strong opinions about everything.

A year later, an expensive diamond ring appeared on her finger. Since she controlled their finances, it didn't matter that she had bought it for herself, after she had apparently proposed to herself on his behalf, and accepted. More bafflingly, a few months later, he found himself standing at the front of a church reciting wedding vows.

When it was time to set up a permanent household, Lindsey contradicted her own opinions even more. Their wedding registry defied all reason. Carpets, curtains, coffee cups, teacups, sugar bowls, salt and pepper shakers, knives, forks, spoons, pots, pans, plates, bowls, serving utensils, juice glasses, wineglasses, water glasses, cordial glasses, martini glasses, champagne glasses, shot glasses, highballs, lowballs, cutting boards, towels, sheets, comforters, pillows, and vases. In particular, she adored the small appliances—the blender, the mixer, the toaster, the coffeemaker, the coffee grinder, the electric waffle iron, the food processor, the pressure cooker, the juicer, the deep fryer, and the bread machine. Cleverly elaborate ways to fulfill your basic survival needs.

Although Lindsey herself was responsible for their accumulation of consumer goods, she still maintained that their hoard was the symptom of their victimization by potent forces stronger than themselves, that their gluttonous materialism was a sociological conspiracy that an individual was powerless to escape, like traffic, tipping, or televisions in waiting areas. To distance herself from the mob of soulless consumers that she belonged to but so abhorred, she took extraordinary pains to ensure that every household item, article of clothing, morsel of food, cleaning product, and service they used was somehow special, not selected from the overabundance of generic products, and contained an embedded signal of her passive participation in a passive rebellion.

Prominently displayed on the sideboard in their dining room was one particular item that fomented her greatest fury, a silver-plated ice bucket, the only wedding gift from David's parents.

"I can't conceive of a more useless or thoughtless gift. It's worse than a toilet seat cover or a tea cozy, which make an ironic joke of their uselessness. But this, this shiny metal thing pretends to have a purpose. Look at it. It has to, doesn't it? It argues for it. It doesn't let you deny it. Why would anyone waste their time designing, producing, marketing, and selling something so well-made if it was completely worthless and disposable? If you were in a panic to save whatever you could because the building was burning down, who wouldn't at least pause and consider this stupid little thing, and regret leaving it behind?"

Hadn't she put this exact item on the wedding gift registry? David liked the design. Curling, lacy vines spiraled up its circumference from its base and burst into glistening silver flowers below its rim, and the entire vessel itself was shaped like a buttercup. Thicker but still delicate vines were soldered on as handles. No, you didn't absolutely have to have such a thing to serve ice or keep a bottle of wine cold. But why not? What was the harm?

David usually didn't express a strong opinion about Lindsey's outrages, but when she found herself wrapped up in the unsolvable paradox of purchasing a new cell phone that was both cutting edge and socially responsible, he surprised the both of them by lecturing her that it probably didn't matter. As long as people refused to reduce how much they consumed, they were merely shifting resources around in the same general places where they had been cut off from more productive uses, like scientific research, medical care, education, mental health, or relief for poverty, famine, drought, and wars. As it was, you had to hope for the wealthy people to share a little bit from their stockpiles. That was like relying on a bucket-brigade with leaky buckets to move water from some distant reservoir to put out a fire. Even when money was available, the amount spilled and lost along the way was equal to the economies of several small countries. It was a matter-of-fact observation, nothing more, but it silenced her on the topic of consumerism and ended the ongoing series of monologues performed for David's benefit.

Three months after their fourth wedding anniversary, David came home from work and found their belongings piled in and around the dumpster. Passersby and neighbors had already looted the best appliances, knickknacks, and small furniture. Their expensive luggage and all of Lindsey's clothes and cosmetics were also gone. His clothes were heaped on the ground, thankfully not stuffed into the trash, and in the middle of one of these piles, carefully wrapped in several of his T-shirts, was the silver-plated ice bucket. He packed his toiletries and as many clothes as he could into the same two large old suitcases he had left his parents' home with and hid them behind the dumpster. He slipped off his wedding ring, put it into his pocket, tucked the ice bucket under his arm, walked to their parking space, and wasn't surprised to find it empty. He then walked to their bank's ATM to withdraw some cash. The screen indicated that their account was deeply overdrawn, and the machine dutifully swallowed his card.

He found out later, when the tax and bill collectors tracked him down, that Lindsey had stopped paying the rent, maxed out all of their credit cards, withdrawn all the money from their bank account, sold their car for cash, and left without a trace.

Their apartment had been on the fringe of an up-and-coming neighborhood, walkable to all sorts of trendy new places, but the old decrepit ones, takeout restaurants, convenience stores, run-down houses, liquor stores, and pawnshops were a few blocks away. A continual irritation for her, that the waves of fashion and progress lapped at their shores but hadn't yet washed over them. They couldn't afford to move anywhere else. He walked to the nearest pawn shop and received for his wedding ring and the ice bucket only enough money to cover two or three nights of cheap lodging.

David returned to the apartment building to find that there had been no miraculous change to the situation. He retrieved his suitcases and headed to a nearby hotel, one of those with a veneer of elegance, designed specifically with the midlevel business traveler in mind. It was as if the executives who journeyed stylishly and comfortably conspired with the hotel chains to develop an experience just tolerable enough so that their underlings wouldn't dwell on the personal inconveniences and disruptions caused by continually being on the road or complain about the unrealistically optimistic expectations for such endeavors, but just intolerable enough to remind them exactly where they were situated in the corporate hierarchy, either to motivate them to redouble their efforts, or make way for someone who would. He brought his suitcase to the front desk attendant and claimed that he had checked out earlier, only to have annoyingly had his flight canceled, and wanted to stow his bags while he killed some time in the lounge. Earnestness and a charming smile also got him a drink voucher.

3

The hotel lounge was sparsely occupied by businesspeople in smart, conservative professional attire with predictable dashes of flair—glimpses of handkerchiefs, blouses, and neckties a little bit daring in color but still safely below ostentation. Most looked a bit stale and wilted from hours of practicing persuasion and days of wandering and drank harder and more than they usually would because, although they would have liked nothing better than to retire to their rooms to rest, hide, do whatever it was they did for relaxation, they were too afraid to confront the silence and loneliness of their strange temporary homes. A few individual packs fraternized politely with not-altogether-feigned laughter. A feast for the insatiable sarcasm of whatever-her-name-was. David tried to imagine something she might say, but he couldn't quite remember what her voice sounded like.

David himself, after a day's work and having had his life fall apart, still looked fresh and alert in his expertly tailored olive-green suit, red Oxford shirt, and burgundy belt and shoes. Overdressed for his occupation, but nobody complained. He wandered through the lounge, unconventionally attracting attention. The responses he elicited were at first reflexive. Something special was happening, and roaming eyes would fixate on him without quite processing what they were seeing. He stimulated no psychological response, no desire, no envy or scorn. Just an indefinite, irresistible curiosity that ceased as soon as he passed from view.

At the bar counter, farthest away from people, a petite woman reposed in either total self-absorption or total lassitude. Her profile was all smooth planes and angles, and her sable hair sprang from her head in long wavy tendrils that flowed back away from her chestnut-toned face, as if the moment of walking into a steady breeze had been frozen. David sat next to her and ordered water. She cradled a glass of wine in one hand and chipped at the nail polish on the thumb of her other hand with her index finger.

"Anything to report?" he asked.

She rolled her eyes and minimally tilted her head toward his voice, scanned the face in her periphery, gave a feeble smile that might be a frown, then looked back at the nothing that was just a place to point her eyes.

He continued, "People waste their evenings. They treat them like they're in a waiting room and fill them with light distractions until it's time to sleep. Even nights out eating, drinking, watching movies, listening to music, dancing, or whatever, are just killing time. The evening hours could be for stillness and examination. The museums should stay open later. Right now, I feel awake and alert."

She responded to blank space, "You're wrong, you know. Nobody examines anything, or thinks about anything. They just want to survive, do enough to check that their self-awareness is still functioning and they aren't just existing, and then be lulled to sleep. Then the things that disturb them, the voices that expose the lies they've told themselves, can be muzzled."

She turned her head to look directly into David's eyes. "I think that's the biggest misconception about artists, thinkers, achievers, innovators, disruptors, or anyone they call exceptional—not that they're visionaries, misunderstood, subversive, chaotic, or rebellious. Everyone understands and can relate to them perfectly but hates them for telling the truth. If people stimulated their brains, like, spending their evenings looking at pictures in a gallery and thinking about what they mean, they wouldn't sleep well that night, or any of the other ones."

"I don't know much about art, but I can appreciate technique—you know, the composition, colors, perspectives, and the materials they use. I'm not an expert about any of it, but I like to look at things like the layers and textures of an oil painting, or the contours of a sculpture and all the little marks left by the sculptor's tools," he said.

"Maybe you've never lied to yourself, so there's no hidden truth you're avoiding. But it sounds like you already look at things deeper than most. Did you know I had a connection to this? How could you? I guess you've gotten incredibly lucky in your choice of pickup material." She had put down her glass and come out of herself.

"It's what came to mind when I saw you," he said. "You don't look like you would be traveling around selling, auditing, advising stuff, or whatever these people do."

"Hmm, I've never been that easy to read," she said. "Or at least that's what people tell me. Maybe they're just bad at it."

"Oh, I didn't read anything about you. Just what you're not, not like them. You could be a million other things, but not them," he said and smiled.

She leaned closer to David, exhaling breath redolent of herself and the wine she was drinking, and continued, "Do you know what I do? I'm the donor relations VP for a large charitable trust that funds museums, galleries, and artists. We like to dole out grant money to the souls who can only create when they're suffering and penniless, and then, when they begin to taste success, cut them off and starve them again to keep the cycle going. I go around begging on their behalf from people who have enough money to spare for vanity causes and people who really don't but think that philanthropy elevates their social status. I know I'm too cynical about this. They don't understand most of what they throw their money at, but I suspect they know that this is how to subjugate these artists who generally ridicule and despise them. That's the point of all this patronage for the arts, as far as I'm concerned. People who have reached the limit of being able to step on and beat people down start using the carrot. But I like what I do, and I'll never do anything else. It's all I've ever done. I'm one of those sick people who are charmed by irony. Oh, look, you've got me spilling all sorts of secrets about myself."

"That actually sounds nice," he replied, and she chuckled. "My name is David, and I don't do anything. That's not an exaggeration." He lied effortlessly. "I used to travel to get grocery stores to stock my company's organic baked goods, like cookies, cakes, or bread. Our owner was bleeding the company dry, cheating on taxes and whatnot. He went missing today, and all the accounts are frozen. They even canceled my plane ticket back home to get a refund on the fare, and obviously the hotel's not going to let me stay."

"Why not just suck it up and pay your own way?" she asked.

"I don't have any money in the bank, and my paycheck is probably never coming," he replied.

"I presume no friends or relatives who can help, either," she said.

"No. Nobody," he said.

"Tsk, tsk. Sounds like *unbelievably* bad luck." She bit the side of her bottom lip.

David said, "What's your name? Wait. Do you ever bite your

lip like that, unbutton another button of your blouse, and lean forward to get someone to write a bigger check?"

"You have a dirty imagination. Absolutely not," she said. "I'm not some hustler. I know my business. I was obsessed with art, but I have no talent, so I settled for art history, and then studied management to have a way to earn a living. It worked out, because here I am. Genius is rare, and it's a privilege, a thrill, to search for it and nurture it. But it's all for the sake of art. Money and people don't matter. You see how honest I am about the whole thing? Probably shortchanging everyone in the process. My name is Diane."

I named her Diane. He called her, "some classical name with a *B* or a *G* or a *D* or something."

Savage yet soft intelligence replaced the tones of whimsy and cynicism in Diane's eyes, mouth, and posture. She said, "There are many ways to apprehend and describe the world. People think all these diverse perspectives compete, but they don't, and they all deserve to be witnessed and expressed. Think about something like a blood-orange sunset. A poet's brain might start uncontrollably firing off all sorts of metaphors. A painter might consider the use of color and texture that captures how that weird light plays over the land-scape. A scientist might just think about the pollution that causes it. Some enraged driver fighting his way home might relax a little. Maybe a couple on some kind of romantic getaway finds that the beauty of the moment permanently brands the trip into their memories and colors all of their impressions of it. A little girl might look up at it and suddenly want to hug her mom or dad because her heart was overcome with the loveli-ness or awfulness of it. Some grimy factory worker gossiping with his girl and their friends over cheap beers might just shut up for a second, sigh, and take a long, slow drink. Everyone gets something out of it, except assholes like this"—she waved her hand around the bar—"who bury themselves in darkness so moments like that don't outshine whatever stupid shit they're talking about."

"It sounds like you've thought about this a lot," he said.

Diane took a deep draft of wine, seeming to see that sunset in her mind. "I'm sorry. Did it come across like I was scolding? Well, whatever. You get the point—one thing, and a million unique experiences of it. All valid."

"I guess that's why people write you checks," David said.

"Maybe. I don't make it seem like their lives are deficient because they don't think and act like some painter or sculptor. It's just things they don't see because they're standing in a different spot. But some of these fucking artists, they spend so much energy bragging about their specialness or superiority. I'm not interested in some publicly or self-proclaimed guru. That's what antagonizes the rest of the world. People used to live in a world of art and imagination. It literally surrounded them and followed them wherever they went. And the creative people mingled with everyone else, drinking cheap wine with their neighbors, the farmers, laborers, craftsmen, and the like, because they were all the same, just creative in different ways. Now there's a gap between these worlds, with the so-called creative class congregating in its own exclusive spaces, and it's getting bigger. But they made it themselves, and then complain that they're fucking poor, starving, and underappreciated, that people aren't smart enough, too smart, too spiritual, not spiritual enough, that the world needs them, really owes them and would die without the beauty they add to it. I shouldn't generalize, but there are a lot of them with entitled attitudes. But I keep these thoughts to myself because I'm more worried about art being driven out of existence altogether. So let all these painters and sculptors have their delusions. As long as the money I get for them makes them produce." She finished off the half glass of wine that remained and wiped her mouth with the back of her hand.

"This is why I often end up sitting alone. I don't care about what any of these people have to say and don't expect any of them to have the energy to follow my ramblings. I probably sound as conceited as the people I complain about. And now I'm wearing out and abusing the first stranger to sit down and talk to me in a long time," she said and frowned. "Were you any good at your job selling sweets?" She giggled.

"I don't know. I didn't try very hard," he said.

"I would guess that, and it doesn't even sound cavalier when you say it. I don't suppose *you* would have to do much to sell anything. That just seems like something you're born with. The rest of us have to work at it because it's obvious that we're always lying. Although I would imagine that even when people know you're lying, they still don't give a damn."

"Honestly, I'm not sure anyone cares about anything I have to say," David said. "I only sat here because you looked interesting. You carefully manage your appearance. You've chosen that style of blouse because the neckline plunges just enough to make any man in this room wonder about loosening one, or two, or all of those pretty little pearly buttons, but there's nothing at all revealing about how you wear it. It complements your nice long neck, and it's loose and tight enough to suggest but not reveal your figure. But sitting near you, I can see this little area of your body you've chosen to share, that breathes your scent we imagine is stronger the deeper down we plunge. All the while, you can still smell your shampoo, a bit flowery and childish, and the baby-powder smell of your deodorant, which is kind of old-fashioned," he said.

"Ha!" She chortled. "How many innocent young girls have fallen for that? I'm not so young and not so inn . . . maybe still innocent, as far as you're concerned. I would normally call something like that ridiculous, but there's nothing ridiculous about you, is there? Say it again like you mean it, and I might believe you," she said. "Oh my, don't we sound witty now?"

David stared at her and blinked.

"I'm sorry, I'm mean because I'm a little tired. Maybe you only meant to say something nice. It was nice, if maybe a bit too intimate. No, that's not fair. People should be more intimate. I miss having grown out of it. You know, when we were little kids, we said anything to each other, like spectacularly nice and personal things," she said.

The bartender came to collect her glass. "Another, please."

"I have this drink coupon," David said. "Could you order something for me?"

"The same for him," she said.

The bartender set out a second glass for David and filled them both.

She raised her glass and said, "Santé."

He raised his and nodded.

"So shall I try now? To tell you something intimate?" she asked.

"If you want," he replied.

"Hmm, you—that's . . . forget it. What did I want to say? Something ferociously honest. I assumed you sat down here because you figured we would talk a bit and then go sleep together. I always assume that. Maybe I think all polished, good-looking guys like you look at women like we're all a little slutty. Oh, and I do that, have done that, I mean let myself get picked up. That's a stupid way to put it. It's a mutual pickup, the only difference being that I've never been the one who sat down and started it. Go sit over there," she laughed and gestured to the other end of the bar, "and wait and see if I come over to you. You might be the first. I don't have a good, like, psychological reason for it. It's all overanalyzed, this whole idea about women's psychology and blah, blah, blah. I'm just lazy, risk-averse, and not very clever. Anyway, I'm in the wrong place . . . wait, this isn't all just me blathering about myself, I promise . . . always the wrong place for something innocent.

There's this seedy feeling sometimes, sometimes all the time, and it's not because you're doing anything wrong but because you're someplace where everyone's guilty—you know, everyone's manipulative and scheming. But you can fuck, even madly and wildly, like innocents. I know what I'm talking about."

Diane poked David in the chest. "You look kind of lost. One time, a little lost boy came up to me in the library, a precocious boy, and just started talking to me. He didn't even know he was lost. I guess it didn't dawn on him. What was he talking about again? How he'd already read a bunch of stuff in the adult book section and how he thought I was like some young lady in an Agatha Christie novel. Speaking of lost innocence, you know about her, right?"

David shook his head.

"Oh, never mind that. Then his frantic mom comes running up and shouting at him, looking at me like she can't decide if she should thank me or accuse me. I don't know why, but you remind me of that didn't-know-he-was-lost boy. There's no frantic woman looking all over the place for you, is there?" she said.

David listened . . . this time just letting listening occupy his mind and ignoring his other senses. He liked her words, the raw rhythm of her language.

She was waiting. The only thing he could think of saying, because saying something seemed obligatory, was, "I don't have any idea what you're talking about."

"Exactly!" Diane exclaimed. She pressed the palm of her right hand into David's chest, just above his heart, and with her other hand seized his. "This talking is so much work. Why are you making me work for this? You, the man, are supposed to be doing all the work. Come on now, I'm tired and lazy."

"It's only six thirty," he said.

"I was planning to go to my room and read," she said. "Not

the worst way to throw away an evening. And what are your ideas?"

"I don't know. I'm not much of a planner. Today's the first day that's ever really been a problem," he said.

"Let's just finish these and go upstairs," she said.

"Do you mind if I grab my things, or are you going to kick me out later?" he asked.

She breathed deeply and smiled. "Maybe, maybe not. How about I say 'probably'?"

Standing, moving, and then leaving that dim lounge weakened the gravity that had been pulling them together. They kept a cordial distance during the short elevator ride to her floor.

David followed Diane into her room. She crouched, unfastened her ankle straps, took off her shoes, and placed them in the closet near the door, where neatly pressed suit jackets, skirts, and blouses were hung orderly. As soon as he stepped out of his loafers, she snatched them and set them next to her shoes. He chucked his bags into the corner by the door.

"Give me your jacket," she said and giggled. "I'm not trying to undress you."

He took it off and handed it to her. She pushed aside her clothes to create a gap, smoothed it, and hung it.

He felt a sense of relief. Odd, because it hadn't been preceded by any anxiety.

"Are you hungry?" she asked. "I didn't have time to eat today. It's really annoying. Nothing I do is so important that I should have to miss doing basic things to take care of myself."

"I actually forgot to eat. I do that all the time," he said.

"We can get something delivered. Or room service, but it looks like overpriced crap," she said.

"I can order some Chinese food," he said.

"Maybe I have more sophisticated tastes," she said.

"You probably do, but it's the only thing I can afford that's not fast food," he said.

"OK, I'm in your hands. I hope you don't mind, but I'm going to get comfortable," she said and darted into the bathroom.

He looked in the phone book for the place he liked. He didn't have an opinion about the food, but they had a huge salt-water aquarium that formed the top half of one wall of the dining room. Many evenings he disappeared there by himself to watch the aquatic life.

"What do you like?" he shouted to be heard over running water.

"Whatever," Diane called back. "Since you can figure out so much about me, let's see how well you do with food."

He phoned the restaurant and ordered randomly.

She came out wearing black gym shorts and a baggy white sweatshirt.

"I hope I don't look scary without my makeup," Diane said. "Jesus, that's a cliché. Let me rephrase. I hope I look better without it."

"It is better, actually. But you don't wear much anyway," he said.

"Just a few enhancements, and I don't even know why I do that," she said.

"So those long, thick eyelashes are natural? That's spectacular!" he said.

Diane replied, "Yep. They make me look permanently like a bright-eyed baby doll." She opened her eyes wide and puckered her lips.

"Oh, and apropos of not wasting the evening, have a look at these." She opened the large portfolio case that was leaning against the dresser and started dealing prints out onto the bed.

"What do you think?" she asked.

There were paintings, drawings, and photographs of sculptures and some full-sized installations. David took his time leafing through them and pulled out prints of six paintings.

"I like that they capture moments," he said.

"Hmm, that's interesting. Two of those confuse people the most. That particular painter suffers because she offers no points of reference or clues about how to approach her work," Diane said.

"What do you mean?" David asked.

"There's a conspiracy of understanding in art. Like language, or any way people communicate. That's all art really is, communication. There has to be an entrance, a path to a work. Otherwise, it's too alien. That's why when we're surrounded by all this supposed creativity, everything still feels familiar, even a little boring. They're only picking apart and recombining elements, maybe dropping and adding a few. But the core is still recognizable. When that leads to some new and unique arrangement, the money really flows. It makes people feel special, like they're the first to learn a secret, and they'll pay for that feeling.

"The problem is that money and the egos of the audience cause art to overemphasize novelty. Artists should operate on two axes, inspiration and technique. You might be able to get away with being less original if your technique is impeccable. And technique can slip a bit—not too much—if you're inspired to produce absolutely new and original things, or at least new combinations. That's why it's still important to demand virtuosity from artists. Otherwise we'll be drowning in creative crap. We already are. The rarest one is someone I'm afraid I'll never find, a person inspired from beyond normal senses and perception and who's also technically perfect."

"So she isn't it?" he asked and pointed to the two prints.

"I have to confess, I don't know. Like I said, she doesn't let you into her work, and she's stubborn. She says she writes visual poems, sight poems. Nobody has figured out what that means yet. She won't even cheat by naming her works. This one's 'six' and that one's 'seven.' She thinks she's been put on earth to test us and weed out the unworthy. It could all be nonsense, though. The colors and tones are appealing, and that's enough for some, but her paintings aren't meant to be purely abstract. It's unsettling to most people that they can't see what she's showing them. People with money don't like to be made to feel stupid," Diane said.

"A swirling mass of a human life from conception to death. You might think she's smudged and blurred it all together, but she's actually carefully built up translucent layers. It's hard to tell from this flat print, but it looks like you could peel them off individually and work your way backwards through the painting. That would be something, right, if she's writing sight poems. With a painting, maybe each image is like a word, and you only have one page, so how do you put all the images of a poem on it? Maybe you can think of it like laying frames of a film on top of each other. That might literally be what she's done. She's taken such a delicate touch to the layers that it looks like you could shine light through the back of them. And wow, if you did and used the layers as filters, like how a film projector works, you would see something a little different. It's tricky to imagine peeling apart the painting, think about the properties of light, and see what the other colors would be. It's two paintings," he said.

"What do you mean by 'other colors'?" Diane asked.

"Paint absorbs light when it reflects it back to you, and the color you see is the light that wasn't taken away. As you mix colors, you take away more light, and when you mix enough of them, you've taken all the light away and get black. When light shines through something, you're adding colors. The only way to get black is to turn off the light, and the colors you get by mixing light can be different than what you get by mixing paint. If you mix all the colors of light, you get white," he said.

"What did you say you did for a living?" Diane asked.

"I liked to sit by the windows in school. There was always something taped to them that tinted the sunlight. I would look down at my desk or my book, or stick my hand into the light and notice something strange happening with the colors. I looked it up. You never noticed that?" he said.

"No," she replied.

"Look at the different regions of the painting and imagine them being different colors. First of all, black and white just get flipped around. See this green swirling area in the middle? Imagine that's also white. These browner areas would be yellow. Many of them are the same, like the orange, the red, and the blue parts. What do you see so far?" David said.

"A white-hot fireball?" Diane replied.

"I'm not sure. I would have to spend a lot more time with the real thing," he said.

"No kidding," she said.

"I can't even look at it anymore," he said.

"What about this other one?" she asked.

"I'm not even close. It reminds me of what happens when you stare at a bright light for a while and then close your eyes," he said.

"That would be too cute," she said.

They discussed the other prints he had picked until the food arrived. Then they sat on the bed and ate while Diane showed him some of the ones he hadn't selected. She mentioned which artists had made big sales recently, although none of their works were in David's pile.

After they finished their food, Diane declared, "I think that's enough of that," and carefully re-sorted the prints and put them back in the portfolio case. David threw away the food containers. They stood and looked at each other. A blank new moment lay before them.

Diane sat on the bed and patted the spot next to her to

encourage him to join her. He did, and she slid closer to him, wrapped her arms around his torso, and pulled him down to lie with her. She removed her sweatshirt and shorts, leaving her in nothing but her panties. She hummed and bobbed her head in time, like you might have done while spending a slow, relaxing time at any light manual task, like cooking or arranging flowers, and removed his shirt, got up, and hung it in the closet. David stared at the ceiling and listened to her music. She returned and unfastened and removed his belt, unbuttoned and unzipped his pants, gently tugged and slid them off him, folded them neatly in half, and hung them. Still humming and bobbing, she took off his socks, T-shirt, and underwear, removed her panties, folded his and her own clothes, and put them all away in a dresser drawer.

Diane turned off the light, lay next to him and clasped his hand. They were silent, letting their naked bodies absorb the interior darkness, the blue-gray dusky haze that seeped in through the window, the sounds of their steady breaths, and each other's warmth.

"We should get under the covers. Hotel comforters are filthy," she whispered.

They got up, she pulled back the blankets, and they lay down again. Diane squeezed his hand and rolled onto her side toward him. She hummed faster and louder as she felt everywhere on his body with her fingertips, working her way down from his hair, brow, eyes, ears, nose, lips, chin, armpits, navel, tracing the lines of flesh and bone all the way down to his toes. She saved his cock for last and stroked it gently to help it become hard.

She mouthed some words he couldn't make out.

"What?" he asked.

"Do you have a thingy, you know, a condom?" she asked.

"Hold on. I should in the little valet bag in one of my suitcases," he said.

"Which one?"

"I don't remember."

"Stay there," she said. She went to rummage through his suitcases, then returned and placed a Mylar condom package on the nightstand.

They wrapped their arms around each other and kissed. She kissed him in a way he had never experienced before. Soft and deep, like their mouths were melting into each other.

David pulled away and nuzzled the soft spot just below Diane's ear.

"Nobody has ever kissed me like that," he said.

"I don't believe you. But I've never kissed anyone like that before," she said.

"Really?" he asked.

"No, not really," she said.

The impressions he gathered through his skin, nose, eyes, ears, and tongue told him more about her than a week of conversation would. Tender, sentimental, vigorous, and strong. Full of youthful passion and energy that had been smoothed and refined. She couldn't have been more than a few years older than him.

She guided his hand to her clitoris, and he rubbed it gently as they kissed and clutched each other more firmly. When he felt that her labia had swelled, she moaned softly and whispered, "Ready?"

David heard the crinkle of the wrapper as she tore it open, and he felt her slide the condom onto him. Diane climbed on top of him, put his cock inside her, and then pressed her body down hard. She made slow, small circles with her pelvis. Her movements were measured and patient. He grabbed her hips and pushed and pulled to accentuate the intensity that was building. As her skin warmed and sweated, the baby-powder scent rained down on him. She gasped, whimpered, and then slid herself up and down to better stimulate him with her contracting vagina. He ejaculated very quickly then. As soon as Diane felt him twitch, she fell on top of him and kissed his mouth hard until his body fully relaxed.

She whispered, "You taste and smell like nothing. Nothing. Did you know that? Maybe I'll claim you. Mark you with my own taste and smell."

With a peculiar indifference to David's past, Diane bought him a plane ticket the next day and took him home with her. It wasn't much of a risk because she was in total control. Whenever she wanted, she could change her mind and let him go as casually as she had acquired him.

Diane made David feel . . . something. It wasn't what she added, but maybe what she subtracted. What was missing was the layer of chatter and distraction that obscured an identity, drew a veil between a person and the world. He encountered no interference or resistance when he reached out and probed for her, and he found something substantial and genuine. Nevertheless, he could never claim he understood her because she, like all the others, was an emotional and psychological mystery to him, but that was a result of his own deficiencies.

Although he hadn't asked her to, Diane gave him a job with no definite responsibilities other to man a secretary's desk and ostensibly help keep her organized, which she was already capable of doing without him.

She rationalized, apparently for her own benefit, "I would really just like your company, but I suppose I'll have to pay you. It would be unethical to pay my live-in lover too well, though. The culture at a nonprofit, especially one dealing with the arts, is a little more flexible with regard to nepotism. Personal connections bind everything together. It would cease to function if we had to be perfectly meritocratic. In the arts, even more so in the performing arts, as a matter of fact, you see husbands and wives, ex-husbands and ex-wives, partners, parents and children, and old friends working together all the time. But I'm still dealing with other people's money, and I don't want any complaints. Nobody is going to object to me paying you the bare minimum. And if I'm being perfectly honest, I would feel awkward having you hang around at home unemployed. There's just the principle of it. It should get you going until you decide what to do with yourself. Obviously, I don't need your money to live on, so you can keep all of it. I know you understand."

He remained the lowest-paid employee and never received a raise.

David also attended local events with Diane and, despite his ignorance, interacted well with donors. Cocktail receptions at galleries, cocktail receptions at museums, cocktail receptions at nightclubs, cocktail receptions at enormous penthouse apartments or suburban mansions of wealthy philanthropists. Men too old to envy him, past regretting their receding youth, reveled in the frank attention given by someone young and beautiful, and the old women were pleased to be proven wrong about the slovenliness of young men these days. The few relatively young and wealthy—and therefore scheming, competitive, and envious—also felt relaxed with him. His apparent poverty and stupidity meant he wasn't competition. Most of the artists despised him, though, and flaunted their contempt. Instinctual antipathy. Their gossip eventually came back to Diane, who related it to him.

"This Alexander, he's come out of nowhere and had great success lately. He's a perfectionist about little details, but he manages to keep a feeling of spur-of-the-moment freshness in his paintings. He's also a real shark. That strangely dressed couple from Toronto you met last week bought several of his works for more than the average person, never mind a painter, earns in years. Nice people, but naïve considering who they're dealing with. What can he complain about? He says something like you fill him with a sense of doom, that you can't help making everyone feel miserable, hollow, and hopeless. Apparently, you're 'oppressive,' whatever that's supposed to mean," she said.

Diane provided all of David's material needs, so he didn't need to spend any of his meager salary. He took care of the household errands, like dealing with the maid, the dry cleaning, and the laundry service, ordering groceries, and getting things repaired. These assignments required trivial effort, so he took up a keen, methodical interest in cooking and carefully studied and experimented with all combinations of her preferred tastes, smells, colors, and textures. He challenged himself to produce new dishes she would like.

Diane traveled often, but when she returned she would vividly describe to David the meetings, the parties, the people and corporations with money to spend, and the new and old artists, interjecting her witticisms about the intelligence, sanity, or talent of the people she had met. They would take their time browsing photos and lithographs. He always found it a pleasure to listen to her stories. When she was away, David went for long walks after sitting at his desk for the required eight hours or took advantage of the evening hours that some of the museums kept. If he had a weekend to himself, he often journeyed to the far side of the city, outside of the boundary of the megalopolis, where modest detached homes occupied by modest families predominated, to an odd museum founded ages ago by a club of hobbyist environmentalists and biologists. It had the largest insect collection he had ever seen, over half a million mounted specimens from everywhere on the planet. So many configurations of antennae, eyes, legs, wings, mandibles, and proboscises. He pondered the evolutionary reasons for such variety. Maybe it was like linguistics, in that individuals had formed groups around their own unique activities, environmental challenges, background noises they needed to make themselves heard over, and distances they needed to make themselves heard across. He recognized and learned the names of many of the hundreds he had found and studied in his childhood. His favorite was a beautiful tan-and-black mottled beetle that had terrified the other children. Wonders from the places he had lived and places he would never visit. It was a pity they were all dead. He would love to have watched how they wriggled, crawled, jumped, and flew.

Diane once told him that because she felt guilty leaving him alone and bored so much, she was thinking of getting him a cat, but she corrected herself, saying, "Actually, I wouldn't mind getting a cat, but you aren't the type of person who would need one. You're kind of a cat yourself. You just need the window to keep yourself entertained."

"Your view is terrible, though. What's the point of being on such a high floor and still having nothing to look at? If you do get one, I would have to take it for walks. And I would want to teach it tricks," he said.

"You what? You want to train a cat? Do you know how hard that is? Have you ever trained an animal? You've never even had a pet, have you?" she responded.

"It can't be that bad. I think you just have to pay really close attention to how it behaves and reacts and then kind of go along with it until you become part of its patterns without it realizing it, so it trusts you. Then you make little adjustments to its routines until it does what you want."

He lived this way with her for several years, but exactly how many was unknowable. The first year was distinct and the second was countable in relation to the first, but after that, his timekeeping broke down.

One evening after they had finished having sex, Diane began crying.

"It's time for you to go. I'm getting married," she said.

Her husband-to-be was a friend from college who had turned up a few months earlier with a large check for the foundation. Since then, they had frequently met in the city, and he had secretly accompanied her on several trips. He owned a relatively small but respected and prosperous architecture and civil engineering firm. His depressed alcoholic wife had crashed through a guardrail two years before and plummeted spectacularly to her death.

"You've even met him and seen us talking. I thought you would have noticed us," she said.

He shrugged.

"Anyway, it was obvious a long time ago that we should be together, but we were young idiots, and I guess thought our choices felt more important if we made them harder than they needed to be. I wasn't pining away for him, although he says he was for me. What kind of person would I have been to torture myself with a hopeless, impossible situation? There are enough lost causes already, right? I mean, he came to mind sometimes. Then all of a sudden, without my even daring to wish, he's mine."

David had no idea what to say, or if he was supposed to say anything. He certainly wasn't stunned or hurt. He felt like he was eavesdropping. The conversation wasn't about him. He didn't need to be there.

"But you—you," she stammered. Tears had been flowing, but she held them back now. "I shouldn't cry, because I'm not sad. Aren't you going to say anything?"

He was fixated on how drastically her appearance had changed lately, as if cleaving to another as an equal or more likely in a subservient role hadn't only psychologically but also physically reshaped her.

"No? I'm not surprised. Well, I don't feel guilty. Nope. I'm putting you back into this world a little better than I found you. You are unchanged, unchanging, unchangeable. I doubt there's a person alive who could have any real power over you."

He was wondering when this discussion would end. Its

purpose seemed to have been exhausted in the opening exchange, and it was devolving into nonsense he couldn't follow.

She paused for a bit and glared at her hands, as if to warn them to stop fidgeting. "Fuck, I didn't think any of this through ahead of time—I mean, what I'm saying to you—and I didn't think I would have to. None of this even matters to you, does it? You would let me do whatever I want. But that's what people do, rationalize their choices even when it really isn't anyone's business. So I'll keep going to check off all the boxes, OK? In case you have any questions.

"You know, you've never burdened me and you definitely added some light to my life. Light, lightness. Can I be honest? I think you ought to know the difference between you and normal people. You're a light, a big blinding bright white light, but people are weak and can't really handle that. They want darkness and color, and to play around mixing their darkness and colors with everyone else's just to see what they get. You're sort of above all this interaction and feedback. Why can't you give and receive? You're in some kind of lamina, where you can't touch or be touched. I think it's incredibly easy for you, to be up there, out there, in there, or wherever you are, and completely impossible for the rest of us. I didn't say any of this to hurt your feelings, and if it did, it would mean I'm completely wrong, which would make this whole conversation cruel and cause me to doubt myself. But I have a lot of faith in your unassailable aloofness. I'm not wrong, am I? Anyway, you should go tomorrow."

He furrowed his brow and grimaced as if in deep concentration. She gasped, thinking she had stung him, and must have felt her confidence waver.

"You know, Diane, if it's the guy I'm thinking of, you're really going to have to get him to buy all new clothes and start getting his hair cut differently, or you won't be able to be seen in public with him. Either that, or you'll have to get a new line of work," he said.

He had intended to lift her spirits, encourage her with this honest, witty gem. She wailed and sobbed. He left her alone in the bedroom. A cat would definitely be great now, he thought. She cried the entire night, and he slept on the couch.

FIRST DIGRESSION

I burst out laughing. His stony, earnest indifference was absurd. It had to be comic understatement. He laughed too.

I said, "When I was in high school, I spent a few days home sick, crying to stupid love songs because a girl I liked told me she liked someone else. Supposedly he was sensitive and I wasn't. I was exciting, interesting, and passionate—of course I was—and she was mistaking his good-natured stupidity for sensitivity. All the guys knew he was like a dopey, slobbery dog. The irony that the girl I was infatuated with would completely misinterpret my best qualities and see them in someone completely devoid of them irritated me until I went crazy. In hindsight, I was railing against fate that had had me fall in love with such a moron, and I was hoping to psychically rewrite her defective personality. But I was the problem. Give up on people! It should be easy, but we waste years fighting with ourselves not to. Life is an addiction. It screams itself hoarse for your attention. Insane old hermits went out into the desert and starved, beat themselves numb, and droned their prayers for hours to blot out the noise of it. But the noise is all on the inside, so no matter where you go, hundreds and thousands of miles away even, you take it with you."

He stopped smiling and slowly rubbed his bottom lip back and forth with his index finger, as if coaxing thoughtful, meaningful words from his mouth, and said instead, "I don't know what you mean."

"Your version of events seems unnatural. People don't just withdraw like that, without any protest," I said.

He reminded me of my grandmother, the one of her many personae that I had interacted with and understood, the one I had known before she had died when I was twelve. Her skin was pale, almost diaphanous, and I remember her in her little apartment, all of her curtains drawn wide and the sunlight streaming in, setting her aglow. Sitting and watching serenely with a little smirk, totally ignorant and oblivious to anything outside the reach of her senses, but in total command of everything in the tight radius of her existence. I'd always reckoned that it takes a lifetime to achieve this kind of composure. Perhaps decades of disillusionment or satiation, figuring out that everything could be categorized as things not worth knowing, things you already knew, and things you should know but would never have time to learn.

Across from me sat a man who presented himself as having no kind of psychological life like any of ours, like he was born detached. Watching us like we were fish swimming around in an aquarium. With someone like my grandmother, it felt fine, because she had earned it, and you knew that might be in your future, to be on the outside of the glass. With him, I only felt like a fish.

He continued staring at me silently.

"Why didn't you try to comfort her or explain that she had misunderstood you? Didn't you love, or at least like this woman?" I asked.

"Well . . . ," he said. "About this idea of hers that I was

unchanging. I had experiences. I aged. I learned things. I adapted to her life. You know, I learned to like cooking. I would like to have had a cat. When I look at you, that's when I see a person who resists change."

This wasn't a new accusation. I've had a lot of battles, many involving screaming and throwing things, on this very subject. I had a polished stock answer. "Is that what you think? You don't know a thing about me." I added, "You can't just go around sizing up strangers like that. Spouting your stupid opinions."

He cut me off. "It's not a criticism."

"I don't care one way or another," I said.

He ignored me and continued, "This idea of who's changing, who's evolving, is pointless. I wonder how many people have tortured themselves and everyone else over it. If you focus on a spot in the distance when you're moving, you can't tell what's moving. And if you look at something moving along with you, it looks like you're sitting still. Like these artists she knew. They were always jumping from one thing to the next, but along with each other and everyone else, so in fact they were always relatively in the same place. The risk was if you were the one who moved first, and you always hoped to be followed and never wind up different and alone. But if I'm deliberately sitting still, and the world is going off in a different direction, then I'm changing with respect to it. My point is that Diane was just making excuses. She really wanted some kind of conformity. Looking at it that way completely nullified her complaint.

"I'd been used to listening to her stories and opinions. I trusted her judgment. She was a careful thinker but could also react quickly because she had amazing intuition about so many things, but I realized how ridiculous she had become. Maybe she had always been that way and hidden it, or I hadn't seen it. I thought I should start paying closer attention to people's personalities."

4

———

For years, David had saved all of his meager pay. He had had nothing better to do with his money, so he had taken an interest in investing. In this endeavor, his lack of ambition, goals, general knowledge, or optimism proved to be beneficial. He was able to ignore the prattle, wishful thinking, and gossip that dominated financial news and managed to double his savings, really a pittance to survive on, but a windfall in light of how little effort he had expended. In addition, Diane told him to take anything she wouldn't have bought if he hadn't been living there, which included many of the kitchen implements, decorations, and linens, thereby resetting her apartment more or less to the way it had looked the first night he had slept there, the chic minimalist apartment of a not-so-young-anymore businesswoman who traveled constantly and who was rarely at home even when she was in town.

For this being the first time in his life he had to take care of himself, and despite not having planned for it, David was exceptionally well set up. He had a mental list of several women and even a few men who had told him that he should never hesitate to contact them for anything, but he reckoned that doing so might lead him into an arrangement like the one he had just been spat out of, and that perhaps this wasn't an experience worth repeating. A hotel was out of the question because he didn't have a credit card—he had never bothered applying for one because he was certain his credit history was still a disaster —or any valid identification, just an expired driver's license.

The only definite idea David had was to find a place with a better view. He set out for a residential area situated on a small, rocky hill that looked down on the rest of the city. The terrain had been too irregular to be fully developed. The winding streets snaked among small and midrise buildings and open spaces of unusable land that had been allowed to remain rough and overgrown, little samples of forests. David liked to walk there because there was more air and light. He entered the first building he came across that had some windows that looked across the rooftops below.

"Who should I talk to about renting a place?" he asked the concierge.

The middle-aged woman who sat behind the front desk had been smiling as he approached but now grimaced to fore-shadow the bad news she was about to deliver. Before she could answer, a younger woman with a teenager's face standing next to her interjected, "I have time. Come on back."

She led him to a windowless office about the size of a pantry. David studied her for a moment. She had a long, rounded jawline and huge swollen cheeks and mouth. It looked as if she had a mouth guard pushing her jaw slightly open and making her lips bulge out. Her limp chocolate-brown hair had been trimmed to a curtain of fringe above her eyebrows, and in the back it fell to her shoulder blades. The tops of her cheeks and nose were speckled with freckles. A face not quite fully developed, stuck in adolescence. She might not age well, he thought.

She dropped into her chair as if she were collapsing from exhaustion. He sat and produced a thick envelope of cash.

"So what are you looking for and what's your timeline?" she asked.

"I would like to rent the cheapest apartment with a city view today. I can pay a whole year in advance," David said.

"You must be new to the area. You sound like me when I first got here. Where I grew up, it was easy to find a place to live. But it's a nightmare in this city, even the suburbs, unless you have a lot of money. As much as I want to help, there's a waiting list a mile long here and everywhere else around. There's no telling when a unit will be available. And anyway it's impossible to move anyone in a day," she said.

"How much is a lot of money?" he asked.

"We do have a penthouse available, but, I don't mean to sound sarcastic, your envelope doesn't look anywhere near fat enough," she replied.

"I'm sorry for wasting your time. I never had to do this before," he said. "On a completely different subject, do you normally wear such conservative clothes? They look weird on you."

She leaned close and confessed confidentially, "They make us wear hotel uniforms. Old people make a big deal about it. I always feel weird in them. I bet I look tired, too. I was out partying until the middle of the night. Hold on, take a look at this." She touched the screen on her phone a few times and held it up to him to show him a shot of her mid-shimmy, eyes closed and arms curled gracefully over her head. "Better, eh?" She flipped the phone around to have a look herself and frowned. "Jesus, my tits are falling out there. Oh my God, why did I just tell you that?" She blushed.

David responded, "Blue's a good color for you, but that dress is too baggy on the sides. I can give you the number of someone who can take it in. She does a fantastic job, and she's cheap."

"Aw, that's sweet. Listen, there's this guy I'm sort of friends with—let me give you his number—who's trying to rent out his place. He had a renter, but that guy was a douche, pissed off the neighbors and trashed the place, and then decided he couldn't afford it, so he just took off, and now he—the first guy, the guy with the place, my friend—is trying to get someone else. I'm pretty sure he's in town, the guy, my friend, Mike. Who owns the place. He's a cameraman dude and he's got a gig now where he has to travel, like, for months at a time. So he's crashing with his friends, me included, to have, like, somewhere to crash, and then renting out his own place full-time. It's a few blocks away. Nice, newer condos. You can probably call him right now. I think he's getting desperate because he wants to get this settled before he hits the road again. But I couldn't tell you when his job's finished and he plans to move back in."

"Thanks"—he read from her name tag—"Angela. But I don't have a phone. Can I borrow yours?"

She smiled, looking livelier than she had a few minutes ago. She scanned the contacts on her phone. "Mike's a good guy. Mike, Mike, Mike. How many Mikes do I know? Ooh, I still have that Mike? Delete. This is the one." She tapped the name of what must have been the right Mike and brought the phone to her ear. "Hey, Mike, it's Angela. No, the other Angela. You really call her that? Never mind. I'm talking to a guy here I think would be a perfect tenant or renter or whatever you're calling them. House guest? Right." She covered the microphone on her phone and whispered to David, "They don't allow rentals." She listened to the person on the phone for half a minute and then interrupted, "Hold up. I know all about that. This guy's a sweetheart." She winked at David. "I do too have good judgment. Point is, is your place still free? Uh-huh.

When's she coming by? Well, I think he can meet you sooner than that. Here, talk to him."

Angela handed David the phone and pretended to give him privacy by studying her nails.

David introduced himself and explained that he was willing to pay a year or however long the apartment was available in advance, in cash, if he could move in today. What happened? He'd just arrived in the city this morning, had a place lined up in someone's basement, and when he went over there to move in, the whole house was gone, burned to the ground. Yes, it really was unbelievably bad luck. He handed the phone back to Angela.

"All set?" she asked.

"Yes. We're meeting at three."

"That's great! I guess you're lucky." She blushed a deep red. "I live around here too, right around the corner, even though I can't afford anyplace fancy. You won't forget, will you? I heard you say your name was David."

"No, I won't forget, Angela. Hold on, let me give you my tailor's number."

"No, don't worry about it now. Next time. Just remember me. Hold on." She wrote a phone number on a piece of paper and handed it to him. "Here. That's me."

David went back to Diane's apartment and made a deal with a couple of the maintenance men who had been hoarding moving boxes. They helped him pack his belongings, or rather, he threw everything in a pile and told them to box it all up, get the boxes out of the apartment, lock up, and bring everything over to the new address in the evening. He next headed to a coffee shop to meet Mike, who took a look at David's stack of cash and agreed to a year, or however long he wanted. By 3:30, David had a new home in a compact one-bedroom apartment that came with simple, clean, adequate furnishings with a dominant color scheme of light grays and white. Sadly, no view of anything but the street and the building on the other side of it.

The unprecedented amount of personal initiative he had used drained him, and he dozed until he was awakened by impatient horn honking. He looked out the window at a utility van double-parked in front of the building. All the accumulated possessions of his life so far could fit in a van. It was nice. He could live in a van if he had to. He went down and led the maintenance men to a service door, and they delivered about twenty large boxes.

When David awoke the next morning, he felt for the first time a faint but unsettling feeling of having put some effort into existing. He disliked the entire experience tremendously. It could have been a nightmare. There were too many rules, procedures, options, decisions, and compromises to accomplish something as trivial as finding a place to sleep. What had happened to people? Thinking about this made him tired again, so he went back to sleep for another two hours.

David learned, although he wasn't surprised, that when relinquishing her claim to him, whatever her name was—that was how quickly he had forgotten it—had blotted him out of existence. He assumed he would no longer have a job, but nobody even admitted that he had ever worked at the foundation. He understood that it would likely be the same for her friends and acquaintances, not that he cared. She had plucked him out of his old life, but she had never gotten around to replanting him. He had only had a half-existence, a rootless life in a role that she had willed into being and that stopped existing as soon as she stopped willing it. A man without a past, a present, a future, friends, or obligations. Nothing but the freedom to do whatever he wanted. A situation people fantasize about. But he continued to struggle to get out of bed as eagerly as he once did.

In such an expansive cosmopolitan city, being unattached

and unemployed but with a decent savings offered an immense number of permutations for how to spend his time. That required choosing, and choices engendered preferences, and preferences led to patterns. He soon developed a flexible routine surveying the teeming organic chaos that hid in plain view. Unkempt parks and landscaping. Seditious branches of trees and bushes pressed against their boundaries, poking through fences and railings. Roots that undermined the walls of their planter boxes and split and warped the surrounding pavement. Hordes of hearty weeds that, much like the city's human inhabitants, overran whatever sliver of land they found convenient. The river lapping at and painstakingly eroding its artificial masonry banks. Animal refugees, opportunists, stowaways, and unfortunates that had lost their way, river and sea creatures, birds, mammals, and insects, that chose the austerity of the outdoors over the tempting comforts of interior spaces.

He didn't have a chance to forget Angela, because she clumsily contrived numerous accidental meetings. She made him meet her on her lunch breaks, or just after work, and he learned that she was a kind, generous, but insecure young woman desperate to submit to someone who could lead her somewhere, anywhere. She bragged to her friends about him, and they ensnared him in their social group. He became an occasional participant in their playacting at debauchery. Long nights at clubs and parties. Dinners they could barely afford. Concerts too loud and crowded to be enjoyable. He was a safe, blissful, restful oasis from the pandemonium these young women skirted in search of excitement. A break from the complex social formulae of men, women, and relationships they were trying to solve. If he slept with one of them, it wasn't because he had a strong desire to do so, but because that was how a particular night had played out. Individuals still bored him, but he was curious about social behaviors, looking at them as he might consider the activities of butterflies flitting around the flowers.

They knew there was no future with him, but he was just so lovely and treated all of them so politely, even when he was tactlessly critical.

5
______

Money and energy limited the amount of time Angela and her friends could spend together, so David still had many evenings to himself. He found a restaurant he liked close to the city's old opera house where he could sit near a window and watch people on the inside and the outside. The exterior was nondescript, and the interior would have been considered dingy and outdated decades ago. But the food was interesting. The head chef was apparently a bit mad and restless. He changed the bill of fare continually, zigzagging among bizarre interpretations of tradi-tional-sounding dishes, completely ordinary staples, and vibrant, haphazard inventions. As soon as the staff got used to a menu, he reordered, supplemented, abridged, or obliterated it completely. Regular diners, mostly older couples who had made a habit of having their pre- or post-theater meals here, were indifferent to its lack of ambience and never bothered examining the incomprehensible, mutating menu too carefully.

The servers were experts at motivating customers to make the start of a performance. They served half-full cups of coffee. When they suggested dessert or an after-dinner drink, they did so in a way that implied you should think better of it—"would you have the time for" instead of "would you like." They always had fully tallied checks ready. Their patrons may not have been aware they were being shepherded like this but subconsciously must have registered that when they ate here, they were always in their seats, with time to smoke a cigarette, drink an over-priced glass of wine from one of the theater concessionaires, and stop at the restroom, at least five minutes before the commencement of the overture.

On such an evening, there lingered an intriguing couple, a comfortable duo that appeared to be exuberantly riding across the high social plateau they had hoisted themselves onto, old enough to have left their worst mistakes far behind, young enough to still have hopes, ambitions, and the energy and enthusiasm to pursue them, and wealthy enough to have few constraints on their choices, but not so wealthy that tasteless extravagance was one of the options available to them. Neither was especially beautiful, but they were both charismatic, modest, and pleasant in a way that powered a potent magnet-ism. You could say that they were superlative versions of ordi-nary people, uncommon types whom he had been lucky enough to observe only a few times before. People who might spontaneously cozy up to another pair of like-minded souls and spend hours in silly, slightly suggestive banter. It was impossible for them to be unaware of the time once the dining room had emptied. Maybe they refused to be hurried, or guided themselves with a more profound philosophy of enjoying a moment to its natural conclusion before rushing off to the next. He overheard, "Oh, it's already twenty after." "We've sneaked in later than that." "But the dirty looks we got." Then spurts of intimate giggles. "Oh, I'm a bit tipsy already." "Drunk, more like it." "Might as well have another bottle." "We can just show up at the start of the second act." After another hour, they were so warm and affectionate that sitting through a show must have been out of the question. Tipping generously after having savored their time, they dashed out into the night to waft to the next scene, perhaps finding suitable companions to complete their quartet along the way.

David would never approach people like them. There was no reason he couldn't. He just didn't want to. They were already whole. He could add nothing. Maybe that woman who had kicked him out had found that with her dopey engineer. What was her name? Maybe the first days David had spent with her had been like this, complete. No. The two people he watched were a binary pair, locked together as they wheeled around the universe. She and David had briefly drifted onto the same path, but the things pulling them apart had been stronger than their mutual magnetism. She always overlooked the present, where he was. Isn't that like artists, or their acolytes? To manipulate moments. Creativity was about nurturing an organism. Watering and pruning, fertilizing, adjusting its placement for the best sunlight. It was logical that she would partner with an actual builder. While they planned the perfect future, millions of moments were happening and racing by unnoticed.

He had learned how some of these artists thought. They could be as observant as he, attuned to their senses, receptive to all sorts of stimuli. But he believed he could better take in a phenomenon and fully experience it. They were compelled to use it as material, synthesize it, and derive abstractions from its substance for the construction of their own super-reality. Their visions could never be experienced, though, and therefore were doomed to ultimately be untrue to the nature that inspired them. That had to have been why David oppressed them. He reminded them of the world they ignored or couldn't see, and that exceeded or contradicted their imaginations.

He must have made her feel that way, too.

At that moment, feelings of not wanting to approach, not wanting to be approached, merged into something stronger and more difficult to overcome than each of them individually. He had often been by himself, but now he felt alone and wanted to be left alone. A moment like this awaits all of us, when we feel like absolute strangers, where the limit of our existential certainty constricts itself to the surface area of our skins, and then we doubt even our own bodies, and what we claim to know shrinks further to the abstract boundaries of our minds.

It was a new psychic experience for David, and not one he found particularly engrossing. He seemed to have traveled the exact middle line between ego and soul, unaware of either. How could he reject the sense of self that he never had or that he was incapable of feeling? Or disavow a soul that had been mute his entire life?

This is how I, biased by having had many more psychological adventures than physical ones, interpreted his next words.

"I felt pretty calm then. A lot of the things that used to catch my attention stopped mattering. I didn't feel like noticing and commenting as much. I'd done it not really caring whether or not there was any point to it, and so I didn't have to care about not doing it either. I think people first hallucinated meaning into the world, and then expected it, and then demanded it. You can't just be a passive observer. I wasn't doing my part to contribute to the delusion and never would," he told me.

Maybe because I was the first person he had shared this revelation with, he paused to let it sink in, or maybe he just paused for no reason. He continued, "To be honest, I realized then that I didn't even know what 'meaning' meant. I think it's the most ambiguous concept in any language. Sometimes it's just an equals sign. Sometimes it's about imposing cause and effect on the past. Sometimes people use it to condition themselves for an emotional response to similar sets of events. Sometimes it's a way for people with the luxury of free time to decide how to spend it. I've even met people who think meaninglessness has meaning. Anyway, I was sure that the last place I was going to find it was in that city."

I've decided to perpetuate the illusion of the orderliness of a story and smooth out the rest of his lengthy, detailed complaints.

A city dams your senses. It hides the world behind a curtain and forces you to look inward, but devises innumerable artificial stimuli to compensate for the information it hides. He had met many people who claimed to be informed in the sense that they had great knowledge and insight into world events, but they were usually secondhand ideas they pulled from a great feedback loop of information that ran through all the cities of the world. This told you nothing about what was happening in the rest of the 99.9 percent of the planet, and was irrelevant on the cosmological scale. What was going on up in the sky? Who could tell, because the noise of the city lights drowned it out? Sitting in some dewy glade, immersed in the sweet smells of leisurely decomposition and growth, the sounds of night creatures, the chirps of the crickets, the whistles of the bats, the hoots of the owls, and the groans of the frogs, whilst scanning the speckled night sky had once provided inexhaustible material for empires of knowledge and insight.

If you're visiting a city from a small town or rural area, you notice the absence of the world immediately. Noise—aural, visual, olfactory, gustatory, and tactile—and novelty create the allure, but the allure evaporates quickly, so the megalopolis must continually manufacture more of them. The entire process is insidious. Whoever heard of somebody with even modest contact with nature—say, a view of a field, a pond, or a small grove—tiring of it? People pay premiums to be near parks, and huge sums to look over the top of the cityscape to see the green-and-blue world in the distance, to view the places where an encounter with the planet can be had for free.

If it's doing its job, a city fulfills all your needs while it lulls you into forgetting about the constraints it imposes. You accept its rules. Life becomes moving from box to box in your home, itself a box within one of many stacks of boxes organized into blocks on squares of land connected by a grid that leads to other squares with blocks of boxes in boxes. This arrangement was once for convenience and defense, but its purpose is inexplicable now. A tautological reality, perpetuating itself, existing for its own sake.

David had held out longer than anyone and had searched for the spots where the light from the rest of the world still seeped in. It would have been easy for him to gather his inconsiderable number of possessions, or simply abandon them, and head for a place where biology thrives and compulsively, relentlessly propagates itself into unlimited sensory contours. He could, in fact, start walking and reach it in a few days. He just couldn't summon the motivation. His will wasn't something he had exercised much, and it had atrophied and weakened. He had always allowed himself to be carried places, and to be swept along by someone else's initiative. Now he was stranded.

It's a mystery why a particular person stands out to us. One who elicits a flash of recognition of a version of ourselves and makes the otherness of all accessible again. Our being aware of them is often simple chance.

One evening while David dined late, he looked up and spotted an older woman, someone he would have never bothered noticing if not for the fact that he had never seen her before, nor seen her enter. But there she was, approximately at the center of the dining room. Her face, full and cheerful, indicated sixty, he reckoned, but her hair, shorn close to her skull, was of someone much, much older, white, without a touch of gray or the lingering color of her younger days, a pure white that seemed to magnify the weak restaurant lighting and glow with it, like glass filaments. She wore a simple black dress buttoned to the collar, baggy to hide all of her stout figure. Across from her sat a man, presumably her husband, with a stern face that was covered in irregular red blotches and that drooped unevenly like wax accumulated at the base of a candle. He cut his steak angrily while he talked, making all his loose skin, even the flesh beneath his eyes, quiver. She occasionally nodded slightly or rounded her mouth in an "oh," with the serene, patient smile a grandmother who might have been listening to a child breathlessly blurt out a day's worth of accumulated impressions. From the distance, David somehow could suppress the din of other conversations and identify their words.

"Not their best, don'tcha think? For a muse, they certainly could have gotten a prettier mezzo. Nobody gives a shit about the singing—all in the heads of these egotistical bitch divas. Diva bitches. You know all this opera started as a meat market for aristocrats? I've told you that, right? Now we're stuck with chubby middle-aged women pretending to be princesses. No prince is going to want to take any of those fat bitches home to fuck. You would have looked better up there. No wonder Hoffman drank so much fucking wine."

He belched a throaty, gurgling laugh, and his wife turned up the smile on her lips a bit more and nodded.

"Still, sang good. I won't argue against that. But they don't let the movie starlets and whatnot put on the pounds. They've got plastic surgery for that, and for what we're paying for that box these days, I gotta think these chubby singers can afford it. We're entitled to some nice tits and asses.

"That Hoffman has turned into a bit of a porker, too, hasn't he? The muse don't got a lot to worry about losing him to some other woman. He used to be a real charmer, years ago, singing to the fat old ladies. Remember? He had to lift one of them up that time? I guess you either get fat or starve to death in this town. He was on top of his game tonight, though."

"Your food is getting cold, my love," she replied absently. He stopped talking, ate a few scoops of the now-pulverized mixture of food, and resumed noting the performance's other deficiencies. She calmly proceeded to eat everything on her plate and, when she was finished, placed her fork and knife down gently, then looked directly at David, as if she had been aware of him the whole time. Her vapid serenity vanished, and she tilted her head slightly, her face looking plaintive and profound. David had usually been the one with the overpowering stare, but he could only meet her eyes for a few seconds before unease welled up. He lowered his head and ate his own neglected food. He peeked again, and she was still watching him, smiling and blinking rapidly, as if she had been lost in thought and staring blindly, and he just accidentally happened to be in her line of sight.

"Am I boring you? I'm sooo sorry I'm not as sophisticated as you," the man grumbled at his wife when he noticed that she seemed not to be paying attention.

"I was listening, my love," she said. "I only had something in my eye."

Her husband dropped his cutlery contemptuously, signaled the nearest waiter, who was trying to take another table's order, and tapped his foot impatiently. When their waitress brought him his bill, he snatched it from her hands, threw it and some crumpled bills onto the table and then stood and strode out hastily, his fleshy face bouncing with each step, expecting his wife to hurry along after him. She got up lazily, followed a route to the door that detoured past David's table, and said as she passed, "Next Friday night. Here. Please."

"What?" he asked after her, but she continued walking calmly to the door her husband had already stormed through.

6

The weather was temperate. A mild breeze blew away the smog and city stench and provided the residents sorely needed fresh oxygen. The ballet and opera seasons had ended. An old, dimly lit restaurant was the last place you would go on a perfect spring evening, but David waited inside that next Friday night. He was the only customer, and the staff, having polished all the flatware it could find, folded every napkin crisply, and set every table for the next busy service, whenever that would be, stood idle. David felt all the more conspicuous and anxious.

There was nothing to look at but the door, yet he missed her entrance completely. Here she was, and almost seated before he noticed. Dressed as drably as possible, as if she had put extra effort into it. A baggy gray button-up wool cardigan, prodigiously pilled, over a plain white blouse fastened up to her neck. She planted on her lap an enormous black handbag, cheap fake bonded leather, judging by how the material was cracked and peeling, and clutched the handles with a pair of flaccid white hands. She wore no jewelry or makeup. Her short hair was disheveled, like tangled cobwebs matted against her head. Her eyes were underlined with thick bags of loose skin, folds of neck fat bulged from her collar, and her bosom sank well below her purse. If that was all one noticed, she looked slatternly, like a thrifty old matron who had thrown on whatever she could find to pop out to the post office. Nevertheless, her frumpy demeanor struck him as deliberate, a costume, a dissimulation of an elderly reversion to infantilism rather than a true state of decline. Did she revel in it, mock you by looking like this? You would have difficulty taking her seriously. Her unblemished white skin and strange eyes that modulated dark green hues like sequins, however, imbued her with a mischievousness that signaled it was perfectly natural for a dowdy, plump old woman to be having a strange and tacitly intimate meeting with a handsome young stranger.

"So here we are. My name is Maeve. I have a photographic memory for faces. You came here many months ago, and I didn't think anything at all about it. I saw you again a few nights later, and I thought you were a tourist traveling alone who was too lazy or uninterested to try out different restaurants once he found one he liked. I do that. Once I find a good one, I eat there all the time. Then I saw you many more times, and I thought you might be looking for someone. Not a fixed meeting, but as if once upon a time a momentous random encounter had occurred here, and the best chance you had of finding that person again was by waiting in exactly the same spot. Then it seemed to me that you were just passing the time on the odd night when you had nothing better to do but didn't want to sit around at home. Finally, I understood why I kept noticing you, so I asked you to meet me."

"I don't think you could have seen me so many times. You had never been here before. I'm absolutely sure of that. And what do you mean you understood why you kept noticing me?"

Maeve waved her hand dismissively. "Is it important?" She

leaned closer to ask confidentially, "What are you really doing here?"

"Here? Where here?" he asked.

What he was doing here at that specific time? Or here in general, a minor participant in a moment of human civilization?

Maeve scrutinized him with her wide, glossy viridian eyes.

"I'm a challenging woman. I—" she started.

He interjected, "I doubt it. I've noticed that people allow themselves to be stymied and frustrated. I've never understood why. To have someone to blame? It shouldn't be so hard to avoid a person who's trying to provoke you. I don't know you, but I wouldn't guess that you're that difficult."

"Well, good. But as for difficult people, suppose someone has something you want, something you can't live without, or is blocking the only path to it? Or a person attacks your sense of identity, your self-expression, or your personal space?" she asked.

"What?" he responded.

"Don't worry about it. As I was trying to say, I don't mind doing the talking. I was once gorgeous. Many old women say this to console themselves because they've suppressed memories of their ugliness, and the only pictures they've held on to are the good ones. They state this with conviction, and when they look into the mirror, they can't believe they always looked like that. But I was truly stunning. Effortlessly, so much so that people feared me, and I was a little lonely."

Her words were an invitation for David to search for the elements of beauty that had once been there, and still were. Her eyes, of course, when her skin was taut, must have dazzled. If that was all you did, stare into her eyes, maybe she could still stun you. Her white skin would have been more effulgent and a creamier. She was not unattractive for her age and size; clean and comfortable looking, she could have been cast in some kind of inspirational family drama as the gentle, wise, charismatic matriarch whom everyone runs to for advice and hugs. The echoes of an elegant jawline were manifest in her expressions and gestures, and the neck around which accordion pleats of fat were gathered was long and could have been thin and graceful. The figure that had sagged and come to rest wherever it would could have once been lean and curvaceous.

"Please tell me your name," she said.

He did. His dismay abated, and stillness enfolded them. She smirked while he looked her over.

A waiter interrupted, "Would Madam like to see the menu?"

"Oh, just bring me coffee. Plain old coffee. Aren't you having anything?" she said.

"No. You asked me why I'm here. I had nowhere to go, and someone brought me and left me here, and now I have nowhere to go again," David said.

"Hm, you make it sound simultaneously mysterious and banal. It happens to women all the time, to follow someone who abandons them, so I suppose it really must be banal. A woman will want to possess and be possessed, really desired. That second tendency can be a leash that pulls her all sorts of places. A man only wants to possess, desperately to own someone. Women and men are odd things, the first wanting to be suffered for, the other wanting to suffer, and when that little drama has been played out, the man will become bored with having been caught by the woman he caught, and then the woman will do the suffering and scheming to retain possession while the man enjoys being suffered for. At least, I believe this is true, but I have no idea why. After all my decades, the only plausible answer I have is brainwashing. I can't imagine how the gene pool is ever going to be refined through this idiotic system of pairing people by their insecurities. I have a theory about what really is going on," Maeve said.

"Which is?" he asked.

"Oh, I can't talk like that with you quite yet," she said and grinned deviously, not in the way you would expect to see from a cozy grandmother.

David couldn't help himself, and laughed.

"Why are you laughing?" Maeve asked.

"It's a bad habit of mine," he said. "When somebody starts to sound philosophical. It's funny. It always sounds a little crazy to me."

She couldn't help smiling herself and said, "I used to be quite wicked to anyone who blathered on like I just did. You obviously didn't love this woman."

"I did like her. She was quite lovely, you know, physically, and I guess she was pretty smart. She cared about a lot of things but wasn't obnoxious or pushy when she talked about them. I thought I was kind to her and made her life easy and pleasant," he replied plainly. "But frankly, because I had nothing better to do. She needed, what's the word, 'pathos' or something. Always had a lot of feelings. She said a lot of things. It was hard to follow. But I think that was the point."

"And did this hurt you? I don't . . ."

"I'm not sure what that means, Maeve. No idea what people would feel or think if they were me. Wait, that's not one hundred percent true. I mean, people have told me how they would react or imply how I should by asking me if I felt a certain way, just like you did. Apparently, I don't know that I'm the victim in a tragedy. I don't see the point. I guess I'm just not made like that. A person who thinks someone is living for them is actually trapping both of them. And what if you wind up changing your mind? Maybe they start having weird ideas, getting their hair cut in a stupid way, dressing funny, or wearing a perfume or cologne you don't like. You're stuck because you've exaggerated the relevance you have to each other." He felt himself speaking freely, as if he were talking over these ideas with himself.

"Sounds philosophical. Boring," she said.

"Definitely," he said.

"I'm luckier, being a woman. I can get away with a lot of things as long as I agree to be had. In fact, once a man gets a hold of something and takes ownership, it's almost as if he prefers that it leave him alone. Men collect trophies. They don't even know why. I don't actually feel lucky because I'm not concerned about being alone or not. My life happened. But I can't complain about being attached to someone's whims. I don't have to worry about a will that frankly I lack or not getting to make decisions about things I couldn't care less about, as long as the choices that determine who I am and what I think are always mine. Speaking of exaggerating the importance of someone else, some people even give all that up and let someone else tell them who to be. When it comes to regular everyday tasks, I have no responsibility or accountability if I don't want it, and I don't. There's a long line of men willing to let a woman live like that. It can be extremely liberating."

"What about having children? Isn't that often expected?" he asked.

"Easily avoided," she said with a dismissive wave of her hand again.

She leaned in as if to tell another secret. "I know I'm not supposed to say things like that, with all the paranoia girls carry around with them these days. Just imagine, a woman could have a man running around waiting on her hand and foot, and the price she would have to pay for it is to be willing to do next to nothing. But our modern women say, 'Oh, but men get all the fame and fortune.' They see accomplishments as personal and social validation and work like maniacs at the same jobs men look for ways to shirk and take shortcuts through. Men compete out of a biological imperative, not because it actually adds meaning to their lives. They're collectors, and money, fame, and power are merely the tools to get the rarest things. And ironically, it's usually women goading them on."

"Maybe they like it," David interjected.

"What? Who likes what?" Maeve asked.

"Maybe some women want to work on things that stimulate them. Haven't you ever thought of having a career that, I don't know, feels like you're having fun?" he said.

"Have you?" she countered.

"Well, no, but that's because my idea of fun is pretty worthless. But it's not inconceivable for everyone," he said.

"You're talking about children's ideas. We've all had them. The sad truth is that hardly anybody has that luxury. Nobody lets you have anything purely on your own merit. Nothing's free. There are always agreements loaded with conditions, and they're still easily broken or amended. Only money can bypass that. Only the wealthy can do whatever they want and treat work like it's a hobby. So if you want that life, you'd better make getting hold of as much money as possible your first objective," she said smugly.

"I don't know," he said.

"Well, I do," she replied.

Maeve continued, "As I was saying, women began thinking more like this when I was young. Drop-dead gorgeous, don't forget, my dear—other women hated me! I always thought, why want anything so badly, when you're just going to wind up dead anyway, and anyone who could appreciate and admire you should be preoccupied with their own inevitable deaths. Take it easy and enjoy yourself. I'm a horrible person, I know. But there's freedom in being horrible, too. People leave you alone and stop pestering you if you insult their ideas enough. Not that this was my intention. I just couldn't help myself. Do you have a job?"

"She gave me a job, sort of as a condition of my living with her. So that's over, too. Doesn't really matter, though," he said.

"Have a little money, I bet. Good for you. But that won't last forever. You should show me where you live."

The waitress set a coffee in front of Maeve. She opened her purse, rummaged around, pulled out some cash, placed it on the table, and slid the cup and saucer onto it.

Had they lowered the lights without his noticing? Her hair seemed darker.

They took a taxi to his apartment, a silent, slow ride sitting together in the back, and arrived there in the time it would have taken him to walk, but he doubted she could have handled the exertion. He showed her his tidy white-and-gray space. She seated herself on the plain square gray chenille couch, clutching her purse in her lap like she had in the restaurant. He sat in a matching chair adjacent to her. They looked at each other across the corner of a rectangular glass-topped chrome table. Maybe the restaurant chair had been uncomfortable and had caused her to sit awkwardly or too stiffly. She didn't seem to bulge as much now.

"I like this place. It's what I would have expected, and what I would have done," she said. "We have a co-op, the type that is associated with all sorts of snobbiness, over there." She vaguely indicated the direction with a wave of her hand. "Near where they've preserved some of the forest. Upper-class and chic, but quiet, with many open spaces, which are worth far more than all the hip and popular places in town combined. The place for people who are comfortable with their wealth and want to retreat and sequester themselves. Our home is quite cluttered, though. I don't bother with any of it. I wouldn't waste my time changing or rearranging. Just clear it all out, right into the garbage. He holds on to possessions like they were talismans. I can't tell you what any of them mean or where they came from. Maybe something he owns is cursed and he doesn't realize it."

David laughed. "I found this place randomly. I don't own any of this. If it were completely bare, I don't even know how I would have bought furniture. I never have before. Maybe you wouldn't like it as much if we were sitting on the floor."

"It wouldn't bother me at all. I used to have to sit and sleep on the ground. I never grew out of it. The furniture is just for people who come over," she replied. After pretending to think for a few seconds, she continued, "Can I come over here again? It could be quite often, except when I'm being dragged to some show or some other god-awful place, or maybe hardly ever. I can come around the same time and bring over food and we can eat together. You don't have to sit around by yourself at that Italian place anymore, or anywhere else, staring off into space, daydreaming when you have nothing to do."

"I don't really daydream. I—" he said.

"I know. I know," she said.

"Yes, that would be fine," he answered seriously. "But you should try to dress and look different. You may not care, but it irritates me. Nothing suits you, not the clothes, not the hair. It's like you're doing this on purpose! You are, aren't you? You have to start letting your hair grow. I don't know what else to tell you now, but everything has to change."

"Of course," she said. "You'll have to tell me how I'm doing, OK?"

Maeve sighed and said, "I'll go now. Don't try to plan around my next visit. Maybe you're here. Maybe you aren't. It doesn't matter." Her eyes had lost their luster, their green weirdly looking like a dull olive color. She shuffled to the door and let herself out quietly. The latch clicked into its bore, and his mind was completely empty.

SECOND DIGRESSION

Usually when I take up my confessor's post, I quickly get distracted and scan the room for something more interesting. They blather on and on, no longer caring—it probably never mattered—that I stopped paying attention. They're happy my presence makes it look like they're not chatting away crazily to themselves. That's how I've gotten to know so well my decrepit little tavern's unevenly mortared bricks, its greasy, gnarled wooden furniture, its warped, scarred, and stained floors, the soot, grime, and cobwebs accumulating in every edge, ledge, and corner. After I've lurched home drunk and collapsed on top of a tangled pile of sheets and covers, I'll lie reeling with visions of crooked lines of bricks, floorboards, chair legs, contorting and straightening, challenging me to focus and will them to freeze precisely at that moment—a fraction of a second—when they're perfectly ordered. Their distortions nauseate me, but I'm eventually exhausted by my mind's exertions, and lose consciousness. When I awaken God knows how many hours later. I couldn't tell you when I left the bar, how I staggered home, or how long I wrestled with my visions.

This new client kept me engaged. I thought, I had come here because I had given all that up—you know, curiosity, interest in people—and ended all the self-indulgent musings that I liked to bully everyone with.

"Have a smoke?" I asked.

He shook his head and allowed the pause I had inserted to expand while he examined the room and finished his brandy. I doubted he was contemplative. He seemed engaged in the moment as a material fact rather than a psychological experience and greedily ingested as much data as he could.

I enjoyed how smoking could be transformational. It was the smoke, the interaction with something that was both material and immaterial, there and not there. Such an interesting sensation. My companion and I didn't participate in the scene around us, the rancorous atmosphere of inferior cigarettes, stale breath smelling of cheap beer, and pervasive shabbiness that protested anything new, vital, or fresh. Everything seemed decrepit in this wilderness oasis: from the moment of conception, people were on a path of steady decline. I drew in clean, full, dignified drags, wearing a wise old persona I had sentimentally stowed in the attic when it had become threadbare.

I was curious if his reaction to this old woman had changed over time, but no clear question popped into my head. When I look backward now, my past is frozen, settled. I remember when the feelings of embarrassment about things that happened to me in primary school disappeared. A random day when the chasm between past and present became wide enough that I couldn't clearly make out the shapes on the other side. My childhood was no longer a still-lived experience and became a collection of vignettes I told in the third person, chapters in a book, a silly ridiculous book from which I select anecdotes, some dear and some biting and mocking, to entertain friends and impress lovers. How long ago had the ink dried on that first chapter, and the next one, and the one after that?

Could he look into my mind? No, he said himself that he could never penetrate surfaces.

"I knew you weren't from here when I came in. How long have you been here?" he asked.

"I came when I ran out of points to make and exhausted all my arguments. That was a while ago," I said, avoiding the question.

The strange, beautiful, untouched and untouchable young man who had rematerialized through the telling of his story said, "I suppose you don't run into many strangers out here."

"I don't think we're strangers," I said. "I don't like the idea that someone you've never met before is a stranger, or that if you know each other, you aren't strangers. I've talked to a lot of people around here, and we're still strangers, and always will be. A stranger is more like somebody you don't recognize as a peer—you know, someone you have little in common with. That could be someone you've seen every day of your life. But if you recognize a person, no matter how new they are to you, they're not strange and never were. And for that matter, I'm not random. Wherever I am, I've deliberately put myself there. Why choose me? There were about two dozen people here when you walked in. There's a weathered old alcoholic who's passed out in some corner by now. You could talk to his comatose body to your heart's content. There are ladies here. Not gorgeous ones by any culture's definition of that word, but comfortably warm, with decent looks and plump boobs and asses. Filthy minds too, I'm sure. Pent-up filth. It's boring out here and the men are unimaginative. As for the men, they are gregarious and generally aficionados of self-pity. With your poor luck and feckless choice in lovers, you could be their hero."

His mood brightened, and he did something unexpected— he laughed and smiled cheerfully at me. "Ha ha. All right. You have a lot of ideas. I could have come and gone quietly. Your boots are old and pretty well worn, but they must have cost quite a lot new. You can't buy them just anywhere. You yourself used the word *deliberately*. It's not just the boots. You've clearly cultivated a demeanor, who you are, even though you're not trying to look like anybody. You've been somewhere," he said. "But on the other hand . . ."

"Ah, you're Sherlock Holmes, too," I said.

"What do you mean?" he asked.

"You know, how he can draw complex conclusions simply through careful observation," I said.

"I don't know what you mean by complex," he said.

"Anyway, you see, I'm not random. What you're saying is that I look a little less washed up than the rest of these people," I said, gesturing toward them as if I were sweeping them aside.

He continued, "I haven't had a serious conversation with anyone in a long time. There aren't that many people you can do that with, or would want to. You seemed like the right person."

I said, "There are poor souls like me who insist on uncovering meaning, who would try to claw through stone until the flesh has been scoured from our fingertips, until we're scraping bone, to reach the tiniest grain of truth buried deep within. Could you guess this, or do I just look a little less stupid than the rest of them?" I said. "But it turns out it's the opposite! I'm the stupidest one of all. That's one of the benefits of being out in the middle of nowhere. You might be hiding from a lot of things, but you can't hide from yourself."

I felt pride swelling in my chest for these temporary neighbors of mine I fought with my conscience not to hate.

"You know, people around here are pretty self-aware. They aren't going to deny that they don't amount to much," I said, tipsily certain of my profundity. "What rankles them is anyone who claims to be more than nothing."

I hoped any of this were true. I'd known these people to

curse, piss, shit, spit, swear, fuck, bully, drink, destroy, scream, insult, punch, or kick with little provocation. I appreciated that they had little malevolence or evil in their violence. Simple misanthropy. Unrestrained internal chaos. Shooting cats. Trampling snakes. Swatting fireflies. Kicking flowers. If you have to ask where the joy was in any of that, you'll never be able to see it.

He didn't seem to have anything to add, so I continued, "My trouble is that I am easily seduced by just a little intellectual stimulation. But in my life, it's always been just sparks, little sparks that never start any fires. Do you know—maybe you don't have any idea what I mean—those people cursed with sentiment, who stagger from situation to situation continually being abused and let down, dumb and uncomprehending about why nobody reacts like they do? My interest in anything is pitifully biased toward the desire for some kind of beautiful resolution, whether it's comic, sentimental, or tragic."

He responded, "I've noticed that people spend too much time asking why. When I was a child, it annoyed me that the other children were always asking, 'Why this? Why that?' When there wasn't an answer, they made one up, and because their imaginations never matched reality, they would argue and rationalize and wound up pulling conflict out of thin air. I'm interested in things you can verify with your senses. It's stupid to ask 'why' first, and then stop looking."

"But you have to believe what you see," I answered. I understood his charisma, how he captivated people. He had a supreme confidence—humble confidence, mind you—in his senses, an explicit faith in them that few have. Most of us are unreliable observers of our own lives.

I can't remember the last time a conversation stimulated me so much. Maybe I had never had one. My brain buzzed like a threatened beehive when I tried to sleep that night, and for the next several nights. I hastened to jot down everything I had heard before it began to make sense—you know, before my cursed, human, masculine mind had done its dismal job of slowly ordering and processing it, polishing away its authenticity.

"See how nicely we're talking?" he said sweetly. "I can tell you more. Hm, now that I think about it, maybe I haven't even started properly. Sorry about that."

7

D avid wasn't sure when he had met Maeve. The passage of time was never something he noticed. Living and working with the second woman, whatever her name was, had given him a temporary, vague awareness of local time, a rolling window of a few days. He could keep track of scheduled appointments as long as he knew when they were relative to now, tomorrow, or the day after tomorrow. He could reckon what part of the year they were in by the amount of daylight, the temperature, and the condition of the vegetation. Spring, however, has deceptively hot days, and the summer deceptively cool ones, so he could be wrong by several weeks. If he misestimated how much time had elapsed since he had last made an inaccurate mental note of the approximate date, he could easily be off by a month or two. So he had no idea how much time passed until Maeve's second visit.

Not that he waited. David lived as he had always done, without plans or expectations. Angela continually pestered him and dragged him along with her and her friends. If he was out all night with them, he slept most of the day, which muddled his timekeeping even more. She regularly intercepted him on the street—it seemed like she understood his schedule better than he did—and forced him to sit with her on the front stoop of the building she worked in while she ate her lunch, usually a yogurt and a banana because she was often dieting and usually broke.

"The guys at the places we go are just boys, David. Some of them are nice, but there are a lot of creeps. We want to go someplace classier, but they won't let us in. Like the Witching Hour."

David had been there a few times with what's-her-name, some artists, and their rich friends, and he decided to tease Angela about it a bit. She was the type of girl everyone acted a little cruel toward and felt compelled to pick on maliciously without knowing why. He understood. There was something slightly pleading and desperate about her. She evinced a deficiency in self-respect that was probably piped up from a deeper well of anxiety, doubt, and self-hatred. The source of her problems in life.

"The bouncers would probably think you look too lively and pretty, maybe like a little too sweet, for their crowd. The people who go there are pretty depressing, and they flaunt their weirdness. You guys are always baseline pretty cheerful and would be like lambs among rabid wolves. And this place you're obsessing over is really expensive. You'd better hope you find somebody to pick up your tab. I'm not sure you'll understand what creepy means until you learn what that will take."

"What! You've been there? Jen's convinced you're like some kind of secret billionaire or prince or something just pretending to hang out with us regular people so we'll like you for who you are. Like that movie. She's an idiot, right? But you just nod your head, make a call, and it's like 'poof,' stuff happens for you. I bet you can get us in anywhere. You're Mr. Suave when you want to be. But nice, too. Just tell them I'm your little sister and it's my birthday and that I have a bunch of my friends with me. Wait, that's too sweet. Are we like your harem or something? How do we dress for that? It's usually some gross old guy that does that. Yuck. That just freaked me out. You're too young and cute."

David let Angela ramble. Her stories were useless, what she did with herself and what happened to her, and her descriptions of people were poor to the point of absurdity, but he didn't mind her chaotic chirpiness. It could even be pleasant. She was sincere and immediate—different than . . . He had been with people who probably thought too much and had taken themselves far too seriously. And he could tell her frankly anything he noticed about her and she would take it, like that she had gotten fat (which prompted the current diet), that her face was puffy and old looking because she wasn't getting enough sleep, that she smelled bad, that her makeup was all wrong. He did this to her friends, too, and they seemed to genially accept it. They might be insecure and directionless, but they needed the blunt criticism. Better than being lied to and humiliated. He didn't care. It was just a habit, maybe even a skill of his.

The plan to go someplace classier was dropped because David stopped participating in the conversation and Angela moved on to the next topic.

"So Lisa's *older*," she stressed, "sister Rebecca just moved here to teach something sciencey. She's got a PhD or something and is totally sexy-smart. You have to come out with us Saturday night because she'll be annoyed hanging out with a bunch of goofy little girls. I bet she would eat you up."

It was an ongoing mission of Angela's to point out to David someone she knew, someone who knew someone she knew, or even a stranger she had just spotted, and insinuate that he was attractive and should be attracted to her. When she ran out of new matches, she would recycle her friends and acquaintances. At some dreary nightclub, emboldened by a bit of actual or imagined intoxication, her voice would deepen and smoothen, and she would goad him, like the one time, "See how Amina's watching you? Look at how she's touching herself. You could take her home and fuck her. Just fucking grab her and walk out of here. It's nothing. She knows it's just sex." Amina was normally reserved but had drunk too many mojitos too quickly and had been pressured into trying ecstasy. Apparently not a moral dilemma for Angela.

He could tell how much these ideas aroused her. She was simmering right now, talking about this Rebecca.

Angela was far from an ideal beauty but attractive in her own way. Her desirability grew from her honesty, openness, and generosity. A better woman than the one he had been married to, Linda or something, but she was still a winsome little bud that hadn't fully blossomed into a mature woman and might never. It would be simple to have her, probably even right now on her lunch break. That definitely would ruin their merry little conversations, and she would never be able to handle it. She would have to have him all to herself, something she didn't have the resources to accomplish.

The sun was blazing directly overhead. The haggard maple that stretched its limbs out over the stoop was more wilted and wan than normal. Angela smelled of teenage girl's perfume, plain white soap, some kind of coconut-scented shampoo, and the unique biome that fed on her perspiration. Large drops of sweat crawled unpleasantly down David's back. They were sweating like they had been jogging. He remarked to himself that it must be summer, some summer month. He wondered how a woman as fat and old as Maeve dealt with the heat. Certain aspects of her demeanor had left impressions, but he couldn't remember exactly what she looked like.

Angela stopped talking. She ate nervously, sweating more than could be blamed on the heat.

As was her habit, she called to remind him on the morning of the day he'd agreed to go out with her and her friends. David met them at the back of an unremarkable pub Rebecca insisted on because she refused to dress up and found dance clubs revolting. A pop-punk band played passably danceable music in the front window. Angela and Shriya, the friend with whom Angela most often ping-ponged between friend-for-life and enemy-for-life, tried to dance in a center area that had been cleared of tables, with about a dozen other people who mostly swayed arrhythmically. Lisa sat next to a baby-faced, waddling young man who was explaining to her the dozens of varieties of beers and ciders on the menu. He managed a feeble, "Hey, bro," when David approached. Lisa, who had been looking over the room, not much minding her man, stared up at David and smiled dreamily. The scene was pathetically, desperately awkward. If any of them were the least bit assertive, they would have erupted in rage at the wretchedness of it all. He felt like wandering off and never being seen again. He couldn't avoid or ignore Angela forever. Even though she took snubs seriously, she eventually forgave them, even when she shouldn't.

Across the table sat a woman who softly sang the wrong words to the song the band played, made-up words peppered with vulgarities, and peeled the label off an empty bottle of cheap light beer. Two other stripped bottles, surrounded by the confetti of their labels, were arranged in a neat line. Rebecca was about his age, lean, bony, and sun-worn. Her nose, cheek-bones, chin, and ears were sharp and thin. Her hair was arranged in a single thick flaxen braid that fell almost to her waist. Her hands looked like they could clamp like vises. She wore jeans and a short-sleeved checkered blouse with the top three buttons undone, which didn't reveal cleavage she didn't have. She wore no makeup, no jewelry. She looked perfect.

"Hey, we'll scoot over so you can sit down," Lisa finally said. "David, this is Chuck. And that is, um, my sister Rebecca"— who was happily singing and peeling, oblivious to everyone —"and so this is David. Yeah, well, sit down."

As soon as he did, Rebecca staggered to her feet and prodded a bony finger into David's face and asked, "Want something, pretty boy? It's your round. You two want anything?"

"Can you get us both another one of these?" Chuck said and showed her the bottle. Lisa frowned.

"Here." David handed her some cash he pulled from his shirt pocket. "I don't want anything."

"OK, whatever," she said and staggered through the sparse crowd.

It was less murky and noisy than the dark, cacophonous places Angela usually dragged him to. People could see each other and try to have conversations, use their oral and body languages. However, you were too visible and exposed to feel at ease, deprived of a backdrop of dusky natant pandemonium that you could sink and disappear into. And this place had an unsettling turbulence. It was neither jubilant nor relaxed. It felt like an anxious person trying to have fun, like many of its patrons. The only way to smooth over the contrasting tempers was to drink.

David could see Rebecca having an animated conversation with a bartender and a chunky older man with a red, mottled bald head and a crooked smile. Chuck resumed his lecture for Lisa. It was a relief to be ignored.

Rebecca returned five minutes later looking perfectly sober, grimacing and mumbling curses to herself. She held together four beer bottles between her hands and slammed them onto the table, nearly causing all of them to topple.

"Whatever the hell you ordered ain't cheap, Chucky," she said. "It's all just fucking beer, right?"

"Well, no, actually, that's an—" Chuck began.

Rebecca rolled her eyes and cut him short. "Here, drink this." She handed a bottle of the same cheap beer she was drinking to David. "I know you said you didn't want anything, but it's weak as water anyway."

She turned her chair to look outward, away from the table, and took swift sips, each time letting her bottle suck onto the inside of her upper lip, and making loud pops when she pulled it off. David had only managed to wet his tongue once by the time she had finished her beer. Without looking at him, and not seeming to address him, she whispered, as if thinking out loud, "Fuck, fuck, fuck. So fucking stupid. Moron. Ugh. Come on, drink up. I want to take a walk. Get out of here. Ugh." And other thoughts along those lines, berating herself or someone else. He wondered if she knew he could hear her, and then she said, "I know you can hear me. Hurry the fuck up."

He set his mostly full bottle on the table.

"Oh," Rebecca said, in a fluttering, musical voice. "Finished already? I think we're going to get some fresh air. OK, li'l sis? Chuck?"

"Yeah, sure," Lisa said timidly.

"Tell Angela I said hi," David told them and then, realizing how she would interpret their leaving together, added, "Tell her not to bother waiting around." Angela, to whom no one could resist being a little cruel. Rebecca was already halfway to the door.

Outside, she beckoned him to follow and jogged a full block away before slowing down to talk. "I thought I would rescue us. How did you end up with a bunch of losers like that?"

"Where are we going?" he asked.

"We shall drift aimlessly. But not too aimlessly. Because I don't want to get lost, or wind up in some funky neighborhood."

Rebecca made long, swaying, meandering strides that kept her at the edge of David's proximity, and although he was following her course, they weren't walking together. Her head rapidly pivoted from side to side and she mumbled commentary to herself while her eyes took everything in. It was warm and humid, their pace was quick, and they were soon thoroughly sweaty. He thought he could identify her smell, a soft scent of vinegar and yeast traveling with him, through the rotting garbage, street food, vehicle exhaust, piss, soot, vomit, and thousands of unwashed bodies. Not a whiff of perfume, or scented deodorant, soap, or shampoo did she exude, but she smelled cleaner, silkier for it, like how the pungent, musty odor of soil and decaying vegetation can smell delicious. Completely unlike the sweet, intoxicating smells that oozed from most women. What did they do to you? Put you in some sort of dizzy stupor, stimulated the amygdala. Rebecca's smell injected electricity right into your hypothalamus. Made you want to grab and consume her.

David had an impulse to say something obscene to her back, so he hastened to stay within earshot to dissuade himself. He could have asked questions to fill in a basic idea about her. But he didn't feel like talking.

He was suddenly thrown against a glass storefront when a crowd bulged to make way for two lean, hairless, and grungy young men grunting and grappling on the ground. Rebecca fell into the crook of his arm, was pressed into his side, and exclaimed a little "oh" when he caught her. So insubstantial was she that she might dissolve into him and leave nothing but her faint cloud of scent. A potent wisp of a woman.

They continued down narrow side streets clogged with people until they finally pushed onto a main boulevard. Rebecca darted to an open spot on the wide sidewalk where she could stand and look around without impeding the throngs of strollers.

"I can never get over how bright it is," she shouted toward the sky, maybe to him. "It fucking sucks. I wasn't paying attention to your name. My name's Kiddie," she said.

"Kitty? What happened to Rebecca, or at least Becky?"

"How about 'Becks' or 'Becca'? Blech. No, it's 'Kiddie,' like 'kid-duh-ee.' That's what the people I like call me. I don't know if I like you or not yet, but that's what you can call me," she said.

"But your sister . . .," he replied.

"I don't know what's going on with her. She's lost her fucking mind. Getting too many ideas from TV shows about women who drink a lot of overpriced cocktails and sleep around. She's with that goofball Chuck now, I guess until a handsome lowlife sweeps her off her feet. When we were kids, she was the one with poise and presence, even though she was younger. Top of her class in everything by a light-year. Easily the prettiest, smartest, and also the most athletic, artistic, charismatic, and assertive. It was disgusting. I'm only joking when I say that. I was proud of her. We all figured she would come here and conquer the place—you know, get to the top of the heap right away. This town is full of morons and pussies, so I can't figure out what the problem is with her."

A boss who exploited her loyalty, and alcohol, drugs, and pressure to be more cosmopolitan, led to a night of events she remembered, but the how and the why of them she never understood. She had chattered to David about it, but no one else. He had had nothing to say. Chuck was an inferior, but he was safe. That feeling of being weighed down, of not soaring to heights she was destined for, might overwhelm her again, and she would be whipped back into the opposite direction, perhaps wiser or perhaps more naive.

"Too many devious people here. You can't challenge them head-on like that," David said. "No, I mean your sister just calls you Rebecca."

"She does what she wants. When I was eight, I got a baby goat I called 'Becky' because I hated my name. I wanted the goat to have it—not as a punishment, you know. I loved that goat. Anyway, my dad started calling me 'kid' or 'kiddie' since I gave it my name," she said.

"My name's David," he replied.

"That's also a stupid name. We're totally Old Testament. What else do people call you?"

He shrugged. "Just David."

"Not 'Dave' or 'Davey'?" He shook his head.

"I suppose you can keep calling me 'pretty,'" David said and grinned.

"I was being obnoxious. If I really thought you were handsome, I would have called you something so inappropriate that you would have turned purple. There was a good chance you were a dick, so I made a preemptive strike."

Kiddie's words were carried on sweet breath that he could almost taste. She punched him hard in the shoulder, harder than you would ever suspect those lean arms could propel a fist. Her sharp, bony knuckles left a searing pain.

"I live over there somewhere," she said, gesturing to the southeast. "I can find it with my feet. I feel like walking for a while."

He asked, "Have you been out in the heat all day?"

"Yep. I love being outside in the summer. Why, do I smell?" she said and brought her armpit up to her nose. He peeked up her short shirtsleeve and glimpsed perhaps a week's worth of stubble. "Not too bad yet." And she walked away.

———

8

"Wait," David said.

She didn't stop and called over her shoulder, "You can try to keep up. I walk really fast."

"Wait!"

She stopped and turned around. "Well?" she asked.

"The girls had this idea that you were, I don't know, too mature or grown up for them, so they wanted me to come along to keep you company," he said.

She slowly walked back to him and said, "Well, obviously."

"And that Angela is always trying to arrange hookups for me," he continued.

"I figured somebody thought they were doing one or both of us a favor. Whose place are we supposed to go to?" she asked.

"It's a sick preoccupation of hers—theirs. I let them drag me along because I have nothing better to do. I think they're funny to watch. That's all," he said.

"I don't think I'm your type," she said.

"Why don't you forget about that?" he said.

"Maybe I will. Maybe I won't. It's pretty annoying," she said.

"I don't have a type anyway," he said. She was in front of him now.

"I took one look at you and thought you were Mr. Popular, Mr. Player. But I can see I was being too judgmental. You aren't like that at all. You're like a little mouse, Mouse. I bet you don't have a lot of friends," she said.

"I don't need them," he said.

She punched him hard in the shoulder in the exact same spot as before. "All right, what do you want to do? Show me the town? I'll behave, Mousey Mouse," she said.

"No, please, don't do that! There's something I think you would like. I know you would like," he said.

"You already know what I like?" she asked wryly.

"Probably. It's a tiny bit illegal and could be dangerous, though," he said.

"Can we bring some beer along?" she asked.

"That would make it more illegal and more dangerous, so that's probably a good idea," he said.

"I have to pee first. And I'm starving," she said.

"I DON'T CARE what we eat. I only derive a small amount of satisfaction from any meal," Kiddie had said, so they settled in the first cheap diner they came across.

She ordered an enormous cheeseburger accompanied by a mound of French fries. Surprising given her size but unsurprising given her personality. David ordered the same.

"Afraid I'm going to make you look like a wimp?" Kiddie asked.

"No. I forgot to eat. I forget all the time," David said. He sounded annoyed, although he didn't intend to.

"I'm sorry. I need to tone it down. Me too," she said. "I won't remember until I'm about ready to collapse."

They dove into their meals and after they felt their hunger subside started paying attention to each other again.

"At first you look like you completely fit in, but you really don't belong here at all, do you? Where did you come from?" she asked.

"It's an interesting story. I came here with a woman, but she decided to get married. To someone else," he said.

"Wow, you really built up the tension there," she said. They both laughed. "You don't sound that heartbroken."

"It's a free country," he said.

"True enough. So why don't you move somewhere else?" she asked.

"No reason to stay or leave, so the status quo wins out. They told me you're a professor," he said.

"Indeed I am," she said.

"That's it? People usually like to talk about their work," he said.

"Nope," she said.

"I suppose it hasn't been a great conversation starter when you're around ordinary people, but I want to know," he said.

"Brace yourself. Nobody ever has any clue what I'm talking about. I work in an obscure branch of mathematics that deals with critical transitions or tipping points, as they're often called," she said.

"Huh," he said. "Are you interested in biological phenomena like diseases, or bigger things like, you know, extinctions, invasive species, evolution, climate or sociology, or even cosmological events?" he asked.

She inhaled part of the mouthful of burger she had just bitten off, coughed for ten, twenty seconds until tears streamed down her cheeks, and sipped some water to finally get herself under control.

"For real?" she asked.

"What 'for real'?" he asked.

"That you even know what I'm talking about," she said.

"Sort of. Well? Answer the question," he said.

"All of it. I love all of it. I see it everywhere. I go to sleep thinking about it. I dream about it. It's the same basic principles that determine when an avalanche is going to start as it is when an infection is going to get the upper hand and eat you alive," she said.

"I probably would too. Dream about it. If I understood it," he said.

"You could read up on science and mathematics papers for fun," she said. "Somebody should read them."

"No," he said. "That's too abstract for me."

"Fair enough," she said. "Did you go to college at all?"

He nodded, lowered his head, covered his mouth with his hand, and said, "Linguistics," with his mouth full.

"Damn. There might be critical transitions all over the place in languages, too. I hadn't really thought about it," she said.

"Probably," he said.

"It's not too late to go back and study," she said.

He shook his head. "I was a very poor student. Very lazy. I spent all my time exploring things I liked rather than bothering to explain them."

"That's the trouble. I wonder how much more I would know if I were left alone. If I could get everyone to fuck off. But that sort of defeats the point of academia. You collect ideas and discoveries, brag about them, browbeat your colleagues with your brilliance because you're so hopelessly socially maladjusted that you've perversely tied your self-esteem to delusions of intellectual superiority, and then eventually, quite anticlimactically, disseminate your knowledge. Maybe somebody will find a way to directly scan our brains. That would probably free up an extra two-thirds of your life for exploring and learning," she said.

"Well, maybe you can still take some time to explain things to me, if it wouldn't annoy you," he said.

"No, I wouldn't mind. I suspect I would like it," she said.

Kiddie had them grab a six-pack of cheap canned beer. They rode to the end of a subway line and then hiked to a secluded spot in the large nature preserve situated where the bay lapped at the edge of the city.

"The park technically closes at sunset, but I think that's just to keep people from living here. We can keep out of sight. And I read that it used to be pretty dodgy here, a favorite place to dump dead bodies," David said.

"Ooh! Are we going to look for dead bodies? Because I'm OK with that," Kiddie said.

"No. I think they cleaned them all up. I haven't seen anything any worse here than in the rest of the city. It only seems scary to some people because it's dark and it's a forest," he said.

"And they aren't used to that," she said. "Lame."

David led them through the shadows to a little bump of bedrock surrounded by a dense cluster of trees that did a fair job of insulating them from the faraway urban noises. A quarter moon was setting in the canopy in front of them, on its way to meet its shimmering reflection in the rippling black surface of the water. They sat down and Kiddie kicked off her shoes and opened a can of beer for each of them.

"Ah. This is great with the moon," he said. "Couldn't have turned out better. Look there. You see the silhouettes?" he asked.

One of the silhouettes acknowledged them by hooting.

"An owl? No kidding," she said.

"There are at least two of them in the trees right now. And bats flying around, too," he said. "There are a lot more owls, but there's no way you can count them. If you're downtown and look up and pay attention, you'll also spot falcons circling. I guess they're attracted to all the rats and pigeons."

"Hold on. My eyes are getting used to it." The moonlight illuminated her face in blue. She squinted. "You know what kind it is?" she asked.

"No," he replied.

"It looks like a great horned owl. Very cool. They're giants but only weigh like a few pounds. They're literally everywhere if you look for them. Still, it's a shock to see them here," she said.

"Well, this is your night on the town, drinking beer and watching owls," he said.

"Watch out, Mousey Mouse. They love to eat mice," she said.

"I know! We might get to see them catch a rat or a field mouse," he said.

"Where I grew up, I've seen them carry off big fucking rabbits," she said.

"I wonder if they could catch a little dog," he said.

"I think so," she said.

"Do you do this all the time?" Kiddie asked. "I mean to me, it's a killer first date."

"I used to, by myself, but it's been a while. You're the first person I've ever shown this to," David said.

The night remained hot. They lay down, the bedrock slab cooling their backs a little, drinking and watching the secretive alien night creatures. The moon set and Kiddie began to pick out and explain the few constellations they could see through the trees.

"Yes!" she exclaimed and clinked beer cans with David. An owl had swooped in carrying a rat in its talons, alighted in the branches overhead, and begun ripping open the twitching animal until it was still. It then took it in its beak and jerked its head back several times, with occasional pauses, to shift the carcass farther back into its throat so it could swallow it whole. It was amazing how wide it could open its small mouth.

Hours passed, and Kiddie finally yawned and said, "It's cool that you're like me, a little out there, daydreaming. People probably don't appreciate that."

"I don't really daydream," David replied, but she had just fallen asleep.

Kiddie's rhythmic purring was hypnotic and put him to sleep beside her a few minutes later.

There was a melody in his dream. He tried to identify it but realized it was coming from outside of himself. Kiddie was lying next to him with her hands folded beneath the back of her head, singing to herself. Her voice had a mellow, husky timbre, like the upper register of a cello. He could just about feel her sounds as well as hear them.

"What are you singing?" he asked.

"You don't know this song? I guess it's getting a little dated," she replied.

"I don't know much about music," he said.

"Just an old Bowie song," she said.

David stood and stretched. He hadn't felt so well rested in a long time.

The pink and orange hues of the sunrise had almost given way to midmorning daylight. Kiddie smiled up at him.

"Do you think this is the type of thing that you're supposed to kiss at the end of?" she asked.

An urge to pounce on her surged inside him, but he suppressed it because he felt the impulse was unworthy of her.

"I don't know if I can handle it," he said.

"I can. Sit down."

He did. Kiddie got off her back and knelt beside him.

"I'll start with your cheek. Then you turn your head a little and I'll kiss a little closer to your mouth. We'll find where the limit is," she said.

"Maybe you can turn it into an equation," he said.

"Maybe."

She kissed him on the cheek. She didn't linger, but it wasn't a peck either. He gradually rotated his head and she drew a line of kisses to his mouth. The last one, on the crease in the corner of his grinning lips, seemed to last much longer than the others. His hands had under their own volition risen to reach out and embrace her. He willed them back down.

"How are we doing?" she asked.

"Um, uh," he said.

"Uh-huh. I think that's my limit, too," she said.

She added his address and home telephone number to her cell phone contacts and wrote her own information on the back of one of her business cards because he still didn't own a cell phone himself. They walked back to the subway station and went their separate ways home.

9

—————

The air was already intolerable, stifling and humid, the kind of weather that excited the insects but drove any other living creature into the shade. Even the plants looked sick, gorged on heat and sunlight. Anyone exerting themselves outside felt heroic. David decided to make an insane hike all the way home. He felt dehydrated, so he stopped to cool off and buy some food and water. He was soon tripping along rapidly, feeling more energetic and fit than he had in months. And he smelled like a human, not bad, but drenched in the aroma of himself. It was a day when everywhere he went, in fact, humanity celebrated its scent. Whatever precautions people had taken to mask or inhibit body odor would have melted away in minutes.

After the sun had passed its apex, a subtle breeze squeezed between the buildings, dragging along with it clouds heralding rain that would scourge the steamy, leaden atmosphere. But the heat entrenched itself and checked the assault of the clouds and the wind. Undeterred, the nascent storm rallied and began fanning away the scorching air, offering hope of relief. Then the first lashes of cool. A tipping point. The clouds rapidly thickened and the wind intensified. Sheets of rain began tumbling from the sky when David was a few blocks from home.

David left his sopping clothes in a pile on the bathroom floor and showered. Afterwards, he sat on the edge of his bed with a towel wrapped around his waist, lay back, closed his eyes, and immediately fell asleep.

He awoke to the phone ringing. He looked for the time on the clock radio on the nightstand, but it flashed 12:00. Apparently, there had been a power outage. Outside was late-night darkness and a steady drizzle.

"You have a visitor," the concierge told him, "A Missus— excuse me, ma'am, your name again?—Oh, his sister? Your sister is here to see you. Can I send her up?"

He had never had any visitor he hadn't brought in himself, but he smiled thinking of Kiddie. She seemed like the type to stop by unannounced and have this sense of humor.

"Yes, yes," he said enthusiastically.

A few minutes later there was a knock at the door. He opened it wearing only a towel and watched Maeve glide past and take a seat in the same place she had the first time she had visited.

He went to the bedroom to dress and called out, "I wasn't expecting you. You're lucky you caught me at home. I was thinking of going out."

"Oh, that is lucky. Of course you don't mind," she stated.

He couldn't say whether he did or he didn't. What time and what day was it? Late Sunday night? Professors probably went to work early on Monday mornings. But it was summer. Was she working at all now? He had no idea.

"Do you know what time it is?" he asked.

"No. I wasn't paying attention," she said.

David came out dressed in old jeans and a polo shirt.

Maeve patted a large shopping bag she had brought in with

her and set it by her feet. "Well, your life's about to change. I brought you some things."

"Oh, good. I haven't eaten."

"Not food, but we can take care of that too. Come sit over here next to me. I look a bit better, don't I? I hope you approve," she said.

He moved to the couch and studied her while she rummaged in the bag. She was wearing a long black taffeta dress cinched around her midsection with a wide sash. Her waist was not as broad as he would have thought. The thick, baggy fabrics she had worn before might have been misleading. The dress was buttoned up to her chin and had sleeves that came down just past her elbows. Her neck fat was now just a single bulge—maybe this collar was more spacious—that blended into her plump cheeks. The skin on her thick forearms and hands was healthy and taut, and not so pale as before, but more the color of ivory. Her hair, still too short, was now in loose curls, and grayer tones had infected the white. It seemed darker nearer the roots, but he had kept the room dimly lit, and it may have been a trick of the shadows. How long had it been since he had seen her for her to have changed that much?

"Here, how's this?" she asked and unfurled a crisp white linen shirt. "Good, she managed not to wrinkle it when she packed it up. There are beige pants to match. I don't suppose anyone's told you that your wardrobe could do with a bit of sprucing up."

She had purchased several pairs of socks, three coordinated sets of shirts and pants, and a belt.

"There will be shoes too. Maybe next time," she said.

David could only grin.

"Oh, you're mocking me behind those lovely eyes of yours, aren't you?" She placed her right index finger on the side of his chin and gently pivoted his head, so that he was looking straight into her eyes. "Oh, you're not! You seem genuinely pleased, although you don't realize you're a master pretender. I'm glad my trinkets make you happy. I haven't changed with the times—to tell you the truth, I've never been part of the times—but I know what works, what works on you."

"Thank you," he said.

"Shall I take you somewhere to eat, my poor hungry little darling? I'll call for a taxi," she said.

And so went the first of their rendezvous. Subsequent ones occurred irregularly and were never planned, sometimes twice a week, sometimes once in several weeks. David assumed that Maeve continued to go about her life as she was required to and felt like, and he didn't await her return. Yet uncannily, she found her way over on the nights he was home and claimed never to have come when he wasn't there. She usually brought gifts and either took him out to eat or carried with her the essentials for a light meal in case his cabinets and refrigerator were empty, which was almost always the case. Then they would spend slow quiet hours preparing dinner, eating, talking about the things they had seen, and finally cleaning up before she departed.

The gifts Maeve bought for him began to fill up his closet and drawers. Just with a glance, she had sized up his every dimension so perfectly—even his feet—that she was able to have things tailor made for him. Her own appearance changed steadily. After what couldn't have been but a few months, her hair had already grown to her collar and sleek, wavy raven-black strands began to outnumber the dowdy white she had been sporting. Her weight dropped slowly, really imperceptibly as well, and he finally accounted for how much after trying to picture the earlier versions of her, starting with the portly matron he had first met.

Her clothing transformed along with her shape, and she was soon wearing things that fit more snugly over her evolving figure. With each new meeting she revealed more of her legs, arms, and neck. Despite being able to apprise the cumulative changes, he could never recall more than a rough approximation of her appearance.

"I don't understand about your hair, or your—your—" he stammered when he could no longer contain his curiosity, a day when he found a pleasantly handsome middle-aged woman at his door.

"What? That I can be whatever I want?" she responded. "He"—she never spoke his name, or the word *husband*—"has had a pathetic old man living inside him since he was young, before I knew him, probably since he was a child. Don't think that's a cruel, spiteful criticism. I'm being honest. He's quite intelligent, but he can't help being a pig. He's disappointed in a world disappointed in him, but he doesn't have any of the qualities needed to change things, so he and the rest of humanity have been circling, snarling antagonists for decades. When it comes to appearances, he can't be bothered at all. It's better for him to have a white, unassuming old witch to match his personality. It's better for me too. But you're not so young yourself."

"Hm, I haven't thought about my age since I was a kid. And then all of a sudden, I was an adult, with a woman—a wife— and a home full of things. It's hard to believe how long ago that happened," he said.

Conversations about their pasts were infrequent. They could have blinked into being the instant before they had first met with just enough fragments of biographies to plausibly define real people, to give credibility to their existences. They rarely even reminisced about their own brief shared history. Every encounter retained a near-total immediacy.

"And?" she asked wistfully.

"And what?"

"And I'm not so old, am I?" she asked.

David could verify the fact of a woman sitting next to him,

but his inner vision, the faculty that processed into thoughts, impressions, and emotions what the senses took in, struggled to focus on her. Like he was seeing her walk past a large filmy window that showed some parts clearly and distorted others. It was almost as if he were seeing an entirely different woman each time she visited. Her eyes, her voice—they were the same, weren't they? His memory was strangely unreliable, so he resorted to faith, belief. But who knew who was really strutting back and forth behind that translucent glass?

When she wasn't with him, he could envision her only generally, as prominent features, but no more clearly than a person listening to his descriptions of her could. He had many precise memories of strangers, acquaintances, and relations, and better than most he could recognize people long after even brief encounters. But if Maeve were placed in a room with similar-looking women, he doubted he could pick her out.

After another unmeasured passage of time, David went outside one day thinking the temperature would still be in the seventies and found that he needed to go back to his apartment for a sweater or a jacket. The tipping point for another autumn, when the old growth finally withers and falls away.

Maeve came that night. She had cut her hair, exorcising the last bit of gray, and restyled it. Voluminous, silky jet locks snaked down her neck and capered in ringlets that framed her face. Her green eyes blazed a light from within. Was this the beauty that she had talked about, manifest again?

THIRD DIGRESSION

He finished the last of his brandy and pounded down the tumbler. I nodded for the barkeep to get him another. He took a break from his story and waited for his drink.

I had to ask, "What happened with this professor lady? You make it sound as if you two were falling in love. How does she figure into all this?"

"She doesn't," he said.

"Really?" I protested. "Why bring her up?"

If I was to endure a litany of this man's relationships, I would have been most interested in this one. His story of her changed him; genuine warmth, although not heat, radiated from him. I needed to know what tragedy lay at the end of this promising beginning.

"Maybe it was the last thing you could call normal to happen to me," he concluded.

"So what, is this some kind of turning point or something, where if you had followed this girl, your life would have been different?" I asked.

"Don't be ridiculous," he answered, irritated. "What's the

point of wondering about things that didn't happen, as if the answer to all your problems is some choice you never made? At best, you can think about not making the choices you did make, and what does that realistically look like? Just any other normal day where nothing new happened. Either whatever happened, happened, or nothing did. There's never an alternative," he said.

"Yeah, that kind of speculation is certainly overrated," I said, intending to be ironic, but finding myself agreeing with him. "But you didn't just turn your back on her like some jerk, did you?"

"No, no, no. Not at all. Her card was in my pocket and got soaked—my sweat and the rain—and the whole thing disintegrated. I remembered the university, and of course, I had her name. I called the school's main number and asked the operator to transfer me to her extension. Do you know how many times I ever called a woman like that?" he said.

"I'll guess never," I said.

"That's right. There's a reason I never had a cell phone and hardly ever used a regular phone. It's incredibly hard to do. What do you say to a person you can't see, smell, touch, or even hear that well?" he said.

"I've often wondered that myself, and yet people are somehow able to talk on the phone," I said. "They manage to do it quite a lot."

"I left messages on her office line. I hope it was her office. Whatever phone I reached didn't have a personal greeting. I didn't have an answering machine, so I don't know if she ever called back. Although, it seemed like many times I was thinking about calling her, Maeve would turn up and I would get distracted," he said.

"It sounds like you did everything you possibly could," I said.

How much would it have taken, I wondered, for the animal

spirits reaching out between them to latch onto and bind them to each other? Maybe only a little more persistence from him, or her. How strong were these forces? Maybe it was impossible, and their waif-like irresolution was deceptively insurmountable. The night is tricky. It distorts all proportion.

10

O ne October day—David had noticed Halloween
displays in the stores—a tempest swept through the
city, the end of the long odyssey of the year's last
tropical storm. It tore loose scores of leaves that still loitered on
the branches, rent tree limbs from their sockets, rattled signs,
toppled garbage cans, created miniature whirlwinds of litter,
and pelted the city so hard with raindrops that they sounded
like hale when they struck his window. The streets were devoid
of human activity but for a few cars that meekly picked their
way through the turmoil. David, unwashed and unshaven, had
lain all day on the carpet, watching through the window that
ran from the floor to the ceiling and formed the outside wall of
his living room. He enjoyed the wind's sound, imagining how
its tone and pitch changed according to its intensity and the
shape of the structure or entity it was surging over, under,
around, or through. But being out in it he couldn't abide. A
force that penetrated the senses and affected your movements
so strongly but couldn't be observed or described was
intolerable.

David had pondered for so long that rectangle of existence,

a vignette framed on his outside wall, that he felt like he was losing the ability to verify the space and time of the universe that contained it, that the longer he absorbed the details of this patch of reality, the more everything that lay beyond felt like an illusion.

Maeve arrived in the evening in the middle of the squall. Her soft and steady knocking seemed at first to be a new sound coming from the other side of the glass. He hadn't seen her for what felt like weeks. He sometimes glanced at the primitive sketch of her he had tucked away somewhere in his imagination and then went about his life as if she were an old, estranged friend.

His mind resisted coming out from the storm so that he could let her in, but apparently he had left the door unlocked. And then the reflection in the window glass showed a woman who must be Maeve. Saying nothing, she let her overcoat drop to the floor, took off her shoes and tossed them carelessly near the wall, and padded over to him in her stockinged feet.

"What does he think of how you look now?" he asked, still facing the window, addressing the reflection. The question came on its own, without his willing it.

"What difference is there for him to see? Besides, we stopped looking at each other a long time ago. Maybe he only looked at me once, that first time, and has been addressing that old picture ever since. I wouldn't be surprised if that's how his brain works. It would explain a lot. Maybe he never looked at me at all. People are stupid that way, unwilling to rely on their eyes, but preferring to see what they want or what they think they should. More people are like that than you might think," she said, apathetically.

"I want to keep watching the storm," David said. "You can come sit with me." He turned his head to look at her from over his shoulder. "But you've been out in it. How did you manage to stay so dry? Are there many cabs out?" Her hair wasn't the least bit ruffled: It was long, thick, and luxurious now, like a calligrapher had plunged a brush to the bottom of the inkwell and doodled sensuous jet-black curlicues.

She smiled and sat next to him, legs tucked under her, ignoring his questions, and said, "The weather is often extraordinarily beautiful after a big storm. You can understand people thinking it was some kind of apology from God. But if the storm were a being, it would think it was the most beautiful thing in the world exactly as it was and not feel it needed to be apologized for. Perhaps it would find those sunny days that follow, really just the absence of its power, a bit embarrassing."

"It seems clumsy to me, not powerful," David said. "But that's what makes it interesting. There's never been a god of clumsiness, has there? An underrated quality, isn't it?"

"There are gods of chaos and discord, but I think they all have some kind of willful intent to their actions. Common, innocent clumsiness doesn't seem to be represented in the pantheon," she said.

"If you really pay attention to nature, that seems to be the governing principle," he said.

David rolled onto his back. His hand happened to land on the one of hers that she was leaning on. Her thumb stroked the tip of his pinky, and his fingertips traced the ridges of the backs of her fingers. Her skin was soft and warm. Their fingers interlocked, and she leaned over to look down at him, to breathe in his exhalations and for him to breathe in hers.

"I'm not so old, and you're not so young, are you? I'm not so old, and you're not so young," she incanted to him. He inhaled her words too and listened to the storm outside trying to shake the signs free from their posts.

Maeve sat up, pulled her hand free, and pointed to a bag she had left by the door. "I've brought us something to eat, of course. Are you hungry? I'm starving," she said. This cued his brain to recall the idea of hunger, how it felt, and then to realize that he was feeling dazed right now because he hadn't eaten since he had become infatuated with the storm early in the morning.

"Me too," he said.

"You should eat more. You're looking a little pale and gaunt. Not a look that suits you. Is everything else all right? Do you need anything? When was the last time you saw other people, or, say, a woman?"

There was one concern. He would eventually run out of money, and nothing and nobody had appeared this time to rescue the situation.

Maeve would pay for things, pay for everything, but if he wanted accountability to and from her, he would have to demand it. He couldn't, and she would never agree anyway. She was always just the present, a random, unreliable, transitory moment, not the foundation for structure or continuity. He felt like he had the first night he had been away from the last woman—anxious. That was the exact word. He had at least grown enough to stop referring to the feeling euphemistically. Thoughts like this made him feel tired and want to keep staring out the window.

He murmured to himself, "Jesus, I still have so much to do." Voicing those words made his worries real.

"Like what?" she asked. "You're so pretty. I doubt it's important. Whatever you men think up rarely is."

"I don't know. I'm not sure," he said. It was a tepid, simpering response, he knew, and he felt disgusted with himself, but it was the truth. "I can't even focus. It's unusual for me to feel confused."

"Hm, that might just be the hunger. If not, I know what the feeling is. People always overanalyze it because infecting their lives with melodrama covers up the fact that we're all weak and lazy in rather basic, boring, and pathetic ways. Letting irresolution fester is like sleeping too long. You actually feel less well, and it's harder to get up. If you lie there long enough, you feel dehydrated and thirsty, your circulation begins to suffer, and you start to feel achy. Nothing about the day ahead can motivate you at that point. But you end up getting out of bed anyway because instinct takes over and forces you to stop doing nothing."

"I wonder if there are people who can do nothing forever and never care," he said.

"Yes. They're like miracles, if you ask me. Like these people who can sit for years and years watching television and eating, blowing up to half a ton. Everybody thinks they need to be cured of something, but their only fault is that they overindulge in the one elixir that would make everyone happy forever, guilt-free laziness. Imagine how much contentment, peace, and prosperity would come from that," she said.

"They don't seem happy," David said.

"That's because everyone tells them they're not," Maeve replied.

"I know it sounds like bravado, but when you can't decide, your only options are to do nothing, literally nothing, and just go about your business like nothing happened or ever will. Or stop thinking and act on impulse. Do whatever you're in the mood for and leave it at that. The typical person living a typical life doesn't have enough power or resources to get into too much trouble. Everyone exaggerates how much any decision or action actually matters. It's not as if we all have our fingers on the nuclear button."

"Wasn't there something you were going to tell me? What did you say? Something like you couldn't talk to me about it yet?" David asked.

"When was that?" Maeve replied.

"The first time I met you. The first time you came over here," he said.

"Let me think. It's been ages," she said.

"Has it?" he asked.

"Don't be silly. We've known each other quite a while now. What did I want to tell you? I probably was complaining about women. Have you ever noticed—well, maybe *you* wouldn't—that there's a persistent revulsion and indignation within my gender directed against ourselves? It's poisonous and full of suspicion and innuendo. I doubt this ever came from men. More likely from bourgeois mothers, grandmothers, and older sisters nursed on too many fairy-tale princess stories. I never had any of that," she said.

"That's probably changed," he said.

"When I was fifteen, I was interested in a particular boy and curious about sex, so I asked him if he wanted to have sex with me. He told me he didn't know how. I told him I didn't know either, and that we could figure it out together. So we did. We told each other what we liked and what we didn't like, what felt good and what didn't, taught and learned from each other, had a nice time, and kept practicing. Then we found other partners. The end. That's the sentimental, romantic story of my first love," Maeve said. "And I'm sure he's given a lot of pleasure to other people in the world. I hope he never stopped. That should be a virtue we celebrate. Imagine what a wonderful world it would be if we lionized the great lovers, and only them."

"That's all? That's what you thought you couldn't share?" he asked.

"Wouldn't that have been too intimate?" she asked.

She paused to let him respond, but David had nothing to say to any of this. It was unsatisfactory. If he was one of the last people you should get advice from, Maeve had to be the absolute last. Even he could tell that her attitude was absurd, dissolute and naive. Nothing was or ever happened the way she described. You couldn't call her a fantasist because her problem wasn't that she was seeing what wasn't real, but that she only saw a tiny amount of what was, and with incredible insight and clarity.

"I'm sure whatever it is that's bugging you isn't really important, my beautiful one. None of it matters. Who cares? You'll see," she said confidently and kissed him on the cheek.

David shook his head and sighed. He studied her expression. Wistful, blank, patronizing—that is, an impossible brew of expectation, disinterest, and superiority. When he couldn't swear this was the same person he had first met, this singular expression of hers always reassured him.

"I might be getting sick," he said. "I never dress right when the seasons change. And now this storm's bringing such a damp chill."

"See, you don't even have to worry about that. Remember, I bought you several jackets. Now go put out the food. It's my turn to lie here looking mysterious," she said.

She lay on her side, back to the outside world, watching him, eyes gleaming mischievously, stroking a thick coil of black hair that snaked around the bottom of her jawline and dipped its tail into the shadowy cup of her jugular notch.

11

David began having vivid dreams, which meant he wasn't sleeping well. Nightmares, too, the first time he had ever had them. A variety of scenarios that led to the same feelings of confusion and discomfort he had shared with Maeve. He remembered a little about one version: He was dragged slowly by his hair through a field. Painlessly, though. When he reached up, he couldn't touch whatever or whoever was pulling him, and couldn't make it let go. The feelings themselves were bad enough on their own, but they were always followed by lingering shame and self-loathing for his having felt them in the first place. He would lie awake in bed until late in the morning, sometimes until noon.

After David pulled himself out of bed, he would walk. Walk far and briskly. Winter had been what people would call mild, but what he would call bland. After the patches of green withered away, the residents of the city wore even less color. A drizzle fell occasionally, sometimes snowflakes dusted the tops of newspaper stands, garbage cans, and cars that had been parked for a while. The weather was gray, stuck in a gray area, open to interpretation. Maybe it was cold. Maybe it wasn't.

David dressed lightly and warmed himself through physical exertion. His observations and thoughts so enthralled him that they generated their own heat. He thought about love, about what people meant when they used the word. He concluded that people felt a kind of euphoria from giving or consuming. Could people who had no needs and no desire be capable of loving? He couldn't imagine a scenario in which this would occur.

Had women loved him? Had they been generous? Maybe they had been self-centered, focused on their own happiness, assertive in this regard, and yearned for reciprocity. For a while, they received reflections of their own benevolence. That could be a lot, because the world tended to absorb and dissipate generosity. But a reflection provided insufficient feedback about yourself. It couldn't suggest how to be, how to grow, how to live better, how to live less poorly. You can groom only the surface of yourself in a mirror.

Maeve's self-indifference bordered on nihilism. It seemed juvenile, her radical rejection of self, all selves. Other than a portion of his inexhaustible free time and the fact of his purposeless existence, David offered her nothing. And what did he receive from her? He couldn't identify any need of his that she fulfilled. He rarely used her gifts, which must have been worthless trifles compared to her own financial resources. Two people with no demands barely trying. And yet it wasn't insignificant. Time only seemed to be consequential during the infrequent occasions they spent together.

There was also something inscrutable about Maeve. He was overlooking something critical, but couldn't identify it.

Up and down the broad avenues David walked, dissecting the city, block by block. He refined his mental images of each neighborhood. In many places scaffolding cocooned what was being repaired, what was being built, or what was being destroyed. In some neighborhoods, old buildings were obliterated without hesitation. In others, similar buildings were reverently rehabilitated and repurposed. He pondered the connection between architecture and the people, what reacted to what, or if they were reacting to each other. Subtle differences in how people dressed, where they tended to eat, shop, or loiter. How these things were manifest in their demeanors. Could you determine where in the city people lived just by observing them, as if they were members of separate tribes that had their own customs, traditional clothes, traditional dwellings, and traditional food?

Smells changed from district to district. Of different kinds of traffic: The newer cars of certain neighborhoods were mostly odorless. In other places he smelled diesel truck exhaust, the poorly filtered emissions of motorcycles and scooters, older vehicles that combusted oil and antifreeze. The scents of open water, of moving water, of still water, and of stagnant, foul water. The scents of large open patches of ground, of vegetation whose decay hadn't been interrupted by a frigid winter, of sodden earth that harbored mold in the temperate air.

But the sounds were nearly the same. The most critical flaw. So much noise. Too many sounds, in fact, for any one of them to have any poignancy. You couldn't hear anything.

He synthesized all these observations. Was he daydreaming? No, only organizing his impressions. He began noticing something he hadn't paid attention to before: the boundaries. He wondered if civilization had ever been so static and minutely planned before. People had always lived with movement and change. Turmoil had molded us; it was the catalyst for evolution. It was the identity of the supreme deity itself, in fact, the all-encompassing designation for things out of our control and beyond our understanding. Whether or not there was any justice to its actions was possibly an irrelevant question. At some point, something had gone awry, and our endeavors had swung toward control and preventing change, so much so that an incomprehensible and chaotic god had become unbelievable. If our attention relented, how long would it take the natural condition of clumsy destruction and regrowth to reassert itself? Months? Weeks? Days? Hours? How long would it take for the teeming hordes of disorderly life gnawing away at human artifice to succeed in grinding it to dust?

He envisioned the patterns in the rubble should the buildings crash against each other and topple like dominoes. The gaping pits in the earth that would appear, like the holes left where the root balls of fallen trees once clutched the ground. Open, pocked ground on which the sun would get to shine on everyone and everything again, across which people who had once lived universes apart would easily be able to see one another.

David found Angela staring at her cell phone in front of his building, pretending she had randomly chosen that spot to wait in. The waist of her pants was too tight, and it squeezed out large bulges of hip and belly fat that were visible under her sweatshirt. When he had last seen her, she had been on a crash diet that had had little effect other than leaving her fatigued. She was now the fattest he had ever seen her. She looked great, like a happy, healthy, glowing maiden from an old painting.

He considered making her awkwardly hail him by pretending to be lost in thought. But his ideas about the orderly compartmentalization of the city nagged him, and she represented a phenomenon that countered that. Here stood a woman who, no matter how hard she tried, didn't belong. She never would. That might be worth something.

"Hi there," David boomed.

"Oh, hello," Angela said, badly feigning surprise.

"I'm glad I ran into you," he said.

"Really?" she said so pleadingly that she left herself vulnerable to all sorts of humiliation. He could torment her by asking about the money she owed him, the phone number of one of her friends, or a suggestion for a new place to live, eat, drink, hang out, or take someone on a date.

"Yeah. I was wondering what happened to you, if everything was OK," he said, supposing that would be adequate, encouraging small talk.

"I thought you got tired of me . . . all of us little girls," she said.

Odd to say, considering she was staking him out, but he let it pass.

"What little girl?" he asked. "You're a woman. You helped me find a place to live and went out of your way to be friends with me."

"Well, you deserve it. I, um, everyone really likes you," she said. "I'm, um, having a party soon. I, I, I mean, I want to have a party. I haven't had one in a long time. Would you come?"

"OK. Just let me know when it is," he said.

"This Friday," she blurted out.

"That sounds fine," he said.

Angela pulled a pen and a small notebook from her purse, took her time writing on one of the pages, carefully ripped out the sheet, and handed it to him. She had written in beautiful script her address and telephone number and drawn a small detailed map from his building to hers.

"What time?" David asked.

"Whenever you want," she said.

Angela called to remind David on Friday morning. He waited until nightfall, went out to a diner nearby for a coffee, sat at the counter and wasted some time talking to a waitress, and, finally, after noticing a clock on the wall above the grill and that it showed 9:00, went to Angela's apartment.

There were no sounds of revelry coming from the inside when David approached her unit. He knocked once and his knuckles missed the second time because of how quickly the door was flung open. Angela appeared to be alone.

"Am I too early?" he asked. "I must be getting old if everyone arrives so much later than me."

"I bet you're hungry," Angela said. "Would you like something to eat?"

"I'm starving. I forgot to eat today," he said.

"I thought so. Have a seat," she said.

He sat on an unfinished pinewood chair at a small square unfinished pinewood table, the sort of cheap dining set that comes in a flat-pack box from a discount store. Two places were set for soup and a main course. In the center of the table was an empty Chianti bottle with a taper candle stuck in the top. Angela struck a match, lit the candle, turned off the light to the single room that served as her eating area, living room, and bedroom, and went into the kitchen. The tidy space contained an unfinished pinewood futon that she would have unfolded and slept on, an unfinished pinewood desk with a laptop and a small flat panel television on it, and an unfinished pinewood coffee table holding a neat stack of magazines. It looked like you could fit everything in the back of a van. A radiator was situated beneath a single narrow window that looked out at the brick wall on the other side of the alley. A few pictures and posters hung from the walls. One was a multi-panel silver frame that appeared to contain photographs of her and her family. Two rotund but by no means obese parents. A young version of Angela in a white dress receiving some kind of religious sacrament. Angela in a graduation gown with one arm around a girl who resembled her and looked a few years older, and the other around a boy who resembled her and looked a few years younger. That older girl, now a woman, holding a baby with a man next to her. In the top margin a little cross was engraved, and in the bottom the name Angelina.

"Is your name Angelina?" David called to her.

"Yes," she responded.

"Why don't you use that name? I like it a lot better," he said.

"I think it stands out too much. Plus it's already owned by someone else," she said.

"What do you mean?" he asked.

"You know, the actress? Or even the children's book character?" she said.

"I don't know what you're talking about," he said.

"I know you don't. It doesn't matter. Call me Angelina, then," she said.

She came from the kitchen and set out a carafe and two glasses.

"It's fizzy lemonade. I made it myself. Fresh-squeezed. I know you don't like to drink alcohol very much," she said.

"Like Italian lemon soda. I haven't had this in a long time," he said. "I love this stuff. The tart, the sweet, the bubbles."

"I know. You told me that once," Angelina said. "Save some for me. But no, actually, have as much as you want. I made it for you."

"Do you need some help in there?" David asked and followed her into the kitchen.

"That would be great," she said. "I only just started because I wanted everything to taste really fresh. But there's not a lot of space."

"What are we making?" David asked.

"Oh, nothing fancy. White bean soup and lasagna," she said.

He pointed to a ball of pale yellow dough on a portion of the counter that had been dusted with flour. "You make your own pasta?" he said. "Can I take care of that for you?"

"You know how?" she asked.

"Uh-huh."

"Go for it. I have the feeling you'll be very precise," she said.

"You don't mind if I rummage around for what I need?" he said.

"Help yourself," Angelina said.

She smiled. Not the way he had always seen her smile before, that had seemed either exaggerated or forced. Peacefully, serenely now. Not the face of a person you could be even a little cruel toward.

The kitchen was little more than a strip of counter about a yard long bookended by the refrigerator and the cooking range. David and Angelina couldn't help jostling and nudging each other to move around, reach an item, or get the other person to let them by. He realized that he had never touched her before. He had all of her friends, and often more than that, but had never made physical contact with her. Not a hug or a handshake or even an accidental bump.

Fifteen minutes later, David had set aside nine strips of noodles to dry.

"How did I do?" he asked.

"Very nice," she said. "The soup's almost ready. Go sit down."

Angelina set the soup pot on a trivet in the middle of the dining table and filled both their bowls. She sat and spread her napkin on her lap.

They ate in silence. Angelina was the more poised, refined eater, while David was aware of being clumsier and noisier.

"Do you like it?" she asked.

"Yes. A lot," he replied.

"Do you want to know where I got the recipe?" she asked.

"Sure," he answered.

"My grandmother taught me how to cook when she babysat me and my brother and sister. Only me and not the two of them. She told me they were special secrets," she said. "Do you want to know the last time I cooked, I mean really cooked like this?"

"OK," he said.

"Right when I got out of college and first moved here. I thought I would cook all the time. Life would be the same, just in a different place. Then somehow I never had time for it," she said.

"I used to cook," David said.

"I could tell," she said. "It's surprising. You don't seem like you're that interested in food."

"It was for someone else. Just a game I played," he said.

"I always thought when you cook for somebody, it shows you really care. Especially if they enjoy it. It means you paid attention to them and are considerate about their tastes and dietary needs," she said.

"Maybe," he said.

"Have some more soup?" she asked and, correctly gauging how hungry he was, ladled his bowl full again before he could answer.

"This is the only apartment I've ever had. I haven't spent money on anything in it for years. I just keep on paying the rent. The only problem is the lack of sunlight. I want to have plants. Well, there's not enough space for them anyway. If I got going with gardening, I would go crazy. I need a big place. I'm saving up for a house. Obviously not around here. I would never have enough money for that. But someplace way out in the countryside. Maybe the mountains," she said.

The conversation had taken its usual turn, with David being a trusted critic, usually to correct and sometimes encourage her thoughts and ideas. Except he had nothing to criticize this time.

"I think it's a good idea," he said.

"Oh, I know. That it's a good idea and that you would agree with me. My friends, the ones I made here, don't understand," she said.

Angelina continued describing the life she had planned. How much she was saving and how long it would take. That, despite the sacrifices living like this entailed, she could save money much faster here than anywhere else. The amount and ideal type of land, five acres fringed with woods with some open spaces in the middle.

David followed her back into the kitchen and helped her make the lasagna while she continued talking. Since she was already used to tight living conditions, she could start with a small cottage or even a cabin and renovate and add on to it. She enumerated the risks and expenses, such as the lack of good-paying jobs in rural areas, but concluded she would be more qualified than most for one of the rare office jobs, or could work as a store manager or something like that.

How much he used to enjoy her merry little rambling, but this was altogether different. A thoroughly planned life, devoid of abstract ideas, romance, or idealism. Practical and attainable, and actually quite simple. Why had he never thought of anything like that?

The oven timer sounded.

"Ha ha. We still have to let it set up for at least forty-five minutes or it will fall apart. But it's almost midnight, and maybe you don't like to eat too late," she said.

"It's fine. What about you?" he said.

"Oh, David. You know I always stay up too late," she said.

"OK. I can wait," he said.

12

———

"Money," he said. "I wasn't spending a lot, but I figured that I would run out eventually. Soon. It seemed like something I should try to delay. Besides, I didn't have anything better to do. I did a rough calculation and figured that even earning minimum wage would reduce my deficit enough to let me hold out at least for another year."

David had few preferences about employment. He didn't want to be indoors during the day. He would work outside or in the evenings. He didn't want to sit at a desk. He didn't want to write a resume and had nothing interesting to put on one. That limited him to a few simple choices. He assumed he would be able to canvas the city for "Help Wanted" signs and let intuition choose for him.

He marched along without success until twilight, when he was dizzy from hunger and thirst and was spun around by the masses of workers spilling from buildings and subway stations onto the streets. The afternoon sunshine faded, and the true air temperature could be felt. It was close to freezing, and a gentle, chilling breeze wafted across the cityscape, cooling the perspiration on his clothes and skin. He shivered and tensed.

David stopped in a glowing pink square. He looked up at the enormous words "Midland Mediterranean" spelled out in neon. He liked the wordplay. Taped to the inside of the glass door was a plain piece of white office paper with the words "Dishwasher Needed. Evening Shift." written in red marker.

The restaurant's old façade showed that it was one of those places fortunate or unfortunate enough just to break even. The entry door's hydraulic hinge was worn out, so it banged shut dangerously at your heels, and its bottom glass panel was cracked diagonally. If you entered too slowly, it could easily close on your arm or your ankle. A strip of cardboard was taped to the length of the doorjamb to prevent aluminum from slamming against aluminum.

The restaurant smelled of old-fashioned aftershave, onions, spices, butter, grilled meat, and a reminder of old-fashioned cigars. The interior was clad in richly tanned wood that looked like it had absorbed all those scents. A lean young man with curly black hair welcomed him with a friendly, quizzical expression from behind a vacant bar. A muscular, broad-chested middle-aged man emerged through a saloon door from the kitchen. He had the same hair and eyes as the bartender's, but his face was composed of lumps, one for each cheek, the chin, the brows, and the nose. Tufts of black hair peeked out of the top of his shirt, which was open to the third buttonhole, and it looked as if he could barely roll his shirt cuffs up over his bulky, hairy forearms. He sauntered through the dining area, smiling and waving from his waist to the customers. A young olive-skinned girl with a dispirited triangular face stood leaning on her elbows next to a cash register on the front counter and read a book with what looked like mathematical formulae on its pages. She wore a billowy long-sleeved white blouse and snug high-waisted trousers. She had thick black eyebrows, but she had dyed her hair crimson and painted her fingernails to match. She flicked her hand to indicate that he should sit wherever he wanted.

As soon as David took a seat, the girl was next to him, presenting a simple menu printed on thick stock paper. The choices comprised an admixture of Greek, Italian, Lebanese, Turkish, Israeli, and generic Mediterranean and Middle Eastern foods. The middle-aged man walked by again, both arms lined with plates, and delivered them to a party of four seated by the front window.

After a few minutes, the young man from the bar walked to David's table with a pen and small notebook held close to his face and asked, "Yes, sir?" rolling the *r* lightly.

The bartender, apparently not a practitioner of any kind of shorthand, carefully wrote down the single item, having had to scratch it out once when he misspelled it, and walked away. David passed the time watching the middle-aged man walk by several times to deliver more dishes. After about twenty minutes, the young woman came with his order.

"Your cappuccino, man," she said, placing it in front of him. He smelled perfume, predominantly scented with lilac. "Maybe you want something else to drink? We filter our tap water." She exaggerated her *w*'s to make sure they sounded right.

"Thank you. Who should I ask about the dishwasher job?" he said.

She placed her hands on her hips and drummed her fingertips.

"Dishwasher, eh? What do you mean by tzat?" she asked.

"There's a sign on the front door," David replied.

"It's still tzere? You're a customer now. Take your time. Relax and tzen talk to Ivo." She jerked her head in the direction the middle-aged man had just gone. "You see, we're busy now."

"OK. A glass of water would be fine too."

They weren't so much busy as the people working there

didn't seem inclined to hustle. And apparently the clientele had nowhere else to be. A few couples or small groups had quiet conversations. One or two diners sat alone reading papers, tinkering with their cell phones, or staring at the luminous pink world outside the window. David did as he was told and waited. Eventually the few customers began to drift away, while a small crowd gathered at the bar. The young woman reappeared to check on him.

"Maybe I can bring you some more coffee and some cake," she said resolutely. "Don't worry, it is . . . complimentary," she said, carefully enunciating every syllable.

The man who must have been Ivo strode to David's table with a wine bottle tucked beneath one arm, a small saucer with an espresso cup in one hand, and a small plate with a large square of napoleon in the other. He set the coffee and the cake down in front of David, placed the bottle on the table, put his hand in a bulging trouser pocket, fumbled around for a few seconds, and produced a corkscrew. He inserted it into the top of the bottle, screwed it in briskly, and tugged out the cork effortlessly, as if it had been lubricated.

"I will sit with you," he said. "It's OK?"

Ivo was about to pour the wine but, finding no glasses, he raised his hand into the air, snapped his fingers, and swiveled his head, searching the room for the young woman. "Magda, beautiful, bring us some glasses," he said when he spotted her. She was at one of the window tables throwing plates into a bus tub, but she stopped what she was doing and strolled to the bar. "I can call that one beautiful and no one can complain. This is my niece. Her mother—my brother's wife"—he grinned, closed his eyes as if savoring a delicious flavor, and shook his head —"even more stunning. Maybe someday she will be too. Magda is still a girl. But her mother has power. Some men are too dead to see it, but to others she is like an addicting drug they would ruin themselves and other people to get. I don't dare call her beautiful, because it would break the tension, you know, the surface tension that keeps me from sinking and drowning."

Magda brought two glasses. "Thank you, my dear," Ivo said and filled them to the top. He stared at his glass and sighed forlornly. "We had other waitress. Local college girl. Pretty, too, but you know, nothing special. I couldn't say anything. No 'honey' or 'sweetheart' or 'darling.' Same things I tell Magda. Hmph! Can you imagine? The owner can't be polite to his own staff! She also complained about Magda not having to work as hard. 'My niece, my family,' I told her. 'You are not my family.' Simple, right? Drink. *Nazdrave*. Means 'to your health.'"

Ivo raised his glass high, almost over his head, David did the same with his, and they clinked them together. Ivo took a long draft, and David set his glass down untouched. "Oh, if you had seen how her mother had looked at me when she asked me to give Magda a job. 'My dear Ivo,' she calls me. Her body sways like some tree full of ripe fruit you want to pluck. 'But don't make her work too hard. She needs to study,' she tells me. It's a hot sticky day. It makes her hair curly like crazy. Her perfume is mixing with her sweat. I almost faint. It's too much for me. So this is what I cannot explain to the American girl who wants to be treated so seriously about why she has to do what she does and why Magda gets to do what she does." He slapped the top of the table lightly to finish the story and stared, eyes gleaming, at David.

"I just came to ask about the dishwasher job," David said.

"Aha! I heard that and I thought you were joking. But we don't know you yet, other than that you're a patient man. That's good and bad. First, what's your name, and then I'll tell you what's going on here." He told him his name, and Ivo finished his glass and poured himself another.

"So I have this local girl who is making me miserable. Then she complains that Magda is teasing her, and Magda complains how much she hates her. So everyone makes me more miserable. Anyway, she's a good waitress. She didn't like that word, so I have to call her 'server,' like a computer. But she's very good at it, very hardworking and efficient. I suspect she makes more money with her pay and tips than I do. One day, I catch her and the dishwasher in the back, kissing. He has her shirt open and his hands under her bra. Hmph, respect, she is always lecturing me about. He's a good worker, too. Very cheap and reliable. But ugly, ugly. Covered with tattoos and things sticking in his ears and nose and here and here." He pulled down his bottom lip and stuck out his tongue. "He stared at people like he would kill them, and smiled like a crazy person. But he did his work. Always worked all the busy times and the weekend evenings. Didn't mind because he stayed out all night after."

Ivo took another deep drink of wine. "If we finish this, I'll tell Danni to bring us some slivova." He topped up David's full glass.

"I started working here with my father when I was a teenager. He was the chef. Imagine, an engineer in Bulgaria and he comes to this country to cook. But you know, engineer means nothing in a communist country. If you don't know what to do with yourself and nobody knows what good you are, you become an engineer," he said.

"That probably made people resourceful and good problem solvers," David said.

"Hey, that's right. Better than stupid things that kids here who don't know what to do with themselves study. Magda is getting a degree in . . . what is it? Publicity politics? Political economics? She reads the Internet all day and lectures all of us about it. Looks down on us. She can barely do math, and her only technical skill is using her phone! Oh, I'd better not talk so loud.

"My father bought the place when the Greek woman who owned it died. None of her kids or grandkids wanted to run a restaurant. So many nice people have worked here. Not just family, and not just Greeks and Bulgarians. "We came when we were having hard times in nineties. People couldn't buy food. Almost famine. I don't joke. Imagine being surrounded by all these rich fucking countries with people buying whatever they want all the time, getting fat and, God, throwing away stuff when it gets boring, and people are starving to death next door. We're one of those places they ignore and let go wild so they can have a boundary between them and strangers. To hell with all of them. There are more Bulgarians here these days. They're smarter. They don't work in restaurants. Like my brother. My brother is an engineering professor. Very smart. Ha ha, another fucking engineer, right? His wife just gets to be gorgeous. And I work hard, not smart, and I don't have a woman being gorgeous for me. No woman even taking my compliments without complaining."

"Where's your mother?" David asked.

Ivo shrugged and scrunched up his nose. "Nobody knows? I used to think my father lied about this, but he says she gave birth to Stefan and disappeared. I was only five, and the two of us grew up without a woman around. We thought girls were too mysterious. A disaster for us one way or another."

David said, "So you fired the waitress and the dishwasher?"

Ivo replied, "No, no. I wasn't really angry—the number of girls I had kissed and touched in the back room a long time ago is impressive. Well, maybe for me. And let me tell you, that's not even close to the biggest thing I've seen back there. I walked up front and waited for them. Told them I was running a business. That we're all professionals. Expect everyone to be respectful. Same kind of shit she tells me all the time, but, you know, just taking the piss out of them. I hoped she would lighten up, but she's, you know, stuck up. She would have died from embarrassment if she stayed. I wanted to keep the dishwasher. He was smiling. He knew I was teasing her. He was maybe harder to replace. But she didn't let him keep working here."

"So you need a waiter, too?" David asked.

"No, no. We have others who can cover, and you walk outside and trip over girls who can wait tables while they study or try to make their dreams come true. Believe it or not, it's harder to find a good dishwasher," Ivo said.

"Right now everyone does extra duty cleaning up and complains that they're being forced to do other people's jobs and not get paid for it. I told them I can pay them less when they wash dishes. Except Magda. She does whatever she does. She's a good girl . . . she knew she needed to help out more, but one of her test grades was bad, and right away her mother is back in here looking at me like that. And if you could see the dress she was wearing that day!

"So that's the story. You have to understand the soul of any place if you're going to work there. Even tattoo guy, he fit in here. His girlfriend didn't and messed everything up," Ivo said.

"Well, I don't have any tattoos or piercings, I don't want to kiss any of the girls, and I can work whenever you need," David said. "I just don't want to work during the day."

"Bah. Kiss all the girls you want. Just not Magda. I should be asking you all kinds of questions, right? Where are you working now? What's your experience? Are you a criminal? Do you hang out with criminals? Did you kill anyone? Steal anything? Do drugs? Steal things or kill anyone to get drugs? Sell drugs?" he asked.

"I haven't worked for a while . . . since I honestly can't remember when. Before that, I guess you could say that I was a secretary," David replied.

"Not working for a long time? In this city? How is it possible? Everybody works, too much to be healthy. Otherwise you sleep in a closet or on the street. You don't look homeless.

Unless you're beautiful like Magda's mother," Ivo said. He rubbed his chin and looked David over again. "Although . . ."

"I had some savings. And being homeless is what I'm trying to avoid," David said.

"OK, OK. It doesn't matter. This only pays the minimum wage, you know? But we feed you too. And it's not just washing dishes, but cleaning the whole place. You probably won't want to stay very long at that pay, so I'll leave the sign up. Unlike the last guy, I think I'll let you out on the floor, so you can help clear tables, too. You get a tiny share of tips for that. See, I'm already doing you favors. I must like you. Maybe I'll take the sign down after all. Let's say Wednesday through Sunday. You come in at four. There will be mountains of dishes from lunch. We're closed Mondays, and Tuesdays are slow. We can handle the rest of the time, but we want to get the hell out of here on Friday nights and the weekends, so you'll be here by yourself for a few hours finishing up. Terrible and lonely. I can't make it any worse for you, so you definitely won't last long. Maybe I'll leave the sign up."

"OK, that sounds fine," David said. Magda had been clearing tables around them so she could eavesdrop, and she smiled when he answered.

"Hold on, there's some forms. Finish that cake and drink your wine and coffee. No, just take all this stuff into the back with us. Wait, why did you leave your last job?" Ivo asked.

"I wasn't needed anymore," he said.

FOURTH DIGRESSION

During many mornings after nights of drinking, I've regretted the sappy sentimentality I shared with strangers. It's in my nature to be contrarian, but when challenged, I always wind up being agreeable to fit in. I nod my head and yep dumbly to nonsensical personal wisdom and ideas that couldn't possibly be applied fruitfully to any version of life I've experienced or envisioned. Maybe it's impossible to connect with people on anything but the stupidest topics. Try to raise the level of discourse, and you're quickly made an outcast.

This was different. Everything that happened to this man was both eccentric and within the bounds of the absolutely ordinary. His story reminded me that life can be full of benevolent ironies that tip the scales and lift us over obstacles. Had I ever moved forward by walking away? Earned respect by disrespecting people? Obtained greater grace by the greater egregiousness of my fault? Gained friendship by being unfriendly? Won by allowing someone else to win? Lost by being allowed to win? Forged insoluble bonds with those who were fundamentally mismatched with me? Gained long-standing peace through a long-standing grudge?

"I hadn't been lying around miserable, but I hadn't been able to get anything productive to happen," my companion said. "But I think this guy Ivo was in the same boat. Nothing happened for him, either. He probably could have gone anywhere, worked less, lived cheaper, had less responsibility, and wound up in more or less the same place. There wasn't a reason for it."

I said, "People can have a hard time motivating themselves. Me, it's all the time. I think it's usually competition and pressure that get people going. Stress. That's probably what moves civilization forward. In my case, it just makes me lazier. Whenever people apply pressure—social, political, career, or whatever—I shut down. I feel a shackle is being clamped on me and I protest. But I see what you mean. A lot of people keep on for no good reason. Maybe there's just not a reason not to."

He shrugged and replied, "It's weird how much difference there is in the amount of effort people have to put in to get the same things. You know, you can't point to intellectual or physical superiority to determine why some people succeed more than others. It's like human evolution has gone off the rails. Like a few women I knew. I'm not talking about the girls who Angela dragged me around with. Elite women. Beautiful. Shallow. Impossible to impress. Men have to bring them to their tipping points."

"Naturally, I can't claim to have any idea what you're talking about, but I've always imagined that there's a version of a man's world like this. But isn't that a stereotype?" I said.

"You need stereotypes if you want to describe yourself in a few sentences the way everyone demands. Anyway, I also figured out that all men who have an easy time with women hate men and are hated by men. It's primitive. These guys all had their own particular styles, but a basic template. Confident in their looks. Harmlessly roguish. A truly dangerous man who only projected charm—and there are plenty of them, too—would be too inhuman for one of the women I'm talking about to give herself to willingly.

"Anyway, these people don't apologize for getting things easily. They aren't terrible people, and I don't think any of them would do anything seriously evil. One woman I knew cheated on her husband with a bunch of different guys, ran away with one of them, and then cheated on him, too. She then blamed it all on him and his inadequacies, kicked him out, and kept everything he bought for her, like furniture, jewelry, and a luxury car. Apparently he thought he could buy his way into her world, so I suppose in a way, it really was his fault. I'm not saying he was at a disadvantage because he was rich. But there are different ways to get there. Unfortunately, he was the hard-working and ambitious type. The scoundrels I'm talking about basically get money the same way they get women. They assume it's their right, money and women, that they're entitled to it, and it just happens."

"You didn't do too badly. But you don't seem like you're motivated by personal gain. There are a few of you left. Poor little Goldmunds," I said.

"Who?" he asked.

"Forget it," I said.

"Anyway, she was living by herself and taking a man home or going home with one when she felt like it. She figured out that the amount of sex she needed was way below average, so there was no point in having a husband or boyfriend just for that. She was very trusting, always believing in the first, best impression a man made. After that, she thought it was pointless to change him, to make him live up to her expectations, or the expectations he created for himself. She was educated, polite, and generous. Definitely not a criminal. Yet she left a wake of hatred behind her because she seemed to get everything she wanted so easily. She didn't care, though. It was everyone else's problem for being too sensitive."

"I bet you lived up to your first impression," I said.

"As a matter of fact, she told me almost exactly that. She said people had both a good and bad side, but that I didn't have any side. I just was. But—how did she put it?—it was out of place, like finding a simple, clean little Scandinavian chair in an old church. Surrounded by all sorts of drama and flourish. A little unsettling. She also said something like, 'Maybe simplicity is ideal, but in a place like that, it puts to shame even God and the angels.' I could never tell if that was a compliment or an insult."

"It's both. A great compliment to you in isolation, but a criticism for not indulging the rest of us," I said.

"I still don't understand," he said.

13

───

Maeve entered, looking sumptuous.

Her loud impatient knocking had awakened David the Monday morning after his first weekend back in the workforce. He had come to the door wearing only pastel blue pajama pants from a set she had bought him. She was so different than he remembered that he paused to check his senses against the slippery model of her in his mind. She carried paper bags by little paper handles in each hand.

"I wanted to have breakfast with you," she said and looked him over. "You're too thin."

She wore white slacks and a thick red hip-length turtleneck sweater that clung to her figure. Her body was shaped like two firm, fresh tulip blossoms placed bottom-to-bottom. Her waist did not dip in narrowly, but it suited her age, whatever that was. Her face was firm and full, like a bursting ripe fruit at the precise moment when it begins to wither, leaving an excess of skin to collapse and wrinkle. Her green eyes shone intensely.

Maeve continued to have strangely fortuitous timing. David never mentioned that he would be occupied most evenings or what he was doing, but she wove herself into gaps in his schedule, late mornings, always after he had had enough sleep, or the afternoon or evenings when he was home.

So far they had briefly touched and had many moments of intimate proximity. Who counts how often this happens between yourself and another over a lifetime? Such encounters are like seeds. They usually lay sterile and eventually waste away without our ever knowing about them. Sometimes they produce sprouts that, due to want of care, immediately after absorbing the first rays of light, shrivel and die. Other times they're given too much attention and immediately become overgrown and wild and then must be mercilessly cut down before they become impenetrable and suffocating.

A rare seed favored with measured care grows patiently. Maybe another encounter, another touch, to mark the spot where a probing tendril could feel its way forward. Reality was evolving around David, changing at the pace of the seasons, too slowly to notice.

There was never a heady rush of heat and longing. Another time, Maeve came for dinner, and he kissed her on the cheek in welcome. That same evening, ready to leave, she held his hand and looked into his eyes, and returned the kiss to say goodbye. Sometimes they sat next to each other, hip to hip, on the floor looking out his window. When she cooked or set the table, instead of saying thank you, he might give her a little rub on the base of her neck to express his gratitude. A poignantly cold evening when the moon blazed brightly through his window, she had held both his hands and given him a peck on the lips signifying nothing more than care and friendship, a gesture given to someone with whom you've already shared years of familiarity.

One evening, David and Maeve kissed on the lips again as she departed, this time lingering while she placed her palms gently on his chest, exerting the pressure of simultaneously holding and pushing away. Several more meetings passed before they kissed the third time, but this time they pressed their closed lips firmly and squashed their noses together. She slowly untucked her blouse and lifted it up with one hand, lifted his shirt with the other, and pressed her body against his, so that the bare skin of their stomachs touched. Not a moment of sexual arousal for either of them, because the other contained something too immense to enfold. But it did lead to a deeper, more relaxed intimacy in which they touched and stroked each other frequently, didn't mind their etiquette or appearance—that is, revealed themselves as plainly, naturally to each other physically as they had done psychologically long ago. Many times they passed the time together separately in the same close space, an indication of their matured intimacy. She read while he tidied the apartment or sat by the window and watched the street.

Maeve liked to lie on his couch in one particular pose, her back propped up against one of the armrests, reading a book she held in one hand and sipping a glass of water she held in place on the apex of her bent knee with the other. One evening, while she was adjusting her position, she spilled almost a full glass onto her blouse.

"Damn," she exclaimed, sprang up, unbuttoned her top, and removed it.

David came from the kitchen and saw her standing unabashedly in nothing but a bra and skirt.

"Lend me a shirt so I can let this dry out."

Her stomach was blank and flat, almost like a small girl's. An even layer of flesh smoothed away all the definition of her abdominal muscles. It was the first time he had seen her exposed, and he had never imagined what she looked like under her clothes. How much change had occurred? And how long had it taken?

He responded, "Just rummage around in the bedroom. You know what's in there. You bought most of it."

He examined her back as she walked away, and adjusted his position to watch her through the doorway. She wasn't lean, but the flesh from her shoulders to her waist was firm and silky. An age showed in the wrinkles of her elbows. Inscrutably older than him.

Wire hanger hooks screeched across the metal closet bar as she examined his clothes.

"I've bought you so many nice things, haven't I? Maybe you should start wearing some of them," she called to him.

The clasp for her bra wasn't on the back. She was reaching up, so he was able to put his arms around her without her noticing, until his hands cupped the weight of her breasts. He unfastened her bra, removed it as if he were helping her off with her coat, and tossed it on the corner of the bed. He stroked her back with the backs of his fingers, denying himself the greater sensation that could come from using his fingertips.

"Mm." She remained relaxed and arched her back slightly. He listened for her breathing to quicken, but it didn't. "I'll get on the bed, and you can do that as long as you want."

He remained behind her but glimpsed the sides of her breasts swaying as she crawled onto the bed and lay facedown. He sat at her side and she turned her head towards him.

"Do you want to know what I'm thinking about?" Maeve asked. "I'll tell you whether you do or not. It popped into my head all of a sudden. A new idea. Can you imagine? I'm usually rehashing the old ones. It's how love is associated with the loss of willpower. People 'fall' in love, as if they were walking along and suddenly tumbled into some kind of tiger pit. How often are people minding their own business like that? No, they're really walking around a forest full of tiger traps hoping to fall into one. And then when it happens, you're supposed to believe it's out of their control. Something magical, like destiny, was supposedly lying in ambush. You have to be willfully ignorant to think that way, which is really a sham way of not admitting that it's your choice.

"And then people 'listen to their hearts' or whatever cliché they use. After walking into the trap and getting pierced and maimed, they stay trapped and recycle the impulses that led them there in the first place. I'm sure a child feels the same way about his cravings for candy, and eats so much he gets sick. Year after year, I've subjected myself to the same stories at the ballet and the opera. They have more variety than the cheap candies fattening up all the children, but they're made of the same sugar and artificial flavors. I have a sick fascination with watching people consume them.

"But the worst happens later. More often than not, either fast or slow, things unravel and they do get sick of it . . . and years or entire lives are wasted. And whose fault is that? Nobody's! They fell in love and followed their feelings. Unbelievable! Just bad luck. You might find worse delusions, like the lover is so unbelievably cunning as to have actually misled their partner. Or that wants, needs, values, and whole personalities have permanently changed, ruining the relationship. How is it possible for beings who claim to be intelligent to think like this? Nobody chooses their friends this way, or keeps bad ones who annoy or abuse them. Yet it's perfectly reasonable for people to blame forces beyond their control for their messed up romances.

"We have this ridiculous myth that mankind seized the initiative to exercise free will. More likely it was entrapment. Any divine being would have foreseen how much work it would take to keep us in a happy, ignorant utopia. I can't say that we even deserve a god, but people still try to hold him accountable, despite it having been unambiguously clear for millennia that our lives are our own problem. Anyway, it's more like that free will was forced on us, and we've spent most of our time avoiding using it in case we're made responsible for our actions.

"We've turned the candy men, all the people who sell good feeling to help us blot out the reality that life is really our own fault, into millionaires and billionaires. They appeal to our stupidity and cause multiple generations to dangerously misinterpret the universe and our place in it. The Greeks, for example, believed hubris would be punished. Now, we celebrate it."

"What does this have to do with falling in love?" David asked.

"I'm getting back to that. Our archetypes are all screwed up. We believe that Romeo and Juliet are heroes," she said.

"You know, I never read it or saw it performed. I did as little as possible in school. I think I would have liked reading better if more writers spent as much time looking at something as they did describing it," he said.

"They used to. There are marvelous old-fashioned things that you would like. But then they became lazy, and inspiration became more important than perspiration," she replied.

"Hm. You're not the first person I've heard say that. But I guess I know the story, Romeo and Juliet, in spite of everything," David said.

"Isn't that annoying? It's as bad as having a pop song stuck in your head that you've never actually chosen to listen to. I swear there are songs I know by heart that I've never heard. It's like we're forced to absorb all sorts of garbage from some kind of flabby mass of cultural knowledge," Maeve said.

"Anyway, you probably know some idiotically sentimental interpretation of it, that this is some kind of tragic romance meant to make us feel sad about sweet victims of an unfair world. Really, the point of the play is that reality fails to meet expectations. Rather than exercise their rational free will in light of this obvious fact, they close their eyes and tumble together into the tiger pit. They do their best to avoid exercising any self-control. Apparently, it's impossible. How sweet! What kind of pity are we supposed to feel? It's a bit like celebrating drug addiction. How about a story about an alcoholic who drinks himself to death for fun?

"I've always perceived a streak of misanthropy and disappointment in Shakespeare. Actually, of all of his fallen protagonists, I would believe he must have had the strongest point to prove with Romeo and Juliet. Something must have been bothering him, and he treats them with tremendous antipathy. We're used to seeing proud, noble heroes leveled by jealousy, ambition, greed, pride, or whatever brings a person down. Romeo and Juliet don't have much going for them. Rich, spoiled, stupid kids ruined for the mundane reason that they were rich, spoiled, and stupid. Full of feelings, but incomplete people. One rash bad choice follows another to an almost unbelievable crescendo.

"But I seem to be in the minority about this work, in the minority in general when it comes to favoring pragmatism over emotion. Our modern never-ending obsession with sentiment would have us all believe that we're supposed to be understanding and forgiving when it's love that makes people lose control. But in that case, love is just an obsession or derangement like any other. Proper love is a function of all the senses and the intellect. Without your brain, you have infatuation, which is nothing at all like love.

"Almost every staging and film of the work I've seen misrepresents what I think is Shakespeare's intent. We generally see kids who are adorable and pure-hearted, just a little rough and temperamental, like rambunctious puppies. Yet Romeo is reckless, a murderer, and Juliet, a maiden from a rich household, hands herself over as fast as one of your chain-smoking, drug-addled, alcoholic party girls.

"My 'chain-smoking, drug-addled, alcoholic party girls'?" he asked.

Maeve ignored him and continued, "Romeo never pauses to consider the consequences of his actions, and Juliet never considers that she's being led down an unethical path. It's actually the exact opposite of what generous, loving people would do. Lead their beloved to their doom, and not stop their beloved from dooming them. There are innumerable touching stories about people who sacrifice themselves to protect someone, or choose separation to ensure someone's safety or happiness later in life. Those are stories about love. This is not. It can't possibly be."

"Remind me how it ends," he said.

"Suicide! Juliet has taken a sleeping potion, but idiot Romeo thinks she's dead, purchases real poison, and fights and kills her fiancé, who has only come to put flowers on her grave. Now a double murderer with a supposedly dead girlfriend, he drinks the real poison and kills himself. Juliet wakes up and sees the lifeless body of her deranged boyfriend and plunges his dagger into her heart. All because they were confronted with the possibility that life wasn't going to be as rapturous and irresponsible as it had been over the preceding few days. Idiotic!"

"Hm," was all David said.

"Do you agree?" Maeve asked. "I haven't ranted like this in a while."

"I don't really have an opinion . . . I could try to come up with one, but I'm not an expert. You might have a point, though. From what I understand, the story is the opposite of what you were complaining about. Two people are trying to avoid being hounded for a harmless choice. Then they come up against all sorts of limitations, which is ironic because of their families' wealth. Money is supposed to open up more possibilities, but it does the opposite. You would think it was strange that being in a higher class means less choices. The audience might appreciate their own freedom more. I noticed that even though average people have less material certainty, nobody really cares about what they do. I suppose there also might be a paradox in the story, of being a slave to your choices, where your decisions become obsessions, but . . . that's as far as I can work it out. I think there are a lot of stronger, more common motivations than love. It seems to me that people are always choosing something instead of love, and maybe being driven by it is unusual," he said and stopped stroking her.

"You're right. You're not an expert," she said.

"Why are you bringing this up?" he asked. "It's a weird topic."

She said, "I suddenly had an idea about why women might find you frustrating. You don't let them fall in love with you. You don't impose any force on them or lead them anywhere. You don't tie them up or trap them. You don't shower them with flowers and gifts. You don't charm them with poetry or humor. You're not really entertaining and you don't even smile very much. You challenge them to be confident, to assert them-selves, to use their free will, and every moment they're with you, they're aware of having made the choice. A cloud of self-doubt and responsibility hangs over their heads."

He laughed. "Except that I've managed to trap you now," he said.

She reached back and slapped his thigh. "Or it's just because you're a little rat!"

Maeve turned onto her side, back toward him, tucked her feet under, and sat up. She huddled curled up like that, covering herself. "I still need to find a shirt," she said. "Which one do you love the least?"

"Guess," he said and left the room.

Maeve's wet shirt lay crumpled on the couch, where it would never dry. David draped it over the back of one of the dining room chairs, moved the chair closer to the heating vent in the floor, and went to sit by the window. She came out wearing a shirt with small pink and white checks. It was something his wife had picked out for him. Hideous, but just the type of shirt the type of woman she was would buy for the type of man she thought he ought to have been in the type of couple she really wanted them to be, at the same time protesting that she didn't want them to be anything like that at all. He had ignored her purchases for months before she had caught on and stopped buying him things. Seeing this shirt again, he felt some relief about her having left.

Maeve lay on the floor near him and read quietly, too quietly. Her nebulous reflection in the glass showed that she had fallen asleep. David watched her. Her eyes were trembling with REM sleep, and her mouth hung open with her bottom lip curled out. It looked as if she had found something appalling. Maybe she had. Her face softened the longer he watched her, and eventually she smiled, inhaled deeply, and opened her eyes.

"Hi," she said quietly. "Goodness, I haven't nodded off like that in a long time."

Her obduracy had melted away, and she appeared frail and coquettish. She unbuttoned his shirt and took it off, arching her back and then hunching forward. Her breasts hung like two large, full water droplets. He wasn't there to her, or appearing topless in front of a man was the most natural thing in the world. She stood, went to the bedroom, and came back, still fastening her bra. "Where's my . . . oh, there. Thank you." She put on her blouse, tucked it in, and then knelt next to him.

"Goodbye." She kissed him, her lips pressed into his, and then her tongue darted into his mouth. The unexpected sensation of it filled his body. The next thing he was aware of was her gently closing the door behind her.

14

———

Maeve entered looking luxurious. She wore a full-length blue fox coat. She briefly mocked him with her eyes, let her coat slip to the floor, and revealed a simple gown that covered her with layers of shimmering aquamarine silk.

She tilted her head and asked, "Hm, what do *you* want?"

She stepped out of her shoes and sidled across his living room, always facing him, unwound the matching silk shawl that covered her perfumed neck and shoulders, and flung it onto the couch.

The phone rang and David picked up the receiver, but before he could lift it to his ear, Maeve put her hand on top of his.

"Let's not answer this," she said and guided him to hang up.

She reached behind, unzipped the dress, and stepped out of it. She stood in white undergarments, lace brassiere, silk panties, garters, and stockings.

"Just stand there and look at me," she said, unfastening the garters. "Study me, memorize every detail." She raised each knee to her stomach and removed her stockings. "Never forget any of it."

He felt dizzy and breathless, as if air had been sucked out of him and breathed into her, filling her with seductive potency that far exceeded the tender allure she had had before. Her hair was ablaze with a gleaming black, her glistening white teeth were revealed by a teasing smile, but her eyes were subdued, as if coiled to strike, to flare their emerald bolts when he was most vulnerable. Her skin was creamy and every crease in her face had been smoothed away, not to the period of naïveté and youth, but where a woman peaks in her combination of wisdom, experience, beauty, and grace.

David had always been an attentive lover, attuned to the numerous variables that affected the sexual act. The season, the weather, the day, the time, what a woman had been wearing, doing, watching, listening to, ingesting, and the many intangible variables that cause subtle changes to a woman's self-esteem, biological chemistry, and perception of her own sexual attractiveness. Ultimately, the language of her body expressed its needs. When and where to touch, how softly or roughly, how fast or how slow, when to give pleasure by receiving it. As with everything, it was imperative that sex should be a harmonious act, and he adapted to the idiosyncrasies of every partner and every mood.

The poignant, soft scent of perfume radiating from bare skin that had been warmed under plush fur whetted David's senses. They stood, kissing and embracing intensely but patiently, inventing their own slow ritual as they went, then nudged each other to the couch. He sat and she lay across his lap, cradled in his arms. She nuzzled and kissed the corner of his jaw just below his ear while he stroked her thigh and massaged the small of her back.

Maeve's fingers unclasped, unzipped, and unbuttoned whenever they had an opportunity. Both of them drifted into a semiconscious state of total relaxation, floating on a steady, soothing wave that neither weakened nor intensified. She suddenly slipped off his lap and darted into the bedroom, giggling like a small girl. He followed her into the darkness. She attacked him from behind, pulled his shirt off, unbuttoned and yanked down his pants, and shoved him facefirst onto the bed. She sat on his back and pressed her forearms into his shoulders, pinning him, making him fight and wrestle to turn over and embrace her. He twisted sharply and knocked her off, and she fell laughing onto the bed next to him. He rolled onto his side and tried to clasp her toward him, but she teasingly pushed and swatted away his grasping hands. He finally succeeded in slipping an arm under her head, and wrapped the other around her. Her face was smothered into his chest, and she nibbled him lightly and ineffectually tried to wriggle out of his tight embrace. She finally slid upward and stung him with a deep kiss on his mouth. The longer they kissed, the more her mock resistance weakened. He unclasped her bra and slipped her panties off, never parting from her lips. She then rolled onto her back and stretched her arms over her head, and he climbed on top of her. She reached and gently gripped his erect phallus, using it to spread her vulva and position the tip just inside of her. Rather than pushing in, he rolled off her toward the night table, opened the drawer, and took out a condom, but she snatched the package from him and tossed it across the room. She readied him to penetrate her again and pushed her pelvis forward. They lay still for a few minutes. He felt like smiling, which he had never done when having sex.

Maeve gyrated her hips, and David responded to her rhythm. She pulled her head back away from him so they could see each other's faces in full focus. They touched only at their loins. She gazed at him and softly moaned through tight breaths.

Little by little, the tempo quickened until their pelvises met in hard, abrupt movements. Their bodies were tensed. Her breasts swished in pleasing circles. Maeve clenched her teeth and moaned huskily. Her face relaxed and her wide green eyes seemed to blaze. Her body went limp and David continued until he ejaculated. She tightened her vagina, inhaled deeply through her teeth, and held that breath until David softened. She closed her eyes, emptied her lungs, wrapped her arms around him, and pulled him close to her.

"Just lie there. Be still," she said.

A beam of sunlight flared across David's closed eyes. He awoke under the bed covers. To his surprise, Maeve lay asleep next to him naked, the sheet and blanket folded down to her hips. Her skin was covered in a thin sheen of perspiration, and her smell hovered like a fog. After he showered and dressed, he sliced some fruit, made coffee, filled a creamer with milk, and set this little repast out for her on the table. He put on boots and a thick wool overcoat and left her sleeping.

He had nothing urgent to attend to, but his routine was to walk in the morning. He wandered for several hours, following a spiraling and zigzagging route. When the sidewalks became crowded with workers taking their lunch breaks, he returned home. Maeve had left but had tidied the place, made the bed, and cleaned the kitchen and dining table, erasing all traces of herself.

Several days later, David received another phone call. It was Angelina.

"I tried calling before, but I thought I heard a woman's voice and then you hung up on me," she said.

"I'm sorry, there was someone banging at the door right when you called. Food delivery. I couldn't believe how stupid I was to hang up like that. I had no idea you called," he said.

"I wanted to invite you somewhere," she said.

"Like where?" he asked.

"I told you I liked plants. I wanted to go to the botanical garden. Nobody ever wants to go with me. If you think it sounds stupid, we can do something else," she said.

"No, that sounds great," he said. "When?"

"How about next Saturday?" she said. "I'll call you in the morning to remind you."

He thought he heard the phone ringing one morning Maeve was visiting, but it eventually stopped.

Maeve's moments now seemed like darts thrown blindfolded at a clock face. She arrived at all times and sometimes lingered for half a day, other times only staying for half an hour. He never considered or asked her how, but occasionally she managed to sneak into his apartment to surprise him when he returned home from work, or to tiptoe in during the early morning and slip into bed with him while he still slept.

Sex did not become their main preoccupation. Several meetings might pass with them barely looking at each other. They could fall asleep together without touching. They had sex when one of them spontaneously initiated it. Maeve had been quietly reading on the couch, and she threw her book down, joined David sitting by the window, and unceremoniously undressed herself and then him. David walked up behind her as she cleaned up after dinner, unzipped her skirt and pulled it and her panties down, reached around and unbuttoned her blouse and pulled the cups of her bra down so that he could massage her nipples, and had sex with her bent over his kitchen sink. She went to use the toilet, and after a few minutes, he heard the shower running, so he took off his clothes and joined her; she wound up straddling him in the bathtub with the water spraying down on them.

At times, their entire encounter could be sexual. Once, he didn't let her through the door until she had stripped, and they moved from room to room having sex, napping, and then starting again.

And there was the long period when Maeve disappeared altogether. Then one evening she showed up at the door completely nude, unadorned, and empty-handed. She rushed past him and into the bedroom. He went back to what he had been doing—nothing, looking out the window, as usual, eating a bowl of cherries and watching a heavy snowfall erase the seams on the sidewalks, the edges of curbs, and the pits and cracks in the street. After he was satisfied with the thickness of the snow cover, he went to the bedroom, where she lay on his bed waiting for him. They took their time, and then she left naked, just as she had arrived. They never spoke.

He described these moments without any sentiment. Time and intervening circumstances hadn't scoured the feeling away. Their physical intimacy simply lacked emotional content. No anticipation, buildup, or denouement. There was no logic. Every sexual encounter was the result of a naive, primitive, inhuman logic: An opportunity presented itself, and it seemed like the thing to do at the time, rather like absent-mindedly plucking a morsel from a tray of hors d'oeuvres that happened to be floating by. They had their treat and then did something else. Just random flips of a libidinous psychological switch. Even wild animals copulate with more purpose, responding instinctively to hormonal signals and the imperative to procreate. But what they did together, they did well, to the great pleasure of both of them, because it was in their natures to do so.

You might think that only a thin, fragile thread could connect such apathetic partners. Imagine if either of them had the slightest interest in anything else. Even deep, abiding love often finds itself overshadowed by a variety of distractions or compulsions. How, then, were such acutely observant people, who easily found stimulation in myriad details the rest of us take for granted, joined so strongly? It was curiosity itself that was the material from which their bond was woven. Their mutual interest in one another—which they had explored with all their senses—was as strong as for anything else in the world. You can wonder how such deep attentiveness is related to feelings of concern, empathy, or generosity, the pillars of authentic love. Was it some kind of inadequate half-formed version of these emotions? Their antecedent?

Theirs was an unusual but not impossible arrangement, although if Maeve never visited again, David wasn't sure he would have any opinion about that.

15

———————

Life was satisfactory. David kept a comfortable routine of mornings and afternoons to himself for exploring or sporadic moments with Maeve and evenings of physical labor, which he performed ritualistically, with an empty mind, as if it were a set of prescribed meditative exercises completed only for the sense of completion. Work had supplanted empty time, hours that had once been spent doing nothing or uselessly socializing. He hadn't given up anything and had delayed financial problems indefinitely. It was a step, a foundation for surviving on his own. He was how old now?

David was intrigued by the necessity of the humble tasks at the restaurant, how he was integral to an enterprise that was integral to sustaining his existence. The instruction manual job had been one tiny component in a much larger mechanism that he had never been able to see the beginning or end of. He had never considered his purpose, but he himself couldn't remember reading an instruction manual. A joint account that he didn't monitor had absorbed his wages, which were spent on his behalf. In the job he had with the art woman, as he thought of her now, he had merely been an accessory.

Now he could apprehend being part of a complete system. Dishes needed washing, floors needed sweeping and mopping, windows, glass, and stainless steel needed polishing, and carpets needed vacuuming. By him.

The imperfections and flaws in this aging restaurant were a feast for his highly acute senses. He was happy refining his methods and finding new ways to make the place neater. From his first night, he spotted how much work it would take to properly clean and renovate the place.

Ivo wasn't willing to pay overtime, and David already had to scramble to finish by the end of his shift, so he tackled a few problems whenever he had spare time. He cleaned ancient cobwebs from corners. He leveled wobbly tables. He trimmed carpet snags. He straightened crooked pictures. He changed burnt-out lightbulbs. He tightened the screws in chairs. No one had ever had the notion to polish the water spots off the cutlery, so he started doing that, and the waitresses, even Magda, volunteered to help him and liked being near and talking to him.

"My mom always thought this place was filthy," Magda told him. "But she was afraid of hurting Uncle Ivo's feelings."

David eventually compiled a list of every major and minor repair needed to return the establishment to perfect condition. He handed five pages to Ivo and said, "We need to fix all this stuff."

"You can't be happy sweeping and mopping and bumping up against cute girls, can you?" Ivo said. "I was happy not knowing about any of it. You had to make me worry."

"Just give me the money and I'll take care of it myself," David said.

"Do you have any idea how much it will cost to fix all this?" he asked.

"Yes. Do you?" he responded.

"No, but it feels like enough to make me start panicking," he said.

"How about you set aside some money every month? I bet when the place starts looking nicer, you'll get more than enough new business to cover it," David said.

"You really think it needs this much work?" Ivo asked.

"No. You could start selling burgers and fries or pizza and I'm sure it would be fine. But for the prices you charge and the quality of the food, there's no reason you can't have a nice, classy décor. To fit its personality," he said.

David used the small sums that Ivo was periodically willing to provide to buy more cleaning supplies, tools, new janitorial equipment, and carpentry, electrical, and plumbing materials. He had to be frugal and take his time, and he wasn't going to kill himself over any of this anyway. He eventually repaired the front door. He completely renovated the bathrooms a little bit at a time. In the kitchen, he fixed leaky pipes, replaced cracked tiles, filled in rotten grout. He touched up paint throughout the dining room. He hung new pictures on the walls. As he worked, the impact was radical. The atmosphere began to feel livelier and friendlier. New customers showed up, occasional customers became regulars, old regulars became more regular, and everyone ate and spent more. Ivo had to hire additional staff and could afford to let Magda officially do nothing by making her a manager. He also raised David's pay a few times to the point where he was breaking even. He could survive indefinitely.

Magda's parents also began coming around more, which delighted Ivo. Her mother was pretty but lacked any of the sultriness Ivo implied. She had large, childlike eyes and was full of warmth, not heat, smiles, and laughter. She kept her hair up and was a thrifty dresser who preferred modest, effeminate, and rather old-fashioned clothing. Reminded you of those old pictures of typists working in an open floor of orderly grids of small desks. Ivo behaved sheepishly when she was around, not daring to look David in the eye, as if embarrassed by his own gossip.

"When is your other sister-in-law, the sexy one, going to pay us a visit?" David asked one day.

Ivo replied forlornly, "I didn't think you were the type of person who teases people. But I know I'm everybody's fool. I never claimed she, um, slinked around like a seducer. She's an angel, isn't she?"

David seemed livelier, too. He buzzed, hummed, crackled dynamism. People wanted to see him, to hail him in some way. Their eyes could settle on him and engage him. He talked to anyone if he had the time in his usual confident, honest, insightful way, not distinguishing between the customer he saw every day and the one he had seen for the first time. Ivo told the staff that it was one thing to know your customers, but David *noticed* them. People found something compelling about how he went about his humble tasks.

"You're doing all right," Ivo said to David. "You're good luck. You have a special touch. That's good. You also keep a lot in reserve. Sometimes it's better to keep some things hidden, a little bit secret. If people get to know you too well, maybe they end up not liking you as much. That's what my problem is. I show everybody everything."

David couldn't tell you how many seasons passed while he made his way through the repair list—not that he ever kept track—but Magda finished college, couldn't find a job, and continued working there. She showed ambition and dragged David into an ongoing argument with her uncle.

"Uncle Ivo, you need to start advertising. Just let me do it. We can get a food critic in here," she pleaded. "Tell him, David."

"I don't know," was David's consistent reply.

"See, Magda? The man agrees with me. Once you start wanting too much, the world finds a way to knock you down. It takes only one snobby critic to ruin everything. I would be physically sick," Ivo said.

"But our online reviews are fantastic," she persisted.

"Magda, honey, we're as busy as we can be already," Ivo replied.

"So open another restaurant," she said. "I can run it myself."

"I have enough to worry about," he said.

"I think you're afraid of being successful," she said.

"I won't argue," he said.

David overlooked that his preoccupations with work, his exploring, and Maeve had been closing him off more. He couldn't recall the last time he had met anyone new, and he had no circle of anybodies he spent time with. He could barely remember when he had last seen Angelina. She had stopped running into him sometime after she had made him dinner. Whatever happened to her? Such a sweet woman.

One day there was an envelope in his letterbox behind the front desk of his apartment building. It contained a single page of beautiful calligraphy.

Dear David,

I have decided to move back home. You probably would not notice because we have not seen each other in a long time, and I do not think you will look for me anyway. I wanted you to know that I love you. I loved you since I first met you. I actually think you knew that already. I was not crazy. It was not some stupid puppy love or love at first sight. I believed that you were as lost as I was, but you did not know you were lost. I only wanted us to help each other find a path somewhere comfortable, safe, beautiful, and caring. That is why I did nice things for you, and I thought you were nice to me for the same reason. I thought I tried everything, but I realized that I did not try hard enough. I will always love you. You were the one for me, and I was the one for you, but you always seem to miss out on a lot of important things in life, and you did not see it. But that is not why I decided to leave. I already saved enough money and life was not as fun as I thought it should be. So it was time to move forward. I will miss you.

Love,

Angela

She loved him? Had she really shown him that? And was she right about the rest of it, about him? He had never thought much about the future, but this seemingly awkward, aimless young woman had decades mapped out in advance. Not only in specific logistical details, but also in how she thought life was supposed to feel. He couldn't say if this was the best way to live. It seemed like you might be trading enslavement to other people's ideas for enslavement to your own.

The letter had no address or contact information. Somebody must know where she was, but David didn't know how to reach any of her friends. He would fondly remember their merry little conversations.

FIFTH DIGRESSION

I'm generally reverential when I consider those whom I have loved and who have loved me. My greatest weakness is to believe that they are less emotionally flawed than I am. I've never been able to acknowledge how shallow a curious or loving gaze can run, the data gathering and the swift calculations of material or existential gains behind a flirtatious glance. The gleam in an eye that asks questions like, "How will my life be easier or more interesting?" or "Is he fun and can he make me laugh?"

Maybe we should have fewer requirements. I repudiate that having more criteria for choosing a partner makes you a more serious person. On the contrary, it might be indicative of insecurity.

The greatest stories are about some inexplicable rapport that simply is and erases all preconceptions. Where two homely factory workers can be enraptured sitting together after work, stinking and drinking their beer. Where a smart, gorgeous, driven executive who has risen to the pinnacle of success succumbs to the winsome—friends will call it dumb— smile of some disheveled cleaner who shuffles into the office to empty the trash every afternoon. Where an aristocrat abandons everything to follow a penniless, consumptive, itinerant child of a menial laborer. Where love swells to overshadow all selfish feelings and desires when a partner is deformed by a tragic accident.

"You know, when a woman tries to direct your attention to another woman, it's usually a sign that she wants you to protest and notice her instead," I said.

"That's weird," he said.

"It sounds like a lot of women you met left hints for you to figure out something like that," I said.

"Do they all behave that way?" he asked.

I shook my head in disbelief.

"Just finish the story," I said.

16

———

One afternoon, Maeve entered looking regal.

She unwrapped an ivory mink stole from her shoulders and tossed it on the couch. She wore a short plum-colored dress with a small Medici collar that tapered into a plunging neckline, and matching wedge shoes with bows on the toes. Her hair was styled into a pile of glistening black ribbons, and attached to her earlobes were large, simple gleaming white pearl studs, like punctuation marks. A shoe box was tucked under her left arm, a cellophane dry cleaner's bag was draped over her right forearm, and a small paper boutique bag dangled from the fingers of her right hand.

"You look . . . majestic. But . . .," David began.

"Ha. That's the most superlative adjective I've ever heard you use. No criticisms or corrections?" she asked sweetly.

"No . . . but you might be a little overdressed," he said.

"Not at all. You're underdressed," she said. "But I'll fix that. Get up."

He stood and she helped him remove his T-shirt, pulled down his jeans and underwear, and led him naked to the bath.

"Get in and sit down," she commanded.

He did as he was told. She turned on the tap and felt and adjusted the water temperature several times until she was satisfied. On the cool side.

"Don't move," she said. She left and returned a minute later, naked herself, with two washcloths.

"Aren't you getting in?" he asked.

"And mess up my hair and makeup?" she said. "Shh. No more talking. And keep still so you don't splash me."

Maeve wet the washcloths, rubbed soap on one of them, and proceeded to clean him, starting at his head. David closed his eyes while she scrubbed his nose, his cheeks, behind his ears, and the front and back of his neck. She sponged away the soap with the other washcloth, rinsed it, and continued. She washed each of his fingers, worked her way up his arms to his armpits, and then cleaned his chest and back. She then moved on to his feet. She propped one of them up on each side of the tub and washed each toe individually, and proceeded up his calves and thighs.

"Now for the interesting parts," she said.

She let the soapy water drain out.

"Get on all fours," she said.

She washed his buttocks, gently cleaned his anus, and then reached between his legs and washed his scrotum and penis.

"Almost done. Sit back down," she said.

Maeve plugged the drain and left the bathroom while the tub refilled with clean water. She returned with a small saucepan, knelt down next to him again, filled it with water, and doused his head. She then squirted shampoo onto his hair and lathered and scrubbed it vigorously with her fingertips. She refilled the saucepan, rinsed his hair, shampooed and rinsed it again, and then rubbed in conditioner.

"We'll leave it in for a few minutes. You seem to be taking this with equanimity. Not in the least bit curious what's going on?" she said.

"As long as I don't have to think or do anything, I don't care," he said.

"That's the spirit," she said. "But I'm dying to tell you and ruin my own surprise."

"Are you preparing my body for burial?" he asked.

"Yes, but I haven't decided how I'm going to kill you yet," she said.

"You shouldn't have bought me more clothes. I hardly ever wear the other stuff you gave me," he said.

"Oh, you don't have anything like this," she said.

She rinsed his hair one last time, turned off the faucet, opened the drain, and toweled his head dry.

"Stand and put your arms up," she said.

She dried the front of his body, tugged at his waist to have him turn around, and dried his backside. She wrapped the towel around his hips, took his hand, and led him out of the tub.

She closed the toilet lid and said, "Sit down here and open your mouth."

Maeve opened a tube of toothpaste and squeezed a small amount onto his toothbrush. She sat on his lap facing him and began slowly brushing his teeth, making tiny circles along the inside and outside gum lines and over the tops of his teeth, tackling them in six sections, top and bottom, left, right and center. When she was finished, she stood, turned on the faucet, rinsed his toothbrush, put it back in its holder, and filled a cup he kept on the sink with water.

"Rinse," she said.

He took a mouthful of water, swished it around, leaned over the sink, and spat. He repeated once more and poured out the cup.

"Now let's get you dressed," she said.

Maeve took David by the hand to the bedroom. The shoe box, a smaller black box, and her underclothes lay in the middle of the bed. Her dress and the garment bag she had brought were hanging in the closet. She pulled off his towel, draped it over the end of the bed, and pushed him onto it. She put back on the black silk panties and balconette bra she had been wearing. She then fetched underpants, an undershirt, and dress socks from his dresser and knelt in front of him.

"Lift your feet up a little," she said.

She placed the leg holes of his underpants over his feet and pulled them up as far as she could with him sitting. He stood just enough to lift his butt off the bed so she could pull them on the rest of the way. She tapped his feet, he raised them, and she slid a sock onto each one. She then stood and guided him to raise his arms, and pulled his undershirt on.

"Now for your pretty hair," she said.

Maeve left the room and returned with a comb and a tube of styling gel. She straddled his knees and combed through his thick blond hair several times, then combed it flat against his head. It reached about two inches below his ears, his eyebrows, and the base of his skull.

"I'm glad you neglected it. You look more rugged, better for your age," she said.

She squeezed a small amount of gel into her hand, rubbed her hands together, and then ran them through his hair, triggering the tension that wanted to coil it. She adjusted a few areas with the comb and stood to admire her work.

"Ferocious. Powerful. But you're a kitten, not a lion, aren't you?" she said. "Up."

Maeve went to the closet, tore open the garment bag, and separated three hangers. From one of them she took a spread-collar plain-front tuxedo shirt and helped him into it. She picked the small black box up from the bed, opened it, and showed him the contents. Onyx cufflinks and tuxedo studs. She fastened his shirtfront and cuffs. She next retrieved trousers that were nearly the identical plum color of her dress. After she pushed him to sit onto the bed, she pulled the pants over his feet and up to his thighs, he stood, and she pulled them up the rest of the way and buttoned and zipped them.

"Shoes," she said. "Hand them to me."

The box contained a pair of gleaming black balmoral shoes.

"This is where I think I've gone seriously wrong. They're too conservative," she said and frowned while turning one of them to examine it. "I should have taken some risks. Oh well. You're too beautiful for anyone to notice your feet."

She crouched, slipped a shoe onto each foot, and laced them. Finally, she helped him into a jacket that matched the pants, looked him over, and brushed some imaginary lint off his shoulders.

"That was fun," she said.

She put her clothes and shoes back on.

"How's my hair and makeup? Still OK?" she asked.

"Yes. Perfect," he responded.

"Great. We can go," she said.

"Go where?" he asked.

"Are you ready to put your fate in my hands?" she said.

"I have nothing better to do," he responded.

Downstairs, she led him to a black executive car parked in front of the building. The driver, who had been leaning against a lamppost reading a newspaper, sprang to attention when he saw her, folded his paper and opened the back door for them. David's reflection shone clearly in the darkly tinted windows, but he refused to look at it. As soon as he sat down, she grabbed his hand and held it.

"It looks like I've run out of words," she said.

"You've made yourself speechless?" he asked.

"Yes. I feel like a . . . I would say a teenager, but I never felt this way when I was a teenager. I've been wanting to be beautiful with someone beautiful. I admit it. I hate myself for clinging to this fairy tale," she said.

"So this is all for you. I thought you wanted to be extra nice to me," he said.

"Oh, I would never do that," she said. "You wouldn't know how to take it."

The driver took them to a part of the city he didn't recognize. A bizarre bourgeois village with wide tree-lined boulevards, oversized upscale houses with enormous, peculiarly tidy yards interspersed with large immaculate row houses with small, peculiarly tidy yards. Other blocks consisted of boutiques selling superfluities like jewelry, designer clothing, home decorations, pet supplies, luxury stationery, and health supplements. Numerous day spas, nail and hair salons, and yoga, Pilates, cardio-boxing, and fitness studios. Every third storefront belonged to a café or restaurant. Small public gardens and parks filled the gaps between the buildings.

"Where are we?" David asked, irritated.

"You've never come out this way before?" Maeve responded.

"No. It's awful. I mean, I'm used to the city being a bit rough, but good God, this is the opposite and just so tacky," he said.

He wondered if any of these people had purchased something from one of the artists he had met.

"This is what happens when you give rich people too much space to express themselves with. I don't know if they know how little taste they have but push on because they feel compelled to compete with their neighbors, or if they really are deluded into thinking that they know what they're doing. Either way, it's some kind of perverse conspiracy, and then idiots on the next level down in the social hierarchy try to mimic them. Before you know it, society's turned to crap. Don't worry. We're just here to eat. Ironically, at the only restaurant I've found in this godforsaken city that I don't have anything sarcastic to say about," she said.

The décor of Maeve's favorite restaurant was sleek, elegant, and understated. Nothing to distract you from your companion.

The staff were polite but not ingratiating, attentive but indifferent. The terse priceless menu assumed you knew what you were ordering and trusted the kitchen to prepare it well. A reconstruction of a past era.

"This may be the last spot in the world that understands its place, merely to provide the setting for an encounter. They must drill it into the staff's head not to breach the boundary between servant and served. It's wonderful. You can't even get your hair cut, your nails done, or a massage without some impertinent chatty hireling presuming that becoming your friend is part of the service," she said.

They ordered light meals and a bottle of champagne, most of which Maeve drank by herself.

After dinner, the driver brought them back across town a few blocks away from David's building and dropped them off at the opera house. He had never been inside. Burgundy and gold all around, and anywhere there was space for a decoration, there was one. The epitome of baroque. It was incredible that such perfect consonance could emerge from so many individual elements. People these days struggled with and failed to coordinate just a couple of simple details.

She was taking him to a ballet version of *Romeo and Juliet*.

"One of my favorite ballets, and the only acceptable adaptation of the play," she said.

They sat in the center a few rows from the orchestra pit, close enough to see every detail in the costumes and the scenery, every muscle, sinew, and drop of sweat on the performers. David didn't bother following the plot but instead concentrated on how the music, the movement, the lighting, the scenery, the costumes, and even the dancers' physiques were part of a harmonious, unified whole. An achievement that didn't seem so challenging. Merely a product of practice and extreme attentiveness. He again reflected on the gracelessness outside. People were just too distracted to use their senses properly.

The executive car was waiting for them after the performance. The driver ushered them in and proceeded to their next destination.

"You should be happy. We got enough stares. Mostly you," he said.

"I'm sure you've had many beautiful women on your arm before," she said.

"Yes, but they didn't believe it enough, or know how to act like it, like you do," he said.

"That takes experience," she replied. "But did you like the performance?"

"It's the first time I've been to a ballet. I had no idea what to expect. Yes, it was good. I never knew something like that existed," he said.

"I spoiled you with a top-quality ballet performed by an elite company. It can easily go to pieces. It's actually not the most challenging choreography. The choreographer could have gone in a lot of directions, but he chose to simplify the work, which brings out what I think is the real point of the story. He also includes Rosaline, the first object of Romeo's adoration, as an important sympathetic character, and in comparison to Juliet, she's demure and dignified. She's mentioned in the play but never appears. Getting to see the other woman makes Romeo come off more like a pathetic waffler flitting from infatuation to infatuation. Paris is also treated compassionately, and he goes about courting Juliet with dignity and decorum. So even though Romeo and Juliet are the centerpiece, they frequently share the stage with a better version of themselves. But did you notice how insignificant the women are? They recede while most of the men behave like a bunch of strutting peacocks. Rams butting horns. Take your pick of macho metaphors," she said.

He replied, "Like I told you before, I never saw it performed or even read it, so I can't compare the ballet to anything. But I see your point. I've always wondered why men fight over women, or fight about an insult to a woman. Has that ever really made a difference, or improved a situation?"

"Men aren't the only ones doing the fighting. Haven't you ever had women fighting over you?" she said.

"I don't know," he said.

"I'm sure you did. You just didn't notice. But, yes, it's a big deal, to me at least. It does make a difference to know that someone is prepared to do violence on your behalf. But I doubt any woman of real quality is going to let herself be won simply because one rival conquers another," she said.

"Would you? Attack someone?" he asked.

"Not for those reasons. For other ones," she answered.

"I see you're not taking me home," he said.

"I wanted to spend the night with you somewhere else. Of course you're OK with that," she said. "Tomorrow, when we're tired of each other, we can both go back to doing whatever it is we do to pass the time."

The car pulled up to a cube-shaped masonry building with blacked-out windows set high above the street, out of reach of intruders. An old warehouse. The man minding the entrance nodded to Maeve familiarly when she got out of the car and opened the single steel door for them. They were met on the inside by a young woman in a dark green long-sleeved leotard closed up to her throat. Familiar rounded hips, plump breasts, shapely legs, full lips, and raven-black mane, although pulled back tightly. She led them down a hallway and through a curtain to the center of a hazy dining room containing about twenty small tables occupied by shadowed people conversing quietly. Everyone was oriented toward a small stage at the back wall that was raised about a foot off the floor. A drummer, a guitarist, and a keyboardist dilatorily played slow, eerie electronica music, while the spot behind the microphone in the center was vacant. The lounge was lit only by the steady tongues of flames from the small glass oil lamps on each table and the stage's single purple footlight. David glanced at the other waitresses, who flickered into and out of the faint circles of light. Identical outfits, identical hairstyles, similar bodies and faces, but like the hostess, none had the eyes. It would be impossible to find enough green-eyed women who looked like her.

Awaiting them were two glass flutes and a bottle of champagne chilling in an ice bucket. It must have been set out well in advance of their arrival, because large beads of condensation clung to the bottle and the bucket. The hostess pulled their chairs out for them and seated them.

"Order something. You should eat. I promise it will be a long night," Maeve said.

Another young woman, having similar physiognomy to the others and an identical outfit, emerged from the shadows, fought to open the champagne, and filled their glasses. But there was something . . . how she prowled, how she took her time and lingered broke the boundary between servant and served that Maeve had complained about. David looked up into her face. It was efficient, serene, with the optimal amount of bone structure and flesh to perfectly define her cheeks, the bridge and tip of her nose, her nostrils, her lips, her jawline, her brow, her ears. No excess anywhere. Not a single eccentric or underdeveloped feature, nor a single extraneous hair or crease. Set within this graceful visage were two bottle-green eyes with starbursts of chartreuse forming the coronas around their pupils. The rest of her body was a similar miracle of economy and proportion, with every feminine curve formed exactly as much as it needed to be. The ultimate realization of the type patrolling the lounge. Even Maeve at the peak of her beauty, an image he could try to look backward in time to examine, would have been a less refined version of this woman, although their differences would have been so subtle, so marginal, that it would take long, patient study for him to enumerate them all.

Their waitress looked down into his eyes and smiled and instantly dispatched whatever thoughts had been fluttering around in his mind.

Maeve quickly drank her first glass of champagne, and as soon as she set the empty glass down, the young woman wafted into the light to refill it, then quickly retreated again to the shadows.

A singer hidden within a billowy black hooded cloak ambled up to the microphone. David couldn't see much in the dimness and instead attuned his ears. She sang to the melancholic down-tempo techno beat of the backup band and accented the melodies with silky, slinky waves of movement that began at her shoulders and hips and rippled to the tips of her fingers and toes. Her first song sounded like a folk tune in an archaic form of French. She sang one in a language that resembled none he had ever heard, with a refrain of "lule lule" that he picked up after the third or fourth repetition. In another, he thought he could detect elements of Latin, but like the others, it was unintelligible. And the last she sang in some kind of old Gaelic dialect, as best he could tell. She curtsied to no applause, and she and the musicians left the stage.

"What was she singing? Do you know?" he asked Maeve.

"Oh, nothing of consequence. 'I miss you' blah, blah, blah. A song about autumn. That type of nonsense. Everything sounds more meaningful in a foreign language. You should see the drivel in opera lyrics," she answered.

"I meant the languages," he said.

"This and that. She's a collector of dead and dying languages. It's quite interesting. If you listen long enough, you would swear that it sounds familiar, but it's all an illusion. It could mean anything, and sounds like whatever you want," she said.

"Excuse me, ma'am, but Miss Scarlett was wondering if she could sing you 'Happy Birthday,'" their waitress said.

Maeve responded with a withering look of contempt.

"I told her it wasn't a good idea," the woman continued.

Maeve wasn't listening and glared at the blank spot at the stage where this Scarlett had stood.

"Sir, would you like to order anything?" the young woman asked, undaunted.

David wondered if in answering he would irrevocably choose a side in the bitter little skirmish that had just occurred. He suspected this was a situation in which a woman's companion should say something comforting, but he was apathetic toward what had just happened, and anyway, Maeve wasn't the type of woman who needed sympathy. Besides, he was starving.

"I'm too hungry to decide. Just bring something filling and healthy. You pick," he said.

She smiled and again transfixed him with those eyes.

"Sure," she said and was engulfed by the shadows.

"I suppose they thought you wanted to make a big deal about your birthday," he said.

"I do. I love my birthday. It's the greatest day of the year. The day I was given the chance to exist. But it's mine. My day. I get to choose how to spend it and whom to spend it with," she said. "And being congratulated by strangers is out of the question."

"What did you do last year?" David asked.

"I spent it with you. The same thing I did for, God, I would guess at least the half dozen or so years before that. I just never told you," she said.

"What?" he exclaimed. "That can't be right! It hasn't been that long."

"How would you know? You daydream and sleepwalk through your days," she replied.

"That might be partially true, but I don't daydream . . . no, I can't believe that it's—"

"David, darling," Maeve interrupted, "why would I lie?"

The band returned to the stage and the singer dryly announced, "It's nobody's birthday today."

"Bitch," Maeve muttered.

They resumed their set of somber songs showcasing the singer's broad repertoire of languages.

The young woman twice more reappeared to refill Maeve's glass, emptying the bottle. Maeve snatched David's untouched champagne flute. The waitress returned with two snifters and a bottle of cognac and splashed a little in Maeve's glass, but he waved her off when she tried to pour him some. Maeve zealously drained glass after glass of cognac, each time pouring a little and holding the glass in her hand to warm it before she drank.

"Aren't you hungry? Why didn't you order anything?" she said.

"I did," he replied.

"The staff here is pretty useless," she said.

As if responding to her cue, the waitress returned and set out an enormous bowl of mussels, a crock of some kind of mix of potatoes, ham, and cheese, and a cheese board.

The quartet finished their set and the stage immediately went dark.

Hidden in darkness, the singer breathed "shh" into the microphone. The conversational murmurs sputtered to silence. A pink footlight came on and showed her holding a small set of chimes. She sounded them three times by running her fingernails across them.

"The time of the metamorphosis is upon us," she whispered.

17

T he singer set down the chimes and threw back the hood of her robe. Her blond hair was cut to about an inch long. She smiled mischievously, looked over the crowd with her heavily kohled eyes, untied her cloak, and let it fall to the floor. She wore nothing but a fishnet leotard with embroidered dragons that covered her breasts and black thong panties underneath.

"That means you, too," Maeve said to the waitress. "Do it here."

The young woman took a deep breath, smirked, and shook her head.

"Why are you always so mean to me?" she said.

"You know you're my favorite. Why else do you think you get away with being so terrible at your job?" she said.

The waitress stepped out of her heels, stretched open the collar of her leotard, pulled it down to the tops of her breasts, and peeled each sleeve off her arms. She smiled and winked at David.

"Oh, stop that," Maeve said.

The young woman scowled and pulled the leotard off the

rest of the way. She left her clothing on the floor, put her shoes back on, and strutted away in a black halter bra and panties. All the waitresses were making rounds in the same lingerie.

Maeve said, "I intend to drink myself silly. Maybe you can try to enjoy yourself."

The guitarist switched to a bass, and the keyboardist set his synthesizer to sound like an electric piano. They performed old cabaret jazz the rest of the evening.

Sweet-smelling smoke filled the room. A few tables were sharing water pipes that were now being brought out.

"I can have them bring us a hookah. We have something special if you don't want tobacco. But I bet what you really want is for her to come back, don't you?" Maeve said.

"Where did they find a woman like that?" David asked.

Maeve nodded to somewhere in the darkness and she reappeared.

"Tamsin, my friend would like you to join us," Maeve said.

"You brought way too much food, and Maeve's not eating, so I need help," David said.

"And I've been drinking for two," Maeve said.

"Go get yourself a chair and whatever you would like to drink. And bring me a bottle of sparkling mineral water," David told the woman, and to Maeve he said, "I am enjoying myself, by the way."

"I could tell. You haven't criticized anything for hours," Maeve said.

"I hope you don't mind getting to know one of the employees," he said.

"She doesn't count. She barely does any work and I've known her a lot longer than she's been an employee," Maeve said.

Tamsin returned with a bottle tucked under each arm, holding a shot glass by its rim in her lips, dragging along a chair with one hand, and carrying a plate and cutlery with the other. She kicked her clothes out of the way and made space for herself at the table.

She shivered. "Brrr. It's a special bottle I hide in the freezer. I think I have frostbite."

"Vodka? The two of you are pretty hard drinkers," David said.

"Not really," Tamsin said. She picked up the bottle and swished it around. "It's only half-full. You can help me finish it." She filled her shot glass to the top and his snifter about a quarter full and giggled.

"Be careful. He's easily intoxicated," Maeve said. "You would normally ridicule a man for that, but you can't apply the normal expectations and judgments of us poor women to him."

Tamsin heaved down the shot while David took a tiny sip. He accidentally breathed in the alcohol fumes too deeply and let out a dry cough.

"Classy," Maeve said and gulped down her glass of cognac. "Pour me some." Tamsin obliged by pouring her half a glass.

"Well, that's half the half bottle already," Tamsin said. "Neither of you has touched the food. You'd better hurry and dig in. I could eat all of it."

"I think I will," said Maeve. "That's impressive even for you, David, that you managed to pick my favorite things from the menu."

"I told Tamsin to choose," David said.

"Ah, of course," Maeve said. "You almost make me feel bad for teasing you."

"You both look amazing, by the way," Tamsin said. She turned to David and asked, "How did you like the ballet?"

"I was impressed," he said.

"I bet you aren't easily impressed," she said.

"David was married to a famous painter or something. He's a horrible snob," Maeve said.

"Sounds boring. Lucky for you there are so many things to hold your interest tonight," Tamsin said.

David reached over and pulled her hair tie out. Her hair fell into soft waves that framed her face and completed the portrait. That made it easier to meet her eyes.

"He would normally start spouting all sorts of lovely things about you. At first you would think he has a big, mushy heart, but you would quickly realize that he's the coldest man you've ever met. That makes it more thrilling. But I believe he thinks you're perfection itself. I've never seen him so enrapt," Maeve said.

Tamsin stared at him for a few seconds and pouted.

"Sometimes if it's hard to light a fire, that means it will burn longer and hotter," Tamsin said, and Maeve chortled.

The women conversed like old friends, pausing frequently to listen to and comment on the music. They both seemed to have no trouble understanding the lyrics, sung in at least half a dozen obscure languages, as far as David could determine. Maeve told her about the ballet, and Tamsin told her about work and complained about a customer who came in with his wife but spent the whole time flirting with her. Maeve described the largely unused wardrobe she had bought for David, and the women speculated about what outfits would suit him, how they would style his hair, as if he were their toy doll.

David marveled at how much the two of them ate and drank. They finished both the bottles of cognac and vodka and wolfed down the food. The hookah smoke thickened. His head was still clear but all his senses were becoming clouded.

Empty bottles, empty glasses, empty plates. The music stopped. The singer re-donned her robe and backed off the stage. The footlight winked off.

"We'll go now. It's just strip tease the rest of the night. Tamsin, tell them to call us a taxi, and hurry up and get changed and meet us at the door," Maeve said. "You want her to come with us, correct?"

David nodded. Tamsin stood so quickly that she knocked over her chair, and then scampered off into the darkness. Maeve took his hand and led him to the door. Without getting a check or leaving any kind of payment, he noticed. The hostess handed Maeve her stole, pulled back the curtain, and showed them to the steel door. Tamsin jogged up behind them in a sweater and jeans that she hadn't zipped or buttoned yet. She held a sneaker in each hand.

The bouncer rotated a tiny disk of metal and peeked through the hole that it covered.

"Cab's not here yet," he said.

"Pull yourself together, Tamsin," Maeve said.

MAEVE GAVE the taxi driver the name of a hotel, and he took them to the tallest building in that part of the city. She led them to a small suite on the top floor. They entered a sitting area with an L-shaped couch, a coffee table, a large flat-panel television, and a small breakfast table with two chairs. That side of the room was partially separated from the sleeping area by a partition that ran two-thirds of the width of the room from the inside wall. The outside wall was made of floor-to-ceiling glass panels, one of which was fogged up. A sliding door opened to a private terrace. On the coffee table was a silver tray with another bottle of cognac and three glasses.

"I've enjoyed being fancy, but now it's time to relax," Maeve said.

She entered the bedroom and returned a few minutes later wearing a white robe.

"There's a hot tub outside," she said. She grabbed the bottle of cognac and the glasses, walked to the glass door, slid it open with her hip, and left them. Behind the steamed pane of glass, her opaque silhouette cast off its robe and quickly melted away.

"I don't have anything to wear . . . you can get in if you want," David said.

"Don't you understand what she's doing? Creating triangles. I think she thinks it's funny. There's no point except to challenge us, you know, test how we react when we have to face two different directions. It's either the two of us in here together and her alone, or one of us by ourselves. Why don't you see if there's another robe and get in with her? That way I won't see you naked. I'll come out and join you in my underwear. You've already seen me in it," Tamsin said. "Wave to me when you're ready."

David did find another robe in the bathroom, took off his clothes, and put it on. He carried two fluffy white towels out with him and tossed them to Tamsin, who had already undressed, and went out to the terrace. Maeve was submerged to her neck in a thick-walled barrel-shaped wooden tub, with one hand poking out of the water holding a glass of cognac. The bottle and other glasses sat on the wide lip that ran around the circumference. She had leaned back and closed her eyes, and was humming one of the jazz songs from the cabaret. The air was clear and the sky moonless. You could follow the city lights out for miles until they merged with the stars at the horizon and then follow the celestial lights back to a spot overhead from where you stood. He took off his robe, got in, and waved to Tamsin, who was beside the tub in an instant.

"There are still so many hours until morning for us to enjoy," Maeve said.

She twisted behind herself, poured the other two glasses, and handed one to each of them.

"They say you shouldn't get drunk in a hot tub. You could pass out and drown," Maeve said.

"We'll have to keep an eye on each other," Tamsin replied

and giggled, each of the four notes cascading downward in pitch and ringing sweetly and clearly as if they were being sung by the finest bel canto soprano. Maeve burst into a smile.

"Ah, that laugh of yours. Completely enchanting," she said.

"It's perfect. You can't even describe it," David said.

"Come on," Tamsin said. "We're supposed to be drinking ourselves silly, not melancholy."

"Speaking of silly, here we are in what you could call an 'erotically charged' situation," Maeve said, "and one of us manages to completely dissipate the heat of the moment. The water got colder the second he got in. I'm actually shivering now."

"I like it. Him. You," Tamsin replied, directing the last word at David, her eyes alive, flashing like pulsars. "There aren't any constraints or expectations with you, like there's unlimited space for a person to let their identity expand into. It feels . . . I can't say more natural, or even supernatural, because that still implies a point of reference or context. More like beyond natural, outside of reality."

"You might be the most philosophical cabaret waitress in the world," David said.

"That's mean," Maeve exclaimed and splashed water at his face. "I used to work at a cabaret, too, and not just waiting tables. And by the way, what do you do for a living?"

"I'm not as young as I look," Tamsin said. "You would be surprised what I know." She sounded another perfect, musical laugh and splashed water at his face too.

The warmth of the water, the gentle caresses of the bubbles, friendly, sweet faces, the clear night sky, the lovely sounds of feminine talk and laughter, and the aroma of cognac hovering above the water beguiled him.

David looked up, pointed to the sky, and said. "I never thought you would be able to see so many stars in the city. I guess you have to go up higher."

He told them about the constellations, sharing information he had retained from Rebecca, not just their mythological significance, but also scientific facts about where the planets were, what stars were actually galaxies, where there were black holes and super bright quasars that crowned them, the massive supernovae, the neutron stars and pulsars that were the remnants of these cataclysms, and the supergiants thought to be ready to explode.

"Where did you pick all this up?" Maeve asked.

"That's where he's from, Maeve. The stars," Tamsin said with mock seriousness.

David then told them about the night animals, the day animals, the plants that he had seen and mentally cataloged in the city. Maeve continually filled glasses. He lost track of how much time passed, if any did at all.

Maeve poured the last drops for him and announced, "That's the bottle. I'm going inside. I'll have them send up something else."

She climbed out, stood still for a moment, proud of her nudity, put on her robe, and padded away. David made a rough estimate of the impossible amount of alcohol the two women had drunk and couldn't explain how they could be so sober and steady on their feet.

"First in, first out," Tamsin said teasingly.

"You go. I've been the corner of the triangle all night," David said.

Tamsin pushed herself onto the top of the side wall, kicked water at him, and pivoted her body out. She shook some of the water off her limbs and head, put on his robe, and skipped inside. The women laughed merrily, and switched off the lights. He glanced around the outside of the hot tub. Tamsin hadn't brought out the towels he'd given her.

David's head was reeling. He had sweated out a lot of fluid and the alcohol had certainly soaked up much more. The dangers of drinking in a hot tub were quite real. Yet he was so comfortable and blissful that he didn't care about passing out and drowning. Drowning unconscious. It could be the most painless way to go, the most humane way to be put to death.

He was shaken from his stupor by the pop of a champagne cork and more laughter. Then their voices joined in raucously singing an old jazz song. He slipped out and walked stealthily to the door. They sat adjacent to each other, obscured in darkness. A cone of lamplight illuminated two pairs of feet propped up on the cocktail table, wiggling in time to the music. He couldn't tell which ones belonged to whom. Both sets of toenails were painted indigo, and both sets of feet were shaped prettily. Identical delicately tapered wedges with a contour from the heels, through the arches, to the balls that followed the same smooth, graceful wave, and the same straight, evenly spaced toes and soft flesh that seemed to have always stepped leisurely through life.

There was nothing to do but flop down in the corner between them. He landed on a stack of terry cloth. He pulled a towel from underneath him, wrapped it around his waist, and spread the other out on the couch behind him.

"Unflappable in any situation. You were born in the wrong time and place," Maeve said.

"Here's some champagne," Tamsin said, and a glass appeared in front of him. "You'll have to do your part. Maeve managed to conjure up three bottles at this hour."

"For as much as I'm paying for this room, there's no such thing as an unreasonable request," Maeve replied.

"How can you both keep drinking so much?" he asked and yawned audibly.

Tamsin replied, "This? It's nothing. Although if I were you, I wouldn't ask either of us to drive anywhere. Or try to walk up stairs. Or write our names. Retaining your self-control when you're drunk is a skill like any other. You just have to practice.

And by the way, this is just spiked juice. I know a Polish guy, who I'm sure is in the mafia, who can drink a couple bottles of"—she paused for effect—"vodka with one of his friends over dinner and then drive home as steady as anyone else. But he blacks out as soon as his head hits the pillow."

"It will be morning soon. We'll be drinking this for breakfast," he said.

"What do you mean? It's still hours and hours until morning. This might not be enough to last the night," Tamsin said.

"Oh, ignore him," Maeve interjected. "For him, time moves too slow, too fast, or not at all. He's got no head for it. I've never seen anything like it. It might be a unique psychological disorder. I wouldn't be surprised if time started moving backwards for him one day."

"There's something called dyschronometria. It's a real thing. But what if time really could be screwed up? All of this could be happening last month or last year, or maybe we'll wake up the day before we started," Tamsin said. "Maeve, my love, you should sing for us."

"I don't have a proper stage," Maeve replied.

Tamsin removed the lampshade, and all of them reeled from the burst of white fluorescent light. She hooked one of the support wires that ran across the top of the shade onto its threaded mounting post. This funneled light onto a spot on the floor in front of them.

"Ecco. You are clever," Maeve said.

She stood, and stepped into the circle of light.

"What do you want me to sing?" she asked David.

Tamsin said, "She has an encyclopedia of songs in her head."

"I don't know much about music," David answered.

Maeve wagged a finger at him and said, "I knew you would say that. You rely on your eyes too much. The least trustworthy, most fallible of the senses, if you ask me. And usually the first to go. You should use your ears more. I know just the thing."

David had never heard Maeve sing before, but she couldn't have had any other kind of voice. She sang in a languid, husky contralto:

> *When the marimba rhythms start to play,*
> *Dance with me, make me sway,*
> *Like the lazy ocean hugs the shore,*
> *Hold me close, sway me more.*

When she finished, Tamsin clapped briskly and asked, "Can you do the Meiko Kaji I like?"

Maeve cleared her throat and began singing in what David supposed was Japanese. Tamsin closed her eyes and mouthed the words along with her, and at the end of each verse, they both sang the sounds "o to ko" followed by words he couldn't catch, spitting them out like venom. When Maeve finished, Tamsin clapped enthusiastically again.

"That's one of my favorite songs," Tamsin said.

"What does it mean?" David asked.

"It's a secret that a man can never know," Tamsin said.

"You shouldn't tease our angel," Maeve said.

"Oh, that gives me an idea," Tamsin said.

She hopped up and whispered in Maeve's hear. Maeve looked flustered, the first time David had ever seen her react like this. Tamsin sat, arched an eyebrow, and glared, as if daring her. Maeve grabbed a glass of champagne, drained it, poured herself another, and drank that down as well. She tottered back to the makeshift spotlight. Tamsin cozied closer to David. Her robe had come untied and her shifting sideways pulled it open on the right side. Evidently, she had removed her wet under-clothes, and exposed was a band of bare flesh that began at her throat and ran through the center of her torso, along the length of her right leg, and down to her toes.

They had both finally crossed the line. The amount of booze it had taken to overcome their remarkable wills seemed like enough to knock out or kill a heavy drinker twice their size.

Maeve turned her back to them, looked over her left shoulder and began singing softly, almost bashfully, as if she were alone and singing to herself. Some kind of burlesque song. Tamsin laughed melodically and clapped her hands with delight, and then slipped her arm around David's shoulders.

Maeve performed for them as if she were before nobody, the ghost of an audience that had vanished long ago.

She whisked herself around and began her dance. She was steady again. With her arms, legs, hips, shoulders, head, and hair, she traced swirling, spiraling lines in the air, leisurely, elaborate movements designed to command a spectator's attention for as long as possible. She put one leg on the cocktail table and slowly tugged the hem of the robe up her calf and over her knee. She hid in the darkness outside the circle of light and flicked a naked limb into it or twirled through it giving the briefest glimpse of newly exposed flesh.

Tamsin poured the remainder of the first bottle of champagne into Maeve's glass. She stood and opened the second bottle, refilled her own glass, and tumbled back onto the couch, causing her robe to fall wide open. David hadn't touched his drink yet. Maeve picked up her glass, and integrated sipping from it into her performance.

"Oh, poor you. We've worn you out already," Tamsin said to David. She laughed and tugged lightly on his hair to get him to turn up his face.

"Open up," she said and poured half her champagne into his mouth, waited for him to swallow, and then poured in the rest.

"Now try to keep up," she said and forced a champagne flute into his hand before refilling her own glass.

Maeve continued with a second, then a third song and gained momentum in shedding her robe, the single article of clothing she had built her strip tease around.

"Maeve's really heating up. Do you see how gorgeous she is?" Tamsin said.

Maeve danced to another song just to loosen the knot in the belt, and her every provocative move and sultry stare now caused Tamsin to blossom into giggles that made her own exposed, naked flesh quiver. She tapped David's hand to force him to drink and continually refilled. When Tamsin stood to uncork the last bottle, she finally shrugged off the nuisance of the robe and let it fall to the floor.

Maeve was accelerating to the climax. She twirled around the end of the sash as she carefully unlaced it, and tossed it across the room. She limply clutched the front of her robe closed and pulled the collar down farther and farther over her shoulders. As she finished the song, she let the robe slip down but arrested its fall just as it was about to pass over her breasts by crooking both arms.

Her final song was slow and melancholic. David had heard it already tonight. It was the "lule" song from the lounge. All it took was minute adjustments to the positions of her arms to let the robe slowly ooze the rest of the way off her figure. As it reached the final points of resistance, the peaks of her nipples, she turned her back to them, sung over her left shoulder like she had when she had started, and let it drop. Tamsin laughed, whistled, and howled.

Maeve turned to face them with her right forearm across her breasts and her left hand splayed open wide to hide her loins. Her face was flush and aglow from the exertion. She widened her eyes, flared her nostrils, and breathed out forcefully, as if to vent the pleasure and invigoration that had built up within her while she performed. She glared with arrogance and pride. She nodded a little bow and sat back down, still covering herself. Tamsin replaced the lampshade.

"Happy now?" she asked Tamsin.

"Very. Why are you still covering yourself?" Tamsin responded.

"The audience doesn't get to see everything. There was never any full nudity. We always kept the bottoms on and at a minimum we had pasties. You should appreciate how classy that little bit of modesty was. You seem fine sitting there shamelessly, though," Maeve said.

"I have nothing to be ashamed of," Tamsin replied.

Tamsin moved Maeve's champagne glass to the edge of the cocktail table farthest away from her.

"Let's see you get that and keep your modesty," she said and laughed hysterically, showing how uncontrollably drunk she had become.

Maeve laughed with her, reached across the table with her foot, grasped the stem of the glass with her toes, slid it to herself, and grabbed it with the hand that had been covering her crotch.

David left to use the toilet. His head felt leaden, not from alcohol, despite the ladies' best efforts, but from lack of sleep, like he had been awake for days. He stopped to look out the two windows that abutted at a right angle on the outside corner of the bedroom, providing a view of three-quarters of the horizon. No lightening of the sky into the pastel purples, blues, and pinks that preceded the dawn. A digital clock radio flashed 12:00, and he had the notion that this wasn't because it hadn't been set, but because time had stopped. After he urinated, he washed his face and splashed water over his head. He lay down on the bed with his legs dangling off the end, closed his eyes and listened to the women's drunken chatter and laughter in the next room. Their voices mingled and blended, swirled around and into each other until they sounded like tinkling chimes. Chimes. He imagined he heard the same ones the singer had rung. He tried disentangling their individual notes and deciphering the conversation.

David awoke naked on the enormous bed between two naked women, their black hair fanned out on their pillows. They were both still and seemed barely to breathe. It was tricky to get out without disturbing them, but he doubted anything would rouse them. He wriggled up the bed until he could sit upright against the headboard and then slowly extricated each leg from under the blankets. He dressed, leaving his tuxedo shirt and jacket behind. The hallway was empty and noiseless, as if it were incapable of conducting sound. It was only after he stepped off the elevator into the lobby that the world welled up and rushed at him again.

18

When Maeve visited next, David noticed a small bruise on her right shin. It looked like it had been the result of her knocking her leg on a piece of furniture or a mild fall, like when you trip going up the stairs. By her next visit, it had healed, but two larger ones had appeared on her left shin. Then others on her back, forearms, and shoulders. Suddenly they seemed to be everywhere, a few fresh ones and many others yellowed in the final stages of healing.

One that looked like it had been made by a bite, a jagged-semicircle of damaged skin and ruptured blood vessels on her forearm, finally forced him to ask, "What's this?"

"What's what?" she responded. "You haven't had a bruise before? Hm, maybe you don't bruise. I've always bruised easily. It doesn't hurt."

Time passed, and when she reappeared, he would have to ask about others.

"What's this?"

"Oh, I don't know. Clumsiness. Redecorating. The place was getting stale. I've decided to do a lot of it myself. I've been softened by too many years of idleness and wealth," she said placidly.

He patiently asked again and again and again. Eventually, Maeve sighed and said, "How stupid I must sound. You must know very well what they are. I forget to exchange masks. Sometimes, he's agitated when I come home. About what exactly, I have no idea anymore. I used to know. Just raving, he is. But there's nothing we can want from each other. Mutual apathy is really the worst. Indifference, not hate, is the opposite of love, they say. I've seen the truth of this. It only creates frustration and anger, contempt and repulsion, without any accompanying conscience or remorse. I put no effort into giving, and during our time together, I've only ever let him take what has little value to me. But I've probably taken so much from him. He had ideas, expectations, and hopes. And who wouldn't? That's what you do when you get married, I suppose. It's nothing to worry about, though."

"Are you making excuses?" David asked.

"No, not for him. I think most people would agree that he's a horrible man. Many times barely human. But it isn't all his fault," she replied.

"I don't think any of that matters. You need to get away from him if he's hurting you," he said.

"Who said anything about *him* hurting *me*? And what about yourself? Haven't you easily endured what would have put others in great emotional distress? Did anyone ask you patronizing questions about your pain? Treat you like a helpless child?" she said.

"I think this is different," he said.

"Well, you're wrong. People know pain in different ways, and physical pain is the least consequential to some of us. I think you yourself are somewhat impervious to it, aren't you? I've seen you cut yourself without even a little gasp. I've been working a lot longer than you at perfecting this icy stoicism.

And I've done that with some injuries you've not experienced yet, and likely never will," Maeve responded.

"Well, what about emotional pain, then? I guess there's a fair amount of shouting and insulting going on," David said.

"Have you met the man? Oh, that's right, you've seen him *one time*," she said, drawing out the last two words sarcastically. "He's always been old and nasty. He was like that when I met him. Nobody understands what fuels it. Sympathetic people who claim to want to understand everyone can't be bothered with the mean ones. Indignation. That's a form of honor, and once upon a time it was considered chivalrous. One of many traits that used to be revered but are now reviled. Weakness and capitulation have become the virtues of a society dominated by cowards. It's now repulsive to beat a man to avenge an insult to a woman. But he doesn't mean it. This is different. There's something very wrong in his head now. It's really not worth discussing. And anyway, as you know, emotional pain is always self-inflicted. It's really stupid of you to ask."

"There are limits," he said.

"Ha ha. You make it sound so heroic. I can't think of anything more boring. If you don't feel anything, it doesn't matter," she said.

"Well, I do feel things, and I hope you do too," he mumbled. Where had that come from?

"Oh, I know," she said, sighing. "The only pain I could ever feel is if you disappeared. I would have nothing to do. Life would become so uninteresting again. I suppose I could tolerate it—I have before—but that's the irony of having anything pleasant happen to you. Your sense of loss when it's gone is greater than the feeling of pleasure it gave you. It's a miracle for rare, strange people like us to find each other. And when we do, we make a little world far from this one where all the tedious people live.

"God, that sounds so dreadfully sentimental," she concluded. "What have you done to me?"

"I didn't do anything to you," he said.

DAVID THOUGHT MORE about her bruises. Their patterns. She never had a mark on her face. Isn't the first instinct to strike the face or the torso? The ones on the legs must be from kicks. But who hits on the arms? Who bites an arm? And there was the fact that she was considerably younger and healthier than her husband.

He remembered a scene in a park he had once witnessed. A frazzled mother had one hand clenched around the wrist of her toddler son and dragged him along while he threw a tantrum. He kicked her shins and rapped his knuckles on her forearms as hard as he could to try to get her to let go.

David wondered what the blows felt like. He punched himself hard in the same places. Fewer nerve endings in many of them, but the shins had to hurt. Something abnormal was going on. Or maybe perfectly normal. What did he really know? It was none of his business.

Maeve had learned to be a dexterous dissembler, it would seem, in order to have total control of her identity. David could easily not care, but she still had to convince others to see what she wanted them to see.

Imagining Maeve's life stirred something. He yearned for her. Gaps in time began to matter. He counted the days between her visits. Two. Eleven. Twenty-eight. Five. One-hundred nine. Forty. One. Was there a pattern? He used to be indifferent to waiting, but now that he felt its sensation, he discovered he had no patience.

He needed her to explain the mystery of herself. Her entire being slid little by little into the pool of his psyche. As it subsumed more of her, the water bulged up over the vessel's edge, barely held in place by the surface tension. But it couldn't hold all of her without the tension breaking.

David studied himself in the mirror, something he hadn't done before. He had certainly taken the time to look at himself, to shave carefully, to arrange his hair, to make sure his clothes looked right. But that face, his own face, wasn't something he had paid close attention to. He had let how other people reacted to him explain it. Outwardly, it was as calm and as beautiful as ever. However, that former lazy aloofness that had ensnared so many was gone. Maybe it was just his eyes that had changed. They seemed to look somewhere beyond the physical space in front of him. They burned with dark, cold, intense energy.

It was a Sunday morning when David felt wearier than he ever had. He was sometimes tired from late nights at the restaurant, but now, after hours of deep peaceful sleep, he hadn't recovered his energy. He lathered his whiskers and mumbled to himself, "Not so young anymore." Unexpectedly, the surface tension of the pool of his psyche finally reached its limit and broke. A single tear streamed down his cheek, a trickle that had unknown volume pent up behind it. The world he had been a part of for years felt utterly unfamiliar to him. The ponderous physical spaces he had explored were a thin, fragile lattice that held fast together millions of lives, and he had merely skimmed across the top of it.

This descent elevated him higher than before. He was difficult to look at, in particular his eyes that shone rapturous melancholy drawn from the most mournful depths of the soul. How seductive that brilliant darkness could have been.

It's a mistake to define human beings as a single species. If scientific classifications were extended beyond the physical to the psychological, as is wholly appropriate, it is evident that within homo sapiens are numerous distinct subspecies. Homo

Stoicus. Homo Romanticus. Homo Melancholicus. Homo Sanguinus. Homo Asinus.

David had long been on the periphery of humanity, circling in his own wide orbit. At the center is a cluster of commonness and mediocrity so incredibly dense that it exerts a gravity that drags more people toward it. There were others out there following their own expansive loops, the rare geniuses of morality, and many of the opposite types, the sick heroes who delighted in their own irony and nihilism but who were terrified by the lonely void they drifted toward and looked left, right, and inward for familiar points of reference, yearned to draw the masses to them, and would eventually be drawn back toward the center. David was neither of these. An outcast among outcasts.

Unbeknownst to him, he had remained a social curiosity, and not everyone he had forgotten had forgotten him. Rumors spread. When he arrived at work one afternoon, Magda whispered, "Looks like you've got a stalker. See tzat lady tzere? She's been in a few times asking about you. I said notzing."

David recognized the woman. He had always thought of her as an incorrigible snob, so she would have had to stoop quite low to seek him out. When he had met her, she had been on the arm of one of the art foundation's wealthiest donors, a man about whom there was no question of his having made his fortune unscrupulously, if not illegally. She was tall, sturdy and trim, and had blond hair, wide, innocent blue eyes, perfect posture, and a flawless smile. She lacked sensuality or sultriness and resonated calm conservatism. She never drank, smoked, cursed, made or laughed at crude jokes, spoke sarcastically, sighed impatiently, or bragged. She exercised regularly but not fanatically, ate balanced, healthful meals, and got the optimum amount of sleep. She smiled a lot, was extremely polite, and made commonplace, positive, encouraging remarks in conversations, like, "Wow!", "How exciting!", "Very interesting!", "You must be delighted!" Simply a quintessential Caucasian woman of Northern European descent.

She had once given David her address and phone number and, even knowing he had a partner, suggested that he stop over whenever he was free. He learned that she was an escort, and that he was her one personal indulgence. Her goal was to find the perfect complement to her own conventional good looks and, in the meantime, make as much money as she could. He had merely been curious at first, but he was always back at her place when what's-her-name was out of town. She was so quiet, so unassertive, so undemanding. They barely spoke or conversed.

She pretended to be surprised to see him. "Oh, hi, David, what are you doing here?" she asked.

He responded, "I work here, uh . . . ." He'd forgotten her name.

She looked exactly the same as he remembered, but also so much older than he remembered. Either his memory was flawed or many more years had passed than he would have guessed.

"Oh, um, I guess I can see that . . . but never mind. Maybe we can chat and catch up. Um, soon," she said.

"About what?" he asked.

"I, I, I don't . . . you know, whatever, anything," she said.

He said, "You look like you're about to cry. Is there something wrong?"

"No. I don't know," she whimpered. She sniffled, trying to hold tears in check.

"Don't cry. There's nothing to cry about," he said.

"I can't help it. Jesus, what's wrong with me?" she said, looking at the table.

David suspected that he saw a woman desperately in love and, based on what he knew of her, possibly for the first time.

"Everything's OK," he said. "There's nothing wrong."

"I should leave. I should . . . would you . . . what's wrong? Why are you looking at me like that? I came to . . . never mind . . . just," she said.

He responded, "Forget it. I have to work. Are you going to order?"

"Please," she said and, finally losing the fragile control of herself, began sobbing. "Please," she whispered again.

"I really have to go," he said.

Ivo called David to the office during his break.

"It looks like you have lady troubles. Beautiful lady troubles. None of my business, but I wish I was you," he said.

"I don't know about that. My problems or you wanting to have them," he said.

"Magda's mother has been asking about you a lot. I both want and don't want that kind of problem. I'm stupid but not crazy, not that I would ever be so lucky or unlucky. That's why I own this place and have a boring life," he said. "I've got a family working with me and living nearby. We're almost right on top of each other. I have limits. But you're too free, my friend. Your life will be better if there's some drama. You need responsibilities, people nagging and arguing with you, and kicking you around. Find some people who will bring you back down to earth. Allies who will stick with you. You don't even have to like them that much. I recommend picking some fights just to stir the pot. You'll find out who you belong to quickly enough."

David laughed. "Pick a fight? Me?"

"Well, you know, it's a figure of speech. You ever been on a rocky beach? You pay attention to each one of those gnarly, ugly rocks. If you don't, you step wrong and hurt your foot. Then you might lose your balance and fall over. You understand?"

David shook his head and said, "No. That doesn't make any sense."

"Never mind," Ivo said.

David meandered home through the intersecting slots between the megalopolis's towering edifices. Time stopped and space was monochrome and flat, a dim hall of mirrors. On and on he walked, hastening to reach the open. Jagged cracks like lightning bolts appeared in the glass walls of his maze, and then they splintered and forked and crossed themselves until they were broken into a mosaic of trillions of bead-sized tesserae. They began clattering to the ground, a drizzle at first, then a torrent, and gradually revealed unending, unyielding white. He walked on, the fragments of the world crunching pleasantly under his chunky-soled work boots. Suddenly they whorled up in front of him and rearranged themselves. Dark letters on a white page streamed past his eyes. Gibberish at first, but soon they organized themselves better, and words appeared, trying to explain something. Phrases, then sentences, paragraphs, and finally pages of a story. About him.

He stopped. He was still surrounded by the reflective facades of skyscrapers that boasted of the power of the institutions they enshrined.

SIXTH DIGRESSION

I asked, "Do you feel different about those times now?" But he looked at me, perplexed.

"Different?" he asked. "You mean my material circumstances? Money? It's amazing how easy it is to get by."

"No, I meant you—if your attitude has changed about your past. If you've grown or see things in a new way now," I said. "How any of this changed you."

His face still didn't register any comprehension.

"I'm very sure of certain facts. What was the story of my life? I'm telling you exactly how things happened. I've never reminisced with old friends or anything like that and let the story change to suit the mood, the point I want to get across, or the people around me. If you want to do that, you might as well invent something the split second before it flies off your tongue," he said.

He continued, "There's truth in rigid facts or total fantasy. Lying and deceit, I would say, is what happens when a person doesn't know what he wants to say and doesn't choose fact or fiction. For a lot of people, if they tell the same story tomorrow, in a different place, a different light, different weather, after having spent the day differently, they'll probably say something different. Conditional truth. I can't do that. I can't think of anything worse than cheating your own senses and memories."

"That is a difficult position to maintain," I said.

"It is? What are your memories like, then?" he asked.

I sucked my teeth and replied, "Everything in the middle, neither fact nor fiction. A thorough set of misrepresentations, slanders, defamations, self-serving revisions, and self-immolating ones. Intentionally. Because I suffer the worst of all character defects, the obsession with life being interesting by virtue of it being grotesque."

19

As David ticked off the days, when he felt a premonition of the next moment with Maeve, it would happen. See her coming tomorrow, let no other thought or expectation intervene, and she would simply open the door and enter. He might come home from work at two in the morning and find her napping on the couch. She usually left before the change of day, as freely as she had arrived, never needing to be seen out. She just slipped away.

He began to make love to her not for himself, but for both of them, feeling how she felt him, thinking every thought for her, reacting to how her skin reacted to his touch, feeling his own kisses from within her. Every quiver, breath, smell, drop of sweat and saliva, hot, warm, and cool spot reported on her emotions and physical sensations. To be connected to a woman like that, you have to be coiled and wrapped around her and wear her like a second skin. It is a delirious sensation that multiplies your own ecstasy, but it binds you like a slave to her, reliant on her pleasure for your own. He slid inside her and swayed gently, patiently building her wave of pleasure until it reverberated back onto him. They touched tighter, closer, tenser, directing energy into each other, desperately trying to pull the other into themselves, to merge forever. But sadly, even such intense sensation passes and becomes a faint echo, merely hollow words pulled from a dictionary explaining the feeling, and no longer the feeling itself.

They lay naked on top of the sheets.

"I wish it wouldn't," David mumbled to himself.

"What?" she asked.

He didn't answer. Maeve closed her eyes and breathed softly, as if she had fallen into a light sleep.

He began again, startling her awake. "Life is supposed to constantly change, isn't it? We can't hold on to anything. It's not in our nature anyway. Our minds wander; we get distracted. It's not our fault. Chemicals finish circulating, our senses go back to work, and our bodies nag us. We feel hungry, need to go to the bathroom, have an itch, smell something, get a cramp, or one of a million other random things. Just like that, the good moments are discarded."

Maeve replied, "The solution is to avoid all that nonsense. Fill your life with satisfying your immediate caprices, but only the ones that don't have—what's a good way of putting it?—a chain of consequences. Like attending the theater. You go, you may like it or love it and come out crying or smiling until your face hurts, or you may wish it better fulfilled its potential and resent wasting your time. But when it's over, it's over. Just treat life like an assortment of performances. That helps experiences seem new."

"Yeah," David said. "I've never been able to describe it well, but for some reason, I realize now that I'm used to letting events come and go without thinking about the past or the future. Nobody's like that. You think that's selfish?"

"Did something happen? Just keep doing that. Selfishness is misunderstood. Choosing nothing and wanting nothing is the ultimate selfishness, but it's ultimately good. What you gain, in fact, is quite small compared to what you give, a little more freedom multiplied by everyone around you. People mistakenly assume that avaricious people are selfish. Behind all their plans to accumulate and consume, or to build and wield power, are people with no individual identities whatsoever. They're simply avatars of collectively valued concepts. You can't compliment them for having human character traits like selfishness. There are no more warrior chiefs, like Alexander the Great or Genghis Khan, who were physically and intellectually superior —you know, unique masters of their clans and the human race. If every entrepreneur, tycoon, or so-called world leader dropped dead all at once, nothing would happen. Maybe there would be brief power struggles among the copycats waiting to take over. Who could have imagined that the pinnacle of human progress would actually be a plateau of mediocrity? Hordes of worthless schemers. So how do they get their power? They plan every action to elicit a reaction from the masses, which makes them completely dependent on them. Their positions are based on a system of quid pro quo, compromise, market reactions, compulsion, and knowing when to be compelled. I'm rambling, but I'll start making sense. They're gears in a system in which everyone, in striving to satisfy themselves, conspires to satisfy everyone else just enough and agrees to validate each other's invalid successes. Prodigious greed, lust for control, you see, is a communal system that requires public consent, which is easy to get because everyone's greedy. The aspirationally greedy need champions and talismans.

"It's brilliant because it's the only mechanism weaklings have to elevate themselves. Almost any exertion of force is outlawed unless it's directed at someone the masses have rejected. We punish and ridicule people who behave like actual human animals. This strips the seriousness from life and makes it all just a game. And people feel it, even if they can't articulate it. Everybody knows someone unjustly imposing their will on them that not so long ago they could simply meet out in the forest and tear limb from limb. It's driving us mad. But the universe is nothing but savage physical conflict. None of these supposedly powerful people would last a second. What's worse, we've been diligently chipping away at intellectual power, too. Imagine, our scientists would have been feared as powerful wizards in the past.

"To choose yourself, to make immediate satisfaction and self-actualization your goal, and to have the courage—it doesn't really take that much courage, but maybe common sense—to remove yourself from the vast social conspiracy, to do it on your own, has to be the most selfish behavior of all, but it's the best path forward. It's the only one left," she said.

"Can two people be selfish together?" David asked.

"You mean besides in brief, one-off encounters? I suppose they could coordinate against any outside concerns. Create a bubble just for themselves. I think it would be easier if one person were a slave, not treated as a human, always serving the pleasure of the other. Otherwise they both have to keep bargaining with each other to maintain the relationship. That means someone gives up something," Maeve said.

"Unless they become one person. So perfectly attuned that they function as an individual," he said.

"Hm, maybe there could be times like this, but it can't be permanent," she said. "Do you suddenly see yourself bargaining yourself away?"

"What do you mean?" he asked.

"With me. Do you feel some sense of give and take, compromise? I could do things differently. Hadn't you thought of this? I can serve your pleasure. Become your slave. Shall I? I don't mind at all. You could do anything you want to me, tell me to do anything. Stop thinking of me as a person. I've done this before for men. That might stop whatever it is you're feeling," she said.

David sighed, kissed her on the neck, and said, "I don't know if you're serious, but you would be doing it out of generosity rather than personal gain. Wouldn't your side of the arrangement be violated?"

He felt both exhilarated and exhausted, as if he were incapable of moving from next to her naked body, and that the sweetest release could come from lying there until their individual existences dissipated.

"Such a devious trap you've set for a philosopher like me to try to get me to admit that I care for you," Maeve said. "Maybe you're nothing special to me, one of the many in the past, present, and future. Maybe you play the same old part that others tried and failed at or gave up on. But anyway, you know, there's an ultimate freedom in total captivity, in sacrificing free will. It's our own wants and needs, not having them thwarted or constrained, that tie us down."

They both napped, and David awoke to Maeve playing with his phallus with her fingertips and her tongue. She giggled when it hardened, and then straddled him and put it inside her. She pinned his arms down and her breasts swayed in front of his face. She pulled away and arched her back when he tried to suck on her nipples, and slammed her palms onto his chest to force him to lie flat. She wanted him to be passive. She moved her pelvis too slowly to stimulate him. So much time passed with no variation in activity that he couldn't feel their lovemaking at all. She seemed to be testing his endurance in keeping focused on the sexual act. His phallus remained erect, but the rest of him, his mind and body, couldn't help drifting. He lost the sense of presence, of whether he was asleep or awake, and her being on top of him floated to the periphery of his perception. Unknown time passed. Her moaning pulled him from his reverie. She was sliding her vagina up and down rapidly now. She held both breasts in her hands and pinched her nipples, and he could feel that the sensation she was giving herself made her tense her vaginal muscles. It was all over in a few seconds, and she immediately flung herself back onto the bed and fell asleep.

David was wide awake now and watched her doze, so lightly that the thoughts swirling in her mind formed impressions of words on her lips. She eventually slept more deeply, and he gently covered both of their bodies.

He was awakened in late morning by the front door closing. In a split second, he decided to follow. He put on the minimum amount of clothes, an undershirt, jeans and shoes, and ripped a light jacket from the coat closet, the first thing he grabbed, snapping its plastic hanger. He opened the door a few inches and listened for the sound of the elevator bell. When he heard it, he counted to ten, and then bolted out. He made a mad dash down the stairs, leaping over the last two or three steps ahead of each landing to try to keep up. There were only two elevators for the twenty floors, and coming down from the fifteenth, she might be delayed several times when it stopped to let other people on. He felt as if he were shaking the entire building. His head hummed from the reverberations of his galloping, and he thought she must notice the rumbling behind her and flee faster.

When David reached the lobby level, he peeked out from the stairwell door. It was around a corner from the elevators, away from the front entrance, so he had no view of anything, but he could hear the clack-clack of a woman's heels in Maeve's cadence on the lobby's marble floor. He had slipped a pair of hard-soled loafers onto his bare feet, and they were already scraping the skin of his Achilles tendons. When the sound of those steps left the building, he emerged and strode across the lobby, walked out, and almost bumped into the back of her. She was hailing a taxi.

"Should I get a cab and follow?" David asked himself. "Does that even work?"

Maeve was looking toward the traffic coming up the one-way street, so he sidled away from her blind side and around the corner of the building. He shivered. He was sweating from his charge down the stairwell. His jacket was too thin, the frigid concrete drew the warmth from out of his feet through the thin soles of his shoes, and a cold wind swirled between the buildings, chilling his ears, face, neck, and hands.

After about five minutes, a cab stopped for her. David watched the vehicle pass. It was unlikely that he would find a second one quickly enough. He patted his pockets to confirm what he had just realized. No wallet.

Maeve's taxi progressed only a few dozen yards before it locked into traffic. Had she looked over her right shoulder, she would have seen David hunched down, hands tucked into his pockets, trying to consolidate his body heat. The next time the driver jerked his cab forward to claim the ten feet of pavement that had opened in front of him, David decided to track her on foot. He didn't know exactly where she lived but reckoned it was only a mile or two, a half hour at most. He could stay close to the sides of the buildings to shield at least some of his body from the weather.

Although the driver didn't seem interested in threading through brief, tiny gaps to save time, he was intent on preventing others from doing so, and frequently accelerated and braked hard to close off openings. David had to alternatively jog and amble to mimic the car's pace and avoid being seen. Blisters were forming on the tops of his pinky toes and the outsides of his big toes, but at least the exertion was warming him. An icy drizzle, partially melted beads of sleet, began to fall. A cold slime formed on the sidewalk, and his smooth leather-soled shoes found no grip when he rolled off the balls of his feet. Then a change in direction positioned him directly into the wind, which sprayed wet, stinging pellets into his face and eyes.

The blisters everywhere on his feet were moist and sticky, and at the many points where his shoes rubbed, his damaged skin stuck to the leather before tearing loose. Free bleeding would almost have been preferred, because it at least would have lubricated his raw flesh.

The taxi turned onto one of the main boulevards and joined a wide ribbon of slowly moving vehicles. It became more difficult and painful to maintain visual contact. David memorized the license plate, but that wouldn't help if the car got a few blocks ahead of him. The situation was looking hopeless. Its illuminated advertising sign was the only distinctive feature he could concentrate on. It was for a film festival from this past summer and had a large hole in it.

The cab suddenly turned left and slipped through a rare gap in the pedestrians traversing a crosswalk. David was stranded on the side of the intersection opposite of where it turned. What he hoped to achieve had already been gnawed away by searing pain in his feet and numbing cold attacking the rest of his body. Transcending the agony and seeing this through became the goal. He was focused and instinctual, a mental state that oftentimes creates a mantle of luck around impulsiveness and recklessness. He dashed across the rows of crawling vehicles but was slipping so much that he could not pull up or feint and was nearly struck twice.

The taxi progressed through two more green lights and receded into the sleet as a yellow smudge, but a red light three blocks ahead held up traffic. David sprinted through the next intersection right after the light changed to green for cross traffic, before any of the drivers had reacted, and passed in front of a police car. The policeman briefly sounded his siren, opened his door, and shouted for him to stop but, having caught a faceful of sleet, reconsidered hassling some heedless pedestrian probably just trying to escape the weather.

Three times David caught up, only for a traffic signal to

change and allow the taxi to dart away. Finally, it had to wait for a throng of pedestrians to clear an intersection before it could turn. They were near the limits, where the city gave way to a large park or, depending on your perspective, a small forest. David followed the car down a side street into a dense residential district.

In this neighborhood, most people could afford to travel by taxi or private car, and dozens of them were picking up or discharging passengers in the blocks ahead. David lost his quarry immediately. The endeavor had been pointless. He leaned against one of the buildings, slid onto the ground, and pulled his knees to his chest.

It was a significant moment, an occasion to take a stand, or rather a sit, for absurdity. What had prompted this chase? It wasn't love, passion, jealousy, or anything you find in innumerable stereotypical stories of relationships. He had simply lost his mind for half an hour. Now he waited for it to return.

I admired his honesty, which he conveyed by not justifying the situation at all. The typical thing is to pull together all the snippets of folk wisdom you've accumulated over the years and use them to extemporaneously fill in holes in your story and make yourself into a recognizable character. Maybe he was right and you really did need a stereotype to explain yourself.

It has become an expectation, a demand, to know why we do anything. Vast industries and academic fields have arisen to study the topic. Courts busy themselves with trying to divine motive or intent. We pretend that purposeful action is much more common than it really is. From time immemorial, however, madness was a perfectly reasonable explanation for much, if not most, human behavior. Question: Why did this person do that thing? Answer: It is unknowable. Perhaps divine inspiration, a witch's spell, a full moon, demonic possession, blind rage, senseless passion, temporary insanity, drunkenness, random opportunistic mischief, hormones, or spleen. All perfectly acceptable. Completely unprovable and the phenomenological equivalent to a shrug of the shoulders.

The temperature dropped. Slush coating the pavement hardened, and the sleet intensified and accumulated as an icy crust. David's hair and clothing froze. The sleet was blinding, and the billions of little ticks it made striking the surfaces of every object and structure blotted out all other sounds. He was visually, aurally, and physically encased, deprived of his senses, and it felt wonderful.

Eventually, the sound of the sleet stopped. Snow fell. David could hear the city again. When he stood, chips of ice fell, like scales of rust. Cold reached into his core. The sores on his feet throbbed and stung. He had never damaged any part of his body so badly before. He supposed there was a subway station nearby and didn't have to walk far to find one. Homeless people bundled in old clothes, blankets, and rags lined the entryway to escape the weather. He remembered he had no money. He thought he could get away with sneaking through the fare gates or talking his way in, but he didn't want to. It was beneath him.

The primitive comfort of warmth seemed a luxury now. David took off his jacket and shirt, wrung them out, and put them back on. He snatched a ruined umbrella lying across the top of a trash can, ripped off its nylon canopy, shook the water off it and stuffed it under his shirt. It kept the frigid dampness away from his skin and served as a good wind block. He immediately felt warmer.

Rather than point himself toward home, he strayed further from it, skinning more umbrella carcasses as he went. There were quite a lot of them; the wind had made a great deal of mischief. One he was able to rip nearly evenly into semicircles, which he wrapped around his feet. He spread another around his buttocks and thighs. A fourth he folded in half and used as a hood. He used others to build up layers around his torso. He managed to make himself somewhat warm and weatherproof.

The snow accumulated rapidly and smoothed over the city's unnatural contours. David had lost count of how many years he had been confined here, but this was the most intense snowfall he had ever seen. When it reached his ankles, he decided to return home. A mechanical army had mobilized to subdue the snow. How much would have to fall to force it to give up? There were some places he had heard about where they barely bothered worrying, and instead acquiesced to winter's months of dominance. Not here. The accumulated will of millions would never allow any force of nature to reconquer it. They had overcome the land, they had overcome the water, and they would try to overcome the sky, never mind the fact that there was so much more of it, an infinite amount, to reckon with.

He collected the spare key from the concierge, ascended the elevator to his apartment, opened the door, stripped off his clothes and rags, staggered into the bedroom, took two extra blankets from his closet, spread them over his bed, slid beneath them, and immediately fell asleep. He dreamed of a new intense appreciation for dryness and warmth.

It was dark when David awoke, the short midwinter day having already run its course. He couldn't imagine when Maeve would return. He didn't feel the rhythm. It had stopped. The present and future of her already yielded to her in the past, the memory of her. The subtlety in her smell and taste, the liveliness of her eyes, how she moved her body, varying its energy and elasticity as a method of expression, to complete her words or to hint at her unspoken thoughts. How she chewed her food, sat on a chair with her legs folded beneath her. How she sweated. The inflections in her voice. Things he would never again witness.

20

How long had he and Maeve been held together by nothing? Were they in any way alike? He had no idea. It had been as if they occupied two tall peaks. Other women had been seduced by the challenge of climbing to him, but Maeve had her own perch. High above the world, they could soar, sway, and cant but always had to alight apart because each peak narrowed to a point that could hold only one.

And what was this obscure link between them? Sentiment? Love? No, it was beyond that. A sixth sense, not a psychic sense, but an attuning of all senses toward one another. Maybe such perception is the next stage of evolution, he thought.

A god would act with perfect intuition. That is what makes a god mysterious, unknowable, and terrifying. Because people don't understand this, they complain about discord and chaos all around them and use them as evidence of the absence of the divine. Such a strange argument, to cite the incomprehensibility of an incomprehensible being as proof of the impossibility of its existence.

David was an empiricist, and god was not observable. But

it's an irrelevant question anyway. The critical one should be, "What would god be like?" It would not, could not create an orderly system sensible to humans. Anyone could design something that complied with our primitive customs and rules and what little we understood about the physical laws of nature. A god must make a universe that operates without constraint, in which structures arise out of nothing. That is truly god-like. Ancient wisdom now buried by the ignorance of knowledge.

If people stopped misapplying their mental powers, the world could be a god-like place. Could humanity survive long enough to realize it? Maybe, David mused, a god would have once been like us, would have remembered what it was like to be trapped in an ego and pitied us our tired, overworked little brains and our paranoid, hormone-doped, overactive imaginations and longed to show us the way out. Hadn't we given up paradise in favor of knowledge and then tried to organize our own? But you can never build utopia. It's an approximate state, an attitude, a way of being.

How long does it take a person to attain this insight? When you do, there's usually too little time left to enjoy it or for it to benefit you. Maybe that's part of the fear of death, that all of life's lessons could be wasted, and why people need the afterlife, to finally have the chance to apply them.

Maeve lived in a perpetual state of innocence untainted by any search for meaning. Simultaneously an idiot and a sage.

So much philosophy! He was disgusted with himself.

Maeve was right about the sense of loss being greater than the sense of gain. Returned to a state of no possibility, he saw the value in where they had led each other. To nothing, and the freedom that it offered.

DAVID DIDN'T KNOW what set him onto the next course of

action. It was as if he watched the subsequent events happen to someone else.

He made a habit of walking Maeve's neighborhood in his free time. He didn't know why or what he was looking for. One time, he thought he saw her husband step out of a cigar shop. Was that her husband? He couldn't remember. He had once seen a man who was already a shell of a man, but this man looked like that one's ghost. Could he have declined so much more?

David paced the sidewalks in front of different buildings, waiting for her to appear. Approximately eight buildings per block and nine square blocks to canvas. He had no idea what her habits were, when she might come and go. He couldn't patrol at all hours and at all places. A hopeless preoccupation.

David switched to wearing a jacket, then a short-sleeved shirt, then a jacket again. His apartment's owner notified him that he was finally resettling in the city and reclaiming his home. David found a month-to-month sublease in a tiny unit with a single small window facing a brick wall. Like Angela's apartment. He forgot to cut his hair, shave. He wore out his clothes and shoes. His habit of forgetting to eat worsened, and he shed significant weight from his already lean figure. He seemed always to have been that way, thin, ragged, obsessed. He looked like the dishwasher now. The light in his eyes and his charisma were snuffed out. And for what, he asked himself now?

When David was wearing a thick winter coat again, he finally found himself in the right place at the right time. He didn't so much recognize her as he did her movement. Her legs, how they lifted a foot, swung it forward, and lazily planted it on the ground. How her hips swayed and her waist undulated with the precise amount of energy, neither too stiffly nor too loosely, to offset the brief moment of risk and imbalance when one foot hovered above the ground. How her arms hung totally relaxed and gently rocked in reaction to her body's movement. A woman in total mastery of herself, strutting as if the other lives around her were utterly inconsequential. Unmistakable from any angle.

The woman got into a taxi and was driven away. The long gap between her visits had just been the most severe eccentricity in her capricious schedule. It would be today, though, and dozens more days in a row to revert to the average. But for once, she wouldn't find him and would never visit again. David could still run ahead, get in another taxi, do anything to get back home in time to meet her. But he only continued his pacing. Ten minutes later, a car pulled up and discharged her. She carried an enormous bouquet of flowers that obscured her face, but he was sure it was her. It hadn't taken as long as it should have. She hadn't gone to him.

She entered a building with a glazed terracotta art deco façade that extended upward roughly twenty stories. Atop the first high tier were second, third, and fourth tiers set in from the preceding levels. Judging by similarities in window treatments, he reckoned that each apartment in the lower levels must take up at least one-twelfth of a floor, and that each corner of the top tier was one unit. Massive homes.

The entrance was attended by a doorman who allowed passage as far as a locked vestibule that was guarded from a desk by a concierge, a man who looked more like a bouncer, a massive grizzled man who had over decades perfected this primitive, unskilled, but critical trade, achieving a sort of omniscience about the comings and goings of every resident and their regular visitors, who belonged there, and who didn't.

David pressed the door buzzer and was looked over and reluctantly admitted.

"State your business," the concierge said inhospitably, having already determined that David was an undesirable.

"I'm a friend of the woman who just walked in with the

bouquet of flowers. I was talking with her at the flower shop, and she, um, dropped her credit card," he said.

"What woman?" the concierge asked.

"She walked in a minute ago . . . but . . .," David responded.

"I'm not sure who you mean. Leave it with me. I'll see that whoever it belongs to gets it," he said.

"No offense, but I can't just leave someone's credit card with a stranger. Can we compromise? If you give me her apartment number, I can mail it to her," he said.

"Put her name on it and have it addressed to the building. The postman will either know which box it's supposed to go in, or he'll ask me or one of the other concierges," he said.

"I don't know her last name," he said. He had never asked.

"You don't know her address or last name? You must not be much of a friend, then," he said. "Please depart the premises."

"Don't you think things like last names and addresses are a little too formal these days? Who needs an address? When was the last time you wrote a letter? I doubt everyone in this building knows or remembers your last name, and probably very few, if any of them, know your address. Yet you could say you all know each other well. If you dropped dead tomorrow, I bet many of the residents would attend the funeral or at least send flowers."

"What the . . .? Listen, I won't tell you again," he said.

The security door opened and admitted the uncoordinated shuffling steps and guttural wheezing of a man with a face permanently creased from scowling all the time.

"Ah, Mr. Karpman," the concierge said. "Recognize this guy? He came in a little while after your wife and says he knows her."

David glanced back and forth between the gargoyles who flanked him.

Karpman frowned, his gray eyebrow tufts in full plumage. He grunted to clear his throat, mumbled something to himself, and growled to the concierge, "What did you say to me, fuckhead?"

The concierge rolled his eyes and replied slowly and pointedly. "This. Guy. Here. Says. He. Knows. Your. Wife."

"That old witch doesn't know anybody like him. She keeps away from faggots. What's this about? Do we need to get the police down here? Beat up the little faggot?"

David said calmly, "I think I'm in the wrong place. My friend's husband is much younger. My mistake. I lost my glasses this morning."

"Whatever, fucking idiot. Fucking idiots everywhere, always wasting everyone's time," Karpman grunted.

As David walked out, he heard behind him, "What the fuck was that about? I thought you blacks were supposed to be tough guys. Can we get that big Hispanic maintenance guy up here next time? You're getting slow and old and fat, Jesse. You gotta toss these losers."

The concierge said, restraining his anger, "Sir, I keep telling you my name's not . . ."

The closing doors cut off the rest of the conversation.

David had a last name and a building. Thwarting the dragons guarding Maeve might not be that difficult, but what then? Maybe he could leave her a note. Send her flowers, a box of chocolates, a balloon, or a teddy bear? Drop in and whisk her away for dinner and a show? Absolutely pathetic. Break their unspoken rules. What did he want to say to her? Nothing. She would never respond anyway. He had to see her and be with her. As long as it took to understand who she was.

Her husband was right. He was a fucking idiot.

David continued prowling Maeve's neighborhood. Oftentimes, he sat in a coffee shop with a view of her building entrance, pretending for hours to read or be lost in thought. As weeks passed, he saw her troll of a husband plenty, but never her. Then he finally stopped even seeing Karpman.

After many fruitless weeks, David decided to try the computers at the public library. The Internet, however, wouldn't admit to her existence. He entered every combination of keywords from the little information he knew. Presumably she and her husband had lived in the same apartment for a long time, so David should have been able to find their property records or some other public information that contained an address with her unit number. He found many Karpmans, but none he could link to the building.

On many nights he didn't work, David stood watch outside the opera house. He searched for the cabaret Maeve had taken him to. Finding no online trace of any place like that or its polylingual singer, he made a list of every club in the city, painstakingly examined websites, online reviews, and satellite and street views of buildings, then visited the dozens of them that had any characteristics of the place Maeve had taken him to. Nothing matched. He tried to identify Maeve's favorite restaurant and wracked his brain to recall a name or how they had gotten there. There weren't that many ugly nouveau-riche enclaves. He visited all of them, but none of the neighborhoods looked familiar. She might have taken him to the suburbs that night. He had so rarely been in a car since he had been brought to this city that he had no sense of the passage of time and space inside of one. He looked for the hotel, which should have been easy to find. It was enormous and iconic, and he had made his way home from it on foot. Yet when he tried to retrace his path, he immediately became confused and disoriented.

After he had exhausted every possible strategy, he repeated them all in case something new landed in the vast heap of information he was sifting through.

Seasons cycled. Then one day, there was a new Karpman in the search results, mentioned in an obituary for a gossip columnist. Ages ago, the reporter had written a humiliating piece about a premiere party for some terrible musical this

Karpman had bankrolled. Karpman had responded by ambushing the writer in front of his office but wound up flat on his back with a bloody nose. That little anecdote had become a part of the writer's legend.

The article hadn't named the musical, but it had given the year of the fight. David searched the Internet for Karpman-produced musicals but found nothing in any list or database of productions from that era, not even among the cult followings that revel in the irony of carrying the torch for the absolute worst of popular culture.

David reckoned his best chance would be the paper that columnist had worked for, but he immediately discovered that it had folded ages ago, and gone along with it were all of its archives. David visited the lonely microform room in the library, where so many obsolete newspapers and old phone books survived in miniaturized form, but that old gossip rag wasn't among them. One of the few things not worth remembering.

David broadened his search to entertainment reviews for that year in all the papers, hoping that the show would have been so bad that it would have provoked a few opinionated reviewers into flaunting all of their wit, humor, and verbal acumen in a lengthy panegyric. He had noticed in the art community that the worst, most detested works elicited significantly more words of condemnation than the good ones did of praise. It was as if critics believed that the ubiquitous dross and mediocrity inflicted upon humanity could have insidious after-effects, rather than dissipate harmlessly like all foul air. These lengthy rants and negative reviews were like barrels of disinfectant, hyperdoses of antibiotics, buckets of dirt to comprehensively cleanse the world of, kill off, and bury these aesthetic profanities. Or perhaps a complaint is easier to articulate than a compliment.

The sun had made the city seethe under its insouciant glare

for many weeks, but finally it gave a languid sigh and yielded to hospitable breezes and feathery clouds that had patiently waited their turn. But unexpectedly you could still wander into pockets of old, hot, noxious air that concentrated the smells of industrial, human, and animal filth, pinned in place by the cooler, heavier atmosphere and shielded from the cleansing autumn wind. It haunted random places: the last car on the subway train, an underground passageway, a bench in a little forgotten park dedicated to an obscure civic hero, a service entrance, an alleyway, or a narrow side street.

He finally had a breakthrough. The only extant remnants of a worthless, forgotten history. He seemed to have memorized sections of these articles as if they were important passages in a narrative of his own life.

. . .

X features a cast of totally unknown performers, the type who come to the city with dreams far larger than their talent. Underwritten and produced by a newcomer to the world of musical theater, a Miles Karpman, whose name might be an anagram for words that describe his artistic judgment, it's a bizarre erotic vision devoid of any beauty, joy, or actual eroticism.

We're presented the picaresque tale of a fresh-faced young rake named Seth. Seth is an everyman who arrives in the city convinced that he'll make his fortune and find the love of his life. However, he isn't a flawed but essentially appealing hero trying to navigate a corrupt society. He's a depraved and cruel manipulator who is himself the source of corruption.

Seth's two objectives are to destroy the lives of all competitors and to acquire a gorgeous, servile feminine accessory worth the money he's accumulating. He pits against each other three equally beautiful and conniving young women who hope to share his ruthlessly acquired fortune.

They encourage him to exercise even greater cruelty toward his peers and vie for favor by attempting to outdo each other in enduring his increasingly elaborate sadism. In one rousing scene, after getting the play's lead love interest, Anastasia—played by M—e (a print error, an ink smudge that obscured the name in the copy that was scanned into microform, but David could tell that it clearly contained the letters *M* and an *e* where they would fit the name *Maeve*) Blood, a smolderingly sweet young actress who's also scandalously rumored to be the producer's very underage paramour—to agree to undress to her brassiere and panties for his inspection, Seth rushes her to his tenth-story window ledge to hide her from another potential mate who has unexpectedly shown up at his door. As it begins to rain, which on stage involves showering the nearly naked girl with cold water, effectively rendering her undergarments transparent, she breaks into a sultry number fantasizing about the expensive clothes, opulent mansion, gaudy jewelry, and handsome, groveling servants she dreams of having. Meanwhile, inside the apartment, the hero explains to his other suitor what her rival is enduring for him, and prods her for her own act of self-flagellation by telling her that if the poor woman outside eventually tires and falls to her death, she will have proven her worth more than the others.

. . .

In this pit of theater, the story we're meant to see might be more than the one that has been staged. The musical seems almost to be a mechanism for publicly torturing its own aspiring actresses, who some would accuse of being stereotypically shallow social climbers themselves.

. . .

A poor-quality promotional photograph. A handsome young man grinning smugly with a woman kneeling in front of him and flanked by two others whose heads were turned to whisper in his ears, one of them a curvaceous woman whose profile was obscured by a wave of raven-black hair that glistened even in a grainy scan of a blurry picture from long ago. Unmistakably Maeve, young and smolderingly sweet, as described.

David found one other review.

. . .

I believe we're seeing an inadvertently ironic work that depicts ideologies that a larger portion of our population than we care to acknowledge lives, breathes, and believes. The lifestyles of another culture, a foreign culture always among us, oblivious to judgment and criticism, full of figures who are unapologetically amoral and focused on personal gain. We could almost consider this musical a nature study, a human nature study. That makes the work compelling in a way, a kind of materialistic pornography that exults in itself, doesn't view itself in relation to anything else, and seals itself off from its own consequences and conclusions. A creation without self-awareness. Is it tragedy? Dark comedy? I don't think we can know, and that uncertainty is maybe a healthy challenge for audiences. It's reality, and doesn't allow the theater to be a refuge from it.

Unfortunately, in order to come up with these positive sentiments, we have to grant an overly generous amount of good will and expend more creative energy than went into the production itself. All of the standard elements of a work of musical theater, such as the acting, singing, dancing, songwriting, dialogue, sets, lighting, and costumes, are amateurish and unskilled.

. . .

21

David reviewed property records for Maeve's building again. One of the apartments belonged to a Blood Trust, a curious name he hadn't followed up on, having assumed this was some sort of cult society or a medical research charity. That had to be it. What could he do with his new knowledge? Nothing. For the remainder of the summer and through autumn, he spent his new free time sitting at home alone, staring out the window.

One evening, cold polar air meandered south; from the sky fell big soft flakes that glowed in and softened the glaring streetlights and glazed the pavement an oily black. An unearthly, cosmic phenomenon, like sparks of light pulled into a black hole.

Across the surface of this void, an insubstantial form drifted into a luxurious apartment building, past an ox of a doorman and a hulk of a concierge who supernaturally didn't notice him, to a door he had found by uncountable months of diligent searching.

A man opened the door who scowled just like Karpman. David grabbed his shoulders and pushed him inside as effortlessly as if he were lifting a child. He scanned the apartment. Spacious and uncluttered. A few simple, elegant pieces of furniture were neatly arranged within the broad open floor plan, and sparse high-quality print reproductions of impressionist paintings were hung on the mostly bare walls.

"You won't get a thing, you cunt," the man said, then pulled away and backed to a console table situated across from the doorway, his terrified eyes fixed on the intruder. He flung open a drawer and pulled out a revolver. "Now I'm going to blow your balls off, you little fairy," he said. But the fierceness relaxed from his face and the weapon fell from his hands. Weary, lifeless eyes encircled by bulging, misshapen folds of skin drooped sadly, showing decades of exhaustion that had long been suppressed by anger and cruelty. "Oh," he said.

The heavy crystal vase that David had slammed into his head fell to the floor and shattered into a carpet of glittering beads dusted around the old man's collapsed body. David noticed a pool of urine at the man's feet and the smell of feces. There were several long scratches on his neck, as if fingernails had raked across it. He stepped backward toward the threshold.

A beautiful coal-haired woman sprang into the foyer, picked up the revolver, and fired a wild shot that grazed David's shoulder. She pulled the trigger again, and again, and again until she had ratcheted through the cylinder two, three times. All but the first chamber had been empty.

A stout white-haired matron, her bare feet cut and bleeding from broken glass, threw the gun aside. Her eyes were a dull, drab green, like the color of a wilted spinach leaf.

She moaned, "Why? Who would do such a thing to a sick old man?"

The woman walked calmly across the room, her feet smearing blood across the black-and-white checkerboard tile, to the telephone. She picked it up and appeared to dial.

"I just shot an intruder who murdered my husband. He's standing right in front of me, watching me make this call."

David turned and walked out. The hallway was deserted. No curious faces poked their noses out from partially opened doors. He pressed the down button for the elevator. He wasn't bleeding much, not really in any pain. He wondered how badly he was injured. He wanted to poke his finger into the hole that must be in his shoulder. A tiny drop of blood trickled down his arm and splattered onto the floor. He put his hand in his pants pocket to keep from making a mess. No mechanical sounds emanated from any of the elevator shafts. He supposed he should leave quickly, run down the stairs, but he remained passively rooted to the spot. He focused on the feeling of more blood slowly dripping down his arm and into his pocket. It felt as if the building had deliberately paused to consider its next course of action. Finally, he heard the groan of ancient machinery. He stepped onto an empty elevator car, rode it down, and walked coolly out of the lobby.

The murder received a couple of minutes of attention on the local television news and was covered in the newspapers for a day or two and then forgotten. The building surveillance camera footage was vague and distorted at the time of the crime and oddly missed David's coming or going. The widow, who in a strange oversight remained anonymous, having been kept nameless and faceless by the reporters, corroborated the description given by the concierge of a man who could be anyone and only implicated David by being something of his antithesis: dark, hairy, short, muscular, and fidgety.

One curious old journalist, canvassing many of Karpman's past enemies, pieced together the dead man's obscure history and published an article a few weeks later, long after the public and the police lost interest. An epilogue. Karpman had exited life with a moderate fortune amassed through residential real estate development, a pittance in comparison to his neighbors, because his ventures had been continually sapped by lawsuits and fines. He had held together his little empire for over half a century with tactless bluster. However, the widow had disappeared, ignoring the decaying business, and the underpaid and indignant lackeys, who undoubtedly were already stealing, became bolder in rectifying their humiliations. Bad deals were made with their own shadowy side companies and business connections, and cash flow was intentionally mismanaged so that asset sales at tremendous losses were required to keep the business solvent. The enterprise was about to collapse in on itself and evaporate.

What followed was an account of a life of ambition, dishonesty, and self-negating behavior. In the early 1960s, Karpman had shown up out of nowhere and begun taking huge risks in nightclubs, restaurants, hotels, shopping centers, residential and commercial real estate, and, oddly, the performing arts. He had failed spectacularly at almost all of them. When an enterprise was on the way to inevitable bankruptcy, though, he bled as much money as he could from it by ignoring health, safety, permitting, and licensing regulations, and failing to pay workers, suppliers, contractors, lenders, and taxes. His business partners made out well by writing off the losses and buying back assets at huge discounts. Where he did succeed was in low-income housing. He couldn't tolerate decay and criminal activity on his properties and built a reputation around providing safe, cheap, simple working-class homes. He even received an award from a civic association for his efforts. He demurred in the crudest way possible by claiming that "peasants" were undemanding and easy to manage, that the stupidity of other landlords in targeting the wealthy meant that his vacancy rate had been near zero for decades, and that soaking up the public subsidies his renters received had been tremendously profitable.

Karpman also had been a scandalous society figure known

for his ill temper, confrontational boorishness, and continual flouting of all rules of decorum. He was always ready to resort to verbal abuse and violence to avenge an insult, in particular if it had been aimed at his wife. His churlishness came to a head in the 1990s, when he was arrested for ramming a beloved local ballet company director's car with one of his properties' utility trucks and then setting fire to it. His rival had made lewd comments about his wife. Karpman then made allegations about his enemy's sexual misconduct, which proved to be true. After several women, some of whom had been harassed or sexually assaulted as minors, were emboldened to step forward with their stories, the director fled the country, and an international manhunt ensued. Karpman's small role was quickly forgotten. Since then, little had been heard from him.

David recited one paragraph from memory:

Miles Karpman lived for decades as a pariah, despised by almost everyone who knew him. Nevertheless, he was in many ways an indispensable minor public figure, seeking out the dirty work that most in his position would have avoided, an integral part of the lives of thousands of people, more than our superficially polite society would ever acknowledge.

IT HADN'T dawned on David that he should immediately flee the city. Instead, he had hailed a taxi, gone home, showered, bandaged his shoulder, cooked dinner, felt a little bored, bought a newspaper, skimmed it without reading anything, still felt hungry, gone out to a café, sat at the bar, and picked up or was picked up by a woman who had caught him quietly admiring her polished ebony skin.

"If you think I'm pretty, you can tell me, as long as you're not corny or rude about it. Although that won't get you very far," she said.

He was taken aback. Hadn't the man she would have been talking to disappeared ages ago? Did she really think who he had become was worth her attention? Or had those few words of hers bridged the gap, reestablished the continuity of himself?

He did remember her name, but refused to give it to me. He held on to it like it was still important to him.

Through his forthright inquisitiveness, he was able to get her to volunteer that she was an emergency room nurse and, as the conversation took shape, that she had spent her entire young adult life in the Navy. Too sensible to be charmed by him, perhaps too sensible to charm anybody herself. He asked her about what she had seen of the world, and she told him. A witness to the things he had been cut off from. She shared his fascination with the stars, some of the only things to look at, she told him, in the many lonely places at sea.

"It's almost like you're out there with them, not just looking up at them," she said.

He went home with her and let her tell him stories until the early hours of the next day, when both of them fell asleep on opposite ends of her couch. He awoke around noon with a blanket on him and a pillow under his head. They went to brunch and came back to her place. She invited him to shower with her, which was when she saw the gouge less than half the diameter of the small-caliber pistol round that had slashed across the side of his right deltoid.

"What the hell happened to you?" she asked.

"Someone shot me," he said.

She laughed and said, "Right. Listen, I'll clean it and stitch it up. Otherwise you're going to have a big nasty scar, and it could get infected."

The subsequent events happened so naturally and easily

that they made everything that had gone before seem completely pointless and inconsequential.

This nurse had to work long shifts that week, but they agreed to get in touch the next weekend. David called Ivo to ask for a few days off and learned he had accumulated three months of vacation. He packed whatever clothes he could fit into his two old suitcases, liquidated his investments, and withdrew all his money from the bank. He left a message for the nurse to call him on Friday when she had a break. She returned his call in the evening.

"Listen, I had to move out of my place all of a sudden. Can I stay with you for a week or two? I only have a few suitcases. I can pay you rent," he said.

"Does this have anything to do with you supposedly getting shot?" she asked.

"Yes, exactly," he replied.

"You don't look like the type of person anyone would shoot at, you know," she said.

"I agree," he said.

"I like you, but you'll have to settle for the couch, and I'm going to have to ask you to cover a third of the rent and utilities. Meet me at the hospital and I'll give you a key. You can drop off your stuff, then come back when my shift is over and take me out to dinner," she said.

A winter passed. When David noticed the first buds in the trees, he told Ivo he wouldn't be working at Midland Mediterranean anymore and left before the owner could ask any questions. The day he first noticed the rustle of fallen autumn leaves, he told the nurse that he needed to get going.

"Ha ha. What happened to you only needing to stay a week or two? I'm glad you stuck around. Hard to find a real person without a head full of melodrama anymore. Let me know where you wind up. I'll come visit," she said.

"Maybe I'll come back and visit you too," he said.

"'Maybe' means I should start looking for a boyfriend," she said.

"I'll definitely visit, then," he said.

"Good," she said.

"I've been wanting to ask you a weird question," he said.

"Coming from you, I wouldn't expect a normal one. What is it?" she said.

"Right. Have you ever been hurt at work? Gotten kicked or punched, or even bitten, or something like that? You know, by a hysterical patient or something."

"Sure, it can happen. A lot of people come in freaked out from the pain or fear or whatever, and there's more than enough who might be on drugs or have psychological problems, or older people with dementia. You sometimes see the person who brought them in freaking out a lot more," she said. "I haven't had anything worse than getting kicked and people grabbing my arms. Got clawed once here on the top of my forearm. Most of the time people are just flailing around, not really trying to hurt anyone. It's definitely an occupational hazard. They say half of workplace assaults happen to health care workers. It's sort of ironic, but I guess it kind of makes sense. What made you ask me that?"

"I was wondering if you were safe at work," he said.

"That's actually really nice of you. You're literally the first guy I've been with who thought about that," she said.

He made his way across the country, taking any low-paying cash jobs that he happened to come across. In response to employers' incredulous questions about why a man like him was getting by doing day labor, he told them bluntly, "I might be wanted for murder," which indicated that he had a weird, dark, self-deprecating sense of humor and therefore was a trustworthy, all-around good soul who wouldn't cause any problems. He's lost track of how long that's been his life.

"THAT'S A HELL OF A STORY," I said.

"Isn't it?" he replied.

He stood, yawned, and stretched.

"Thanks. I've enjoyed the company," he said.

He put some cash on the counter and strode out.

Who knows what the truth is? I've never bothered to check. It's probably not that interesting.

www.ingramcontent.com/pod-product-compliance
Lightning Source LLC
Chambersburg PA
CBHW021149110726
47900CB00002B/487